MURDER IN THRALL

MURDER IN THRALL

ANNE CLEELAND

KENSINGTON BOOKS
http://www.kensingtonbooks.com

KENSINGTON BOOKS are published by

Kensington Publishing Corp.
119 West 40th Street
New York, NY 10018

All Kensington titles, imprints, and distributed lines are available at special quantity discounts for bulk purchases for sales promotion, premiums, fund-raising, educational, or institutional use.

Special book excerpts or customized printings can also be created to fit specific needs. For details, write or phone the office of the Kensington Special Sales Manager: Attn. Special Sales Department. Kensington Publishing Corp, 119 West 40th Street, New York, NY 10018. Phone: 1-800-221-2647.

Kensington and the K logo Reg. U.S. Pat. & TM Off.

Library of Congress Card Catalogue Number: 2013936491

ISBN-13: 978-0-7582-8791-5
ISBN-10: 0-7582-8791-7
First Kensington Hardcover Printing: August 2013

eISBN-13: 978-0-7582-8793-9
eISBN-10: 0-7582-8793-3
First Kensington Electronic Edition: August 2013

10 9 8 7 6 5 4 3 2 1

Printed in the United States of America

For Nellie at SJN; and for all others like her

CHAPTER 1

Her eyes were five centimeters apart. Her face was propor-
tioned perfectly; the wide-set eyes, the spacing between the zygoma and
the mouth, the ratio of chin to forehead to temples. He had taken a pho-
tograph of that face when she was unaware, and he often studied it
after he went home. He could not help himself.

"I am *wretchedly* sorry, sir," Doyle apologized for the fourth
time in the past two hours. She was waiting with Acton in the
unmarked police vehicle, the rain pattering on the roof. Although she was cold and miserable, she would rather be tortured than admit to it, a demonstration of stoic atonement
being needful at present.

"Whist, Constable," he answered without taking his eyes
from the door of the pub. They had been staking it for over an
hour.

Cautiously heartened, she stole a quick glance in the dim
light at his averted profile and wiggled her toes in her boots to
keep them warm—she was fast losing feeling. Surely it was a
good omen for her future prospects that he was imitating her;
he was not one to joke about before lowering the boom. She
stole another glance at his impassive face and recalled that he
was not one to joke about at all, so perhaps it meant nothing.
Or perhaps it did. She was Irish, with an accent that tended to

broaden when she was nervous—the present circumstance serving as an excellent example.

She ventured, "Is there a rank lower than detective constable?"

"Not at present."

He continued his silent perusal of the pub and did not look at her. Snabble it, she thought, sinking into the seat. You're only making it worse; keep this up and he'll push you out of the car, he will.

They were outside the Laughing Cat pub, hoping their prime witness would make a reappearance. Doyle had lost him.

"D'you think he has gone to ground, then?" The words were out before she could stop them. Honestly; what ailed her that she couldn't keep her mouth shut? Acton was going to rethink his ill-conceived plan to partner with a first-year and give her the well-deserved boot—it was a rare wonder she had lasted this long.

It was indeed one question too many, and Acton turned to meet her eyes.

"I'm that sorry," she offered yet again, feeling the color flood her face.

The chief inspector had been most displeased when he discovered she had allowed Capper to trick her. She knew this only because the words delivered in his modulated public-school voice had become clipped. The signs were subtle, but she was alive to them—it was a survival mechanism, it was.

The witness had been a fellow Irishman, from Limerick, who was coming to meet with the murdered man. Doyle was never to discover the purpose of his visit because the aforesaid witness, a man named Capper, had neatly given her the slip. He had thought to show her the tack room as a likely place to search for evidence, all the while expressing his profound shock at the horse trainer's murder. So helpful he was, in his low country manner, that she had abandoned protocol and had gone in before him. The door to the room had then locked with a snap and she was left alone in the darkness, breathing in the scent of worn leather and muttering Gaelic curses. She was forced to ignominiously text Acton on her mobile to request a rescue, and after springing her free, her commanding officer had told her in all seriousness that she had taken a huge risk and was lucky not to have been shot. He never raised his voice nor changed his tone, but she was thoroughly ashamed of herself all the same; she wouldn't care to lose his good opinion. She knew—although she couldn't say how she knew—that she indeed held his good opinion. Or had held it until this latest misadventure in the tack room.

At present he was having her repent fasting for her wayward ways—although she took it as a good sign that he had not sent her back to CID headquarters to submit to yet another session of retraining in basic protocol. Instead, after backtracking for several hours around the racecourse, they had managed to find the merest scrap of a lead that had led them here; a pony boy's tip, given on promise of anonymity while the frightened man looked over his shoulder every other word. Have a look about the Laughing Cat pub in North Hampton, the man had told them. He intimated the murder was not an isolated incident but would say no more; wouldn't even give his name. This was of interest; when Acton had briefed her about the murder, he mentioned Home Office concerns that a syndicate of some kind was laundering money at the racecourse. Her run-in with Capper could turn out to be a case-breaker—if she didn't get the sack, that was. And if they ever laid eyes on him again.

They waited in silence. Doyle didn't dare suggest he turn on the engine so that the heater was engaged, and she didn't like to even think of what the wet weather was doing to her hair after such a ragged day. Have pity, Acton, she pleaded mentally; I'll expire of shame, else.

At long last he relented and turned to face her, his dark eyes meeting her own. "I don't think he's here, but there may be someone who knows where he's gone to ground. Let's have a look 'round."

As was his custom, he opened the car door for her and she declined his umbrella, as the rain was now only sporadic. He was somewhat older than her and always treated her with grave courtesy. It's in the breeding, she thought as she cautiously stood up on stiff legs; he's probably dyin' to give me the back of his hand.

They approached the pub, which was located on an undesirable corner of the working-class area that bordered Kempton Park racecourse. It was late and the street was quiet as they crossed it, their footsteps echoing whilst she tried to keep up with Acton's long strides. He forgot, sometimes, that she was so much shorter. Or he continued unhappy with her, and would just as soon leave her behind. Doyle stepped up her pace.

He glanced down at her sidelong. "You will allow me to take the lead, please."

She blushed again in shame; he was reminding her not to stray away from him as she had done at the racecourse when she had been roundly hoodwinked. "I'll be clingin' to you like a barnacle, sir," she replied in an overly pert tone; may as well be hung for a sheep as a lamb, and perhaps she could tease her way back into his good graces—anything to alleviate her current state of disgrace. She glanced up to observe his response and was relieved to receive one of his half-smiles as he opened the door for her. There now; perhaps she wasn't to get the sack, just be tortured till the wee hours in the hope that she had learned her flippin' lesson. It was a rare wonder the man didn't get sick of the sight of her.

They stepped in through another set of doors and made for the bar, Acton giving the interior of the pub a quick survey and Doyle trusting him to see if their man was present. He was keenly observant; her talents lay elsewhere.

"Not here," he said quietly.

They leaned on the counter and she glanced around; the rain had kept the customers away, and as it was quite late there were only a half dozen or so hardy souls scattered about, drinking in a desultory way as could be expected on such a night and in such an area of greater London. It was a shame their man was not in evidence; if Capper had indeed been present, Doyle would have leapt upon him and strangled him single-handedly for putting her through it with Acton. Sadly, her temper would occasionally goad her into doing things she oughtn't, so perhaps it was just as well.

"Should I ask a few questions, sir?" She was hoping to redeem herself by showcasing her talents.

Acton considered, his elbow on the bar whilst he took a keen look around and then settled his gaze upon her. "Have one of your coffees and we'll see what the barkeeper has to say."

Doyle didn't hesitate and caught the 'keep's attention; coffee was her life's blood. "A latte with half soy and half skim." She threw caution to the winds. "And whipped cream." She was empty as a pocket and in desperate need of sustenance—it was grueling work, here in the doghouse.

The barkeeper lifted his lip and regarded her with undisguised scorn. "Not that kind of place. I can give you coffee with half-and-half."

"Done." At this point, plain hot water would do, if for nothing else than to pour on her poor frozen feet.

When the man brought the coffee, Acton took the opportunity to display his identification. Doyle watched; often the witness's reaction to the warrant card told her a lot, as Acton was well-aware.

Acton asked, "Do you know a man named Danny Capper?"

The barkeeper took a little too long to answer, and while he considered, she noted that he gripped the bar rail with both hands for a moment. "Yeah. He's here sometimes."

"When's the last time?"

"Dunno," said the man in the tone of one who would no longer discuss the topic. "Maybe a couple of days ago."

Doyle brushed her hair from her forehead.

Acton leaned forward, all menacing law enforcement. "Obstruction of justice is twelve months. Shall we try this again or shall we continue the conversation down at CID headquarters?"

Now uneasy, the barkeeper weighed his options but continued defiant. "Look, I don't want any trouble."

"There's trouble enough," countered Acton, unrelenting. "A trainer's been murdered at the racecourse, and we'd like to speak with Mr. Capper."

Thus admonished, the barkeeper decided to cooperate but made a show of sullenness so that there was no misunderstanding his reluctance to cooperate with all persons constabulary. "He stopped in to talk with his girlfriend and asked that I cover for him—to say he wasn't ever here. He left about an hour ago."

"Know where he is now?" Acton tapped a long finger on his warrant card case, just as a reminder.

"No. But I suggest you talk to her." The man jerked his chin toward a woman who sat at a table alone. "She's the girlfriend."

Doyle pulled out her occurrence book and jotted down the barkeeper's information while Acton watched her. He always watched her hands while she wrote, and it made her self-conscious; as a consequence, her left-handed scrawl was even less legible when he was present. No matter; it would all be typed into a report shortly—thinking of the coming report, she paused, her heart sinking.

Acton indicated she was to follow as he walked over to introduce himself to the girlfriend. She was the type of woman who inhabited this type of pub; a buxom brunette of perhaps thirty who looked a little the worse for wear, an empty pint glass before her along with an ashtray full of cigarette butts marked with lipstick. She was texting on her mobile phone, pausing to draw on a cigarette and gaze out the window, a crease between her brows. She appeared abstracted and unhappy until she took one measuring look at Acton and brightened—Acton was tall and darkly handsome. He was also reclusive and unapproachable, which made him all the more attractive to the opposite sex; Doyle had witnessed the phenomenon many a time.

"Do you mind if we ask a few questions?" Acton showed his warrant card and introduced Doyle.

"Sure—I'm Giselle and I am very pleased to meet you." She ignored Doyle and took Acton's hand, looking up at him from under her lashes.

Doyle noted that her eyes strayed for a moment in the direction of the barkeeper but couldn't determine if any unspoken message had been sent or received.

"May we join you?" Acton could be semi-charming if he thought he could obtain an advantage, which was a useful talent in this line of work. Doyle knew she should observe and learn; she was not good at subterfuge.

Smiling warmly, Giselle indicated to Acton that he was to take the seat beside her, and then when he offered to light her cigarette, it gave the woman an opportunity to lean in and show her cleavage to full advantage.

Brasser, thought Doyle, annoyed; you'll catch cold at that. It didn't help that the other's cleavage was indeed impressive and made more so by a push-up bra with the emphasis on push. Doyle was left to seat herself and her less impressive bosom in the chair opposite them.

"Aren't you that detective from the papers?" Giselle put a teasing hand on his arm and blew a cloud of smoke Doyle's way.

Worse and worse, thought Doyle, who may as well have gone somewhere else in search of a decent cup of coffee. Acton was larger than life in the public's eye; the brilliant, titled chief inspector who regularly solved high-profile murders. The newspapers featured him often—not that he noticed. He had little use for the newspapers and tended to give them short shrift, much to the dismay of the detective chief superintendent who knew a good public relations gambit when he saw it. Instead, Acton was reserved almost to the point of rudeness and definitely did not suffer fools—a decided drawback for Doyle at present. In this instance, however, Acton was giving every indication he was intrigued by this two-penny brasser, who was taking full advantage and small blame to her; it must seem like Christmas.

"We are told you know a man named Danny Capper."

"Oh, Danny—" Giselle made a dismissive gesture with her hands that made it clear he was yesterday's news. "We had a falling-out."

Doyle surmised that this remark was meant to convey to Acton that he had a clear field—it was too much to hope for that the woman was truly unhappy with her beau; few things were more helpful to a detective than a disgruntled girlfriend.

"He was here tonight?"

"Yes." She exhaled some smoke in Acton's direction, pursing her bright red lips. "That's when we fell out."

Doyle brushed her hair from her forehead.

"A shame," said Acton, his tone indicating it was anything but.

"I suppose that depends," said Giselle with a great deal of meaning.

Honestly, Doyle thought crossly; they should get a room.

But Acton was as subtle as a serpent. "You wouldn't mind giving me some information about him, then."

There was only the tiniest pause before Giselle rendered a slow smile and drew on her cigarette. "No, I wouldn't mind at all."

Giselle gave Capper's address and explained she had known him, off and on, for over a year—yes, they had dated but it wasn't serious; this said while fingering a curl that rested on her bosom, as though any more emphasis was needed or necessary. Trying to suppress her annoyance, Doyle jotted down the information and sensed that the girl seemed wary, despite her easy banter with Acton.

"Do you know what he was doing at the track today?"

Giselle threw back her head to blow a cloud. "He likes the track."

Acton arched a brow at her. "Did he come home with a lot of cash sometimes?"

Giselle laughed throatily, tapping the cigarette on the ashtray. "Now, that would have been nice."

She is definitely wary, thought Doyle, trying to avoid the scattering ashes. She glanced around the room but could see no one who sparked an interest. The barkeeper was not within earshot.

Acton leaned in to suggest, "Perhaps there would have been no falling-out, then."

The woman stubbed out the cigarette, even though it was half smoked. "Hmm," she agreed, contemplating the ashtray. "Money does talk."

"Did you quarrel with Capper about money?"

She shrugged, and the movement made her breasts shift upward. Honestly, thought Doyle; may as well plant a flag between them.

"No; we have different ideas about our future."

This was true, and although Doyle kept her gaze on her occurrence book, she felt Acton glance at her, to make certain. She tried to gauge what he was about; Acton never asked an idle question.

"Do you know where he is now?"

"Not a clue." She smiled at him as though it was the last thing on her mind now that Acton had come into her orbit, and crossed her legs toward him.

In response, his tone was almost apologetic, having to interrupt their semi-flirtation with the grim facts. "A man's been murdered; Mr. Capper may have information that could prove useful, and I would very much like to speak with him."

"Murder. How shocking." Giselle's heavily mascara'd eyes widened with dismay. She did not ask who had been killed.

Doyle considered as she scratched out some illegible notes while Acton assured Giselle that she was perfectly safe. So Capper came here, needed to see Giselle in person, then did a bunk. He didn't want to use his mobile, perhaps. Or he needed to deliver something to her or to another. He may be the killer or he may be unwilling to tell the police what he knows. Or he may be afraid of the killer. Whatever it was, it had been important enough to lock a police officer in the tack room so he could escape with all speed back to the Laughing Cat. She remembered thinking that his story rang true when she interrogated him—he had been coming to meet up with the trainer at the stables and was brought up short when he saw the forensics tape cordoning off the area and heard that the man had been murdered. He hadn't known the man well, but they had friends in common. Doyle had been in the process of asking him about the identity of the aforementioned friends when he suggested they look around the tack room. Trumped me, she thought in annoyance. Stupid culchie.

She saw that Acton's gaze had shifted to her because she wasn't paying attention. With a guilty start, she proceeded to focus like a laser beam.

"Do you know if Capper had any friends who may know something? Criminals or underworld types?"

Doyle recalled what the pony boy had intimated; there were dangerous people and dark deeds involved. Giselle played with the ashtray for a moment, her lashes lowered. "I can't recall any just now."

There was a slight emphasis on the last two words. Acton pulled his billfold from his jacket's inner pocket. "May I give you my card? If you come across any information, you can give me a ring."

She held the card and stroked it with her long red nails, her limpid gaze on his. "I'm your girl." She looked up at him through her lashes.

Doyle brushed her hair from her forehead and saw Acton hide a smile.

CHAPTER 2

*S*HE LIVED IN A TINY FLAT IN CHELSEA. AFTER SHE LEFT WORK, HE *would drive to her tube stop to watch her emerge and then he would watch her enter the building. He had been inside and knew what it looked like. Her only photograph was of her mother.*

Doyle could read people. It wasn't magic, or a science where physical reactions were carefully gauged—that was more Acton's bailiwick. She was simply good at reading people and could usually spot a lie; one of her ancestors must have been fey or some such thing. The talent had been very useful—she had avoided deceitful boyfriends and steered her very gullible mother away from annuity schemes and the like. Upon reaching adulthood, she had come to the realization that by combining her passion for crime shows with her perceptive ability, she could forge a very satisfying career in police work. "Very discerning; excellent interrogation," her course reviews at the Crime Academy had said, as though it were something at which she had to work. Still, it made up for the fact she was not well educated and positively abysmal when it came to the sciences.

She had managed to secure one of the coveted entry positions at New Scotland Yard and was working very hard to maintain it, no small feat in light of the competition. Or, to be more accurate, she *had* been working hard to maintain it until Acton had plucked her up into his rarefied sphere.

She presumed that it was word of her talent for sorting out the truth that had brought the great DCI Acton to her lowly cubicle in the basement of CID headquarters one fine morning. He had fixed his formidable gaze upon her and asked in his brusque way if she would please accompany him to the docks to investigate a high-profile homicide. As she had never worked a homicide, she was terrified, so terrified that she was beyond words and didn't gabble on as was her wont—which was just as well. By the time she had recovered from her astonishment, she was able to tell him the decedent's grieving wife was shammin' it, and the case had unraveled from there.

For three months she had worked alongside him, and there was no denying that they worked well together; he so smart and she so intuitive. He had never asked her outright about her ability, but she knew he had a very thorough understanding of it—and he blessedly knew she preferred not to speak of it. Despite his reserve, she felt they had a certain connection, an understanding—in a strange way they had much in common; they were both a bit freakish. As a result, neither of them did well with other people; he was famously reclusive and Doyle led a reclusive life in her own way—it was no easy thing to be able to read what one's friends and acquaintances were feeling at any given time. She avoided crowds—and clubs in particular, where literally no one was saying what they meant.

It was she who decided they needed a signal when she wanted to alert him that something was amiss so that they wouldn't have to confer or interrupt an interrogation. They got on well—considering he was who he was—and together had solved some very tough cases in an impressively short time. He used her in his investigations on a regular basis now, and she lived in dread that he would rethink their partnership; it would be devastating to return to the shame of mere first-year misdemeanors again.

They left the Laughing Cat and returned to the unmarked; it was late and cold, and the street was silent, as the rain had stopped. Doyle could see her breath in the chill air and practiced blowing it out as had Giselle the brasser.

Acton opened the door for her. "You think that Giselle wanted to talk to me but couldn't." It was a statement, not a question. He was always quick on the uptake, and Doyle sometimes thought he didn't need her at all.

"Yes—I think so, sir. And there was that hint about talkin' for money. Was she afraid? Who was watchin' her?"

"The barkeeper?" he suggested as he walked around to get in the car. "He wasn't right, either."

Doyle was not so certain; she had not gained the impression that the barkeeper was a threat to Giselle. "Perhaps—but he couldn't hear what she said."

Acton sat for a minute, contemplating the steering wheel and thinking about it with his dark brows drawn. "Do you think she is afraid of Capper?"

"No," Doyle said immediately. "She is worried about Capper."

"But he's not the killer." Acton said it with certainty.

Doyle had come to the same conclusion but didn't know why. "Why so?"

"The scene was clean—the SOCOs couldn't come up with anything. It was a professional hit, and Capper does not fit the profile."

Doyle contemplated the surprising news that the stable area where the trainer had been shot was cleaned of any forensic evidence; if there had been a hair out of place, the Scene of the Crime Officers would have found it. "There'll be a bullet in his head, surely. That's a start."

Acton shook his head. "The shot was a through-and-through and the bullet removed from the scene. Severed the spinal cord but avoided the carotid artery."

She stared at him. "That is meticulous work." She hoped he noted the apt use of the word "meticulous."

"Are you warm enough?" They were sitting in the car, but he had turned the ignition on to run the heater. Apparently she was no longer in the doghouse, thanks be to God.

"Yes, thank you, sir. I don't think it was Capper either, but I'm not sure why. I think it was because she was afraid for him—she was that shook." Doyle thought about it, holding her cold fingers to the heating vent; she had forgotten her gloves. "Can you call her—get her to meet you somewhere? She's in a state, I think, and would tell you what she knows."

She could see he was reluctant as he ducked his chin for a moment. "It's late; I have to drop you."

This seemed a minor consideration, in light of the recent dire events. "I can take the tube, sir—there's a station up a few blocks."

He made no reply and she prompted, "Tell her you'll pay her for information. Or better, let her think she can have her way with you."

At this, he lifted his head to meet her eyes and Doyle had a quick impression of annoyance, or exasperation—or something. My wretched tongue, she thought with extreme regret; I am too flippant by half. "Sorry—I didn't mean to suggest you should sacrifice your virtue on that particular altar, sir. But she was indeed smitten by your *beaux yeux*."

It was a running joke between them; he had once used the phrase when advising her not to be influenced by a handsome suspect's protestations of innocence. At the time, Doyle was forced to confess she didn't know what he meant. When he had explained the idiom, she was heartily amused. "D'you think I'm so desperate, then, as to be castin' my lures at convicts? I thank you for the compliment." He had begged her pardon with his rare half-smile, and now the term was a byword between them.

He put the car in gear and pulled into the street. "It's late; I'll wait a day to see if she contacts me. If she doesn't, then I'll contact her."

Doyle counted her tasks on her fingers. "I will start tomorrow on witness interviews and see if there is *anythin'* forensics can give us—I'll beg them, if necessary. CCTV tape, too. And I'll do background checks on all visitors and employees who had access." She was determined to be very thorough after her earlier lapse—without ballistics or prints they were relegated to fieldwork and it would be a hard slog.

He nodded, thinking. "Add the barkeeper, Giselle, and the pub owner to the background checks."

"Done." She hoped she'd remember—she tended to forget things if they weren't written down, which was why she was constantly scribbling in her occurrence book.

"Would you like to get something to eat? It has been a long day."

She felt as though it was nearly time for breakfast. "No thank you, sir. I'm bound for home—I'm that weary." She was careful never to accept his occasional invitations to dine—she knew he offered out of courtesy, but she didn't need to add more fuel to the resentment that was already rampant among the other fledgling detectives. Very few had ever met Acton, let alone worked a case with him, as he was not one to feel duty-bound to educate the youngsters. By all rights, Doyle shouldn't have come within calling distance of a homicide for at least another two years and as a result, there were some mutterings about favoritism and the usual suspicion when a young female was mysteriously aligned with a more powerful man. As a result, she was careful never to appear overly familiar with him, not that it did much to quash the rumors. It was an unfortunate state of affairs, but Doyle was going to hang on to this opportunity like grim death and everyone else would just have to deal with it. Once, though, an enterprising detective sergeant had taken a different tack and had begun a practice of lunching with her at her desk for the express purpose of finding out as much about Acton's methods as Doyle could relate to him. The strategy must have paid off; he was suddenly promoted and transferred to counter-terrorism and she did not see him again.

They drove back to the Met in what Doyle believed was a companionable silence. At first she had been uneasy around

Acton, even though he was unfailingly polite and considerate to her. There was no denying he was a bit odd, as brilliant men sometimes are. He was one of the few people Doyle found difficult to read, and it threw her a bit off balance, not to be able to guess what he was thinking. He was not one for idle conversation, and sometimes he would study her silently as though she were on a slide under a microscope. It had been unnerving at first, but she had become accustomed to his ways and now she felt they got on well; he had even begun to show glimpses of humor. She believed he enjoyed their work together—when she wasn't muckin' it up, that was.

Reminded, she asked, "Should I start a report, then, sir?" She kept her voice carefully neutral.

"No need. I will report."

There was a pause while she tried to decide if she should apologize yet again or if he would indeed throw her out of the car.

"Constable," he said into the silence, "you are remarkably foolish if you think I am going to grass on you."

She let out her breath in relief; her humiliating episode in the tack room would never see the light of day. "Thank you, sir. I won't be puttin' a foot wrong again, I *promise* you."

He gently corrected her. "I'm sure you will, but you must try to be more careful. This is dangerous work; you must never become complacent."

"Yes, sir." She hung her head like a good penitent.

"Shall I drop you home?"

With a smile of gratitude, she nevertheless demurred. "I should fetch my tablet from headquarters, sir." This was an excuse; she wasn't going to do anything tonight but go straight to bed. The truth was she was embarrassed to show him where she lived—it was that grim. She was still paying off debts from when her mother was sick and was little by little trying to save enough to move someplace nicer. Next year, she assured herself—next year I'll live in a finer place, and I won't be ashamed for Acton to see it.

They arrived at the parking garage where the unmarked vehicles were housed and walked toward the garage lifts—she noted he was heading to the building with her rather than to the premium garage where his personal car would be parked. "Aren't you goin' home, sir?"

"No; I have something to see to."

His office was in the adjacent building across the elevated walkway, so they parted in the lobby.

"There may be some late evenings until we come up with a working theory," he warned as he called the lift for her. "I hope you have no plans." She had the impression his gaze was suddenly sharp upon her.

"No plans, sir," she said mildly, which had the benefit of being mostly true—she had the dreaded church thing three days hence, and she half-hoped the case wouldn't be solved by then so she needn't go. Coward, she scolded; take hold of your foolish self.

"Good—we'll start in tomorrow, early." He said nothing further and she nodded in acknowledgment as the lift doors closed.

As she rode home on the tube, she reflected that whether it was night, day, or weekend probably didn't matter much to him; he was all business and no nonsense. An "ascetic," that's what he was, Doyle thought in satisfaction. She had been trying to improve her vocabulary ever since the *beaux yeux* incident.

CHAPTER 3

*H*ER HANDS WERE BEAUTIFUL EVEN THOUGH SHE BIT HER NAILS TO *the quick. He tried to avoid thinking about her hands touching him; he couldn't risk a rejection, couldn't risk the loss of daily interaction. She had a small mole at the juncture of her hairline and the nape of her neck.*

The next morning Doyle approached her desk and was mentally reviewing the coming tasks for the day when she noted that her supervisor was lurking about her cubicle, awaiting her arrival. Not that Inspector Habib actually lurked in so many words—he was a very precise and dignified Pakistani man who took his job seriously. However, she was aware he was emanating impatience even as he stood and patiently watched her arrival.

"Mornin', sir." She greeted him in the cheerful fashion of a dosser trying to obscure the fact she was aware she was late for work and wondered what could be afoot that Habib would be waiting for her. After mentally reviewing her recent performance, she decided that she probably wasn't getting the sack, as long as Acton held faith. Habib was full of news, however, and wouldn't be waiting for her unless it was important. Of all mornings to oversleep—although surely she deserved it after the late hours the night before. She unloaded her rucksack from her shoulder and awaited events.

"I was unable to contact you through your mobile," Habib began, his dark eyes opaque.

"Oh—I'm that sorry, sir." She dug her CID-issued mobile out of her rucksack. "I had it on vibrate, I'm afraid." Because she needed some sleep, for the love o' Mike. Checking it quickly, she noted there were two calls from Acton and two from Habib. Back in the doghouse, she thought with an inward sigh; I should take up permanent residence, I should.

"DCI Acton came by to leave a note." Habib's careful diction managed to wordlessly convey his disappointment that she had not anticipated such a visit and had instead chosen to be unavailable. "He asks that you meet him at this address."

He handed her a note written in Acton's spidery hand. *Giselle murdered,* it said, and listed an address in Teddington.

Giselle murdered. "Mother a' mercy," she breathed, staring at the paper.

"Indeed." Habib said nothing further but regarded her with an unblinking gaze; Doyle realized he was curious but could not bring himself to ask an underling what the note from the chief inspector meant. He was very punctilious about all things hierarchical (using the fancy words, she was), but on the other hand, he was not going to interfere if one of his DCs was consorting with Acton and thus bringing glory to his team.

Doyle gave him a quick explanation of Giselle's connection with the trainer's murder from the day before as she texted Acton that she was on her way. "We were interviewin' her late last night, and I think she wanted to talk. Someone else must have been thinkin' the same thing."

"That is disappointing," Habib agreed in a grave tone. "But it is also encouraging."

Doyle saw what he meant. "Yes—we were on to somethin'. And this time maybe there'll be some evidence." Even the most careful killer could make a mistake—Acton had once told her it was always best to kill someone with a single shot from a distance, as though this piece of information was something that could be of use, and she had assured him solemnly she would keep such advice close to mind. It was true, though; a murder at close quarters was too hard to contain. The SOCOs were the next thing to magicians—they would find something.

She didn't want to keep Acton waiting and shouldered her rucksack again. "Do you mind if I use an unmarked to drive to the scene, sir?"

Habib blanched and Doyle could hardly blame him. She was not the best driver, having recently learned, and had a spotty record with the unmarkeds.

"If it is necessary," he replied with stoic fatalism.

She spared the poor man with a smile. "Never mind, sir—I'll take the tube. It's safer for the public, an' all." She grabbed her coffee canister and headed for the tube station across the street.

Once standing in the crowded train, she sipped her coffee and tried to concentrate—crowds were always hard for her to handle; too much sensory input at the same time and all the mixed signals always made her a bit anxious. In addition, she was trying to quell a feeling of inadequacy—she should have picked up on something the night before; should have known that Giselle was in danger. It was as though she was given bits of insight that seemed of little use, sometimes, which was extremely frustrating. Perhaps instead of being annoyed that the newly deceased was shamelessly flirting with the chief inspector, she should have been paying closer attention—she may have noticed something that only she could notice. With a mental shake, she took herself in hand; dwelling on perceived deficiencies wasn't productive; she had been given a gift and was trying to do her uncertain best with it. In all things, give thanks.

Upon her arrival at Giselle's building, Doyle noted that a small crowd had formed around the entrance where the police had set up a cordon. It was a questionable neighborhood, and many of the inhabitants did not appear to be gainfully employed, so there were more lookers-on than usual for a weekday morning. She showed her identification to the PC guarding the entrance, and he directed her to the appropriate floor. There was no problem finding it; the flat was crawling with SOCO personnel and swathed in yellow tape. Curious neighbors were congregating in the cramped hallway, abuzz with excitement while Doyle shouldered her way through and as she passed them, Doyle heard little that was flattering about the recently departed. Although she had not been working homicides long, a basic tenet of human nature had emerged; if you were murdered, the immediate reaction was that it was your own fault.

Ducking under the yellow tape, she entered the flat and spotted Acton speaking with the forensic photographer near the windows. Only mild sunlight glinted through those windows, but the place was hot as an oven, the sickly sweet smell of decomposition heavy in the air. She met Acton's eye as she pulled on latex gloves, and a slight nod indicated she could examine the body. She walked gingerly toward what remained of Giselle, careful not to step on the congealing pool of blood and tissue. A violent crime, it was, but Doyle didn't flinch; she had discovered long ago that she was not the queasy type and tended not to think of the sad remains as the person—the person was long departed, and hopefully to a better place. She crouched down and scrutinized the body, careful not to touch anything without Acton's permission.

Her work with the illustrious chief inspector had taught her to observe minute details she might otherwise have overlooked—details that may later turn into case-breakers. He was justly renowned for his analytical powers and would explain to her that humankind had a set number of predictable reactions to certain stimuli; therefore, it was important to notice when the reaction did not make sense, given the stimulus. He was also trying to help her understand the science of it—the physics and the biology that nowadays were just as important as motive and opportunity. It was the forensic evidence that won cases, as she well understood.

Giselle had been shot in the face, so there was little left that was recognizable. Shot at close range with a large-caliber weapon and it didn't look as though there had been a defensive struggle—although the forensics morgue would be definitive on this. She had been dead for less than twelve hours, from the looks of it, which placed time of death shortly after Doyle and Acton had spoken with her. She wondered if Giselle still had his card in her purse and remembered the girl's arch flirtation as she'd held it in her red-nailed fingers. Those fingers were now lifeless, the red nails rather incongruous but intact, which would indeed indicate there had not been a defensive struggle.

Sitting back, Doyle observed the position of the body and its location in the room. No—no sign that she had been trying to flee to an exit; perhaps she had been pleading with the killer rather than trying to fight or flee—it couldn't have been much of a surprise, the weapon was a large-caliber and therefore not easily hidden—especially if there was a silencer, which seemed likely if no one heard the shot in these close quarters. Of course, it was possible Giselle had known about the gun but didn't think it would be used against her; what a terrible moment it must be when you realize you are wrong.

Acton came over to crouch beside Doyle, and they both considered the evidence in silence for a moment.

"I'm sorry you couldn't get through to me this morning, sir." She made the apology as a matter of form; she'd known immediately upon entering the room that Acton was not unhappy with her.

"No matter; you had a late night," he replied in a mild tone. "But I did have an anxious moment or two."

She glanced at him, puzzled, and he indicated Giselle's remains with a nod of his head.

"Oh—I see." He had been concerned she had met the same fate, apparently. "I'd left the mobile on vibrate, I'm afraid."

"Yes—I realized that must have been the case when I checked the GPS unit in your mobile and saw that you were en route to headquarters."

She made a wry mouth. "That is excellent detectin', sir."
Acton was a wily one; mental note.

He continued almost apologetically. "I would appreciate it if
you kept communication open at all times."

She turned her head to meet his gaze and said sincerely, "I
will. I am sorry I gave you a turn, sir." There had been a suppressed anxiety underlying the last words that was rather
touching—he must think her a sorry excuse if he thought she
would let some crazed killer have his way with her.

But the moment had passed and he was back to business.
"No sign of forced entry. The landlord says she had a variety of
men visiting at odd hours over the past few months; he thinks
more than one had an Irish accent."

This was of interest; the witnesses had said the dead trainer
was Irish, and Capper was Irish. Giselle, however, was not—
Doyle could tell when an accent had been erased and Giselle
had not emigrated from the old sod.

Acton indicated the fatal wound. "What do you think?"

"A lot of firepower. And it makes such a crackin' mess; perhaps he didn't plan on doin' this when he came in."

"I think he did." Acton turned the body so that the mangled
mass that used to be the back of Giselle's head was in view.
Doyle studied it. "Where's the bullet, in the wall?"

"Not here."

Doyle met his eyes in surprise. "He took it again. He used a
weapon that was so powerful it would not leave the bullet in
the skull."

Acton rose and pointed to a splinter that was protruding
from the window frame. "Pried it out."

Perplexed, Doyle looked over the murder scene. "Surely
there must be trace evidence left behind; the place is a sham-
bles."

Acton shook his head. "He had plenty of time to clean it up.
He knows his forensics—he even turned the heat up."

"So time of death is obscured." The temperature of the body
would be unnaturally high; they wouldn't have a target time

for witness interviews or review of the CCTV tape; not immediately, anyway. Doyle was silent, thinking it over. There was something a bit chilling about such cold-blooded calculation; a professional killer was a different breed.

They rose to their feet and Acton continued. "We'll have to do it the hard way; I'll have the landlord come down to headquarters to look at some photos of Watch List persons of interest—Irish, as well as track personnel. Show photos of Capper and the barkeeper while you're here. I would also like you to review the surveillance tape of the lobby for the past twenty-four hours and anything available from the CCTV in the street."

Doyle hated reviewing surveillance tape, which was a tedious job usually given to first-year DCs such as herself. "Perhaps I should show her photo around at the track?"

Acton rested his gaze on what was left of the dead girl's face for a moment. "No."

Doyle knew better than to argue. He glanced up at the curious residents who were jostling for position behind the cordon. "Check for witnesses who can place her coming in last night, and find out if she was alone."

Acton then gave instruction for the removal of the body as the forensic photographer took a few last photographs. When the team began to unfold the body bag, he turned back to Doyle. "Where is your latte, Constable?"

Always one for noticing the details, he was. It was true she started her mornings with her favorite latte concoction from the corner franchise—she shouldn't be so addicted to the expensive vice, but there it was and there was no resisting it. This morning, however, she held a travel canister from home, which she lifted in ironic acknowledgment. "It's Sav-Mart's finest generic brew. It's economizin', I am."

He looked at it, then back to her. "You alarm me."

"It is the eighth wonder of the world," she agreed, and took a sip.

But he was not going to let it go and continued to regard her as though she were the next thing to a homeless person. "Is the wolf at the door, Constable?"

Blushing and uncomfortable with this inquiry, she resorted to flippancy, as was her wont when she was blushing and uncomfortable. "Not a'tall, sir. My rental was raised and I can save twelve quid a week if I cut back—it's an unhealthy habit and past time. I'm debatin' whether to go full bore and give up half-and-half, although it may well kill me."

Acton rendered his half-smile at her light tone, and it seemed as though he wanted to say something but thought the better of it. To get past the awkward moment, she pulled out her occurrence book in what she hoped was an efficient manner and made ready to hunt for potential witnesses in the hallway. As she turned, however, he caught her elbow. "Hold for a moment, please."

She waited in surprise while he lowered his head to hers—his hand remained on her arm, and she couldn't remember another occasion when he had touched her. He then said quietly, "If you ever need anything—a loan, or—anything; you need only ask. I would be honored."

Mother a' mercy. She could feel the hot color flood her face as she protested, "Oh no, sir—I have plenty of money. I am rigorously savin' a down payment for a condo—almost there." They looked at each other, and she couldn't help but reflect that his coat alone was probably worth two months' rental. "But I do thank you for the offer, sir—I'd have no back-up plan, else."

The coroner's team had hoisted the body onto a gurney, and so there was a general movement out the door as the clean-up phase began. Doyle took the opportunity to recover her equilibrium as she moved toward the group in the hallway—Acton had always shown little interest in her personal life and so she was thrown a bit off balance, although she had managed to use the word "rigorously," so there was that. And to offer her money, of all things—she was certain that protocol forbade him from offering a loan to a subordinate. It surely was a sign of the apocalypse.

To take her mind off it, she spent a very patient hour listening to tales of the Jezebel from the neighbors who vied to outdo each other with the result that much of what they told her was not true. Doyle found it rather sad—there was nothing like getting one's self killed to find out what everyone thought of one. She dutifully jotted down all variety of wild theories while reflecting that it was a terrible thing to be murdered; all foibles and weaknesses were brutally exposed to public scrutiny, and yet no matter the weakness, no one deserved to die in such a way. She showed a photo of Capper around, and one neighbor identified him as the current boyfriend. No one was sure if he had been visiting over the past few days, and overall, the consensus was that the victim had got no less than what she deserved.

Acton came out to join her and indicated she was to finish up, which was just as well as she was learning very little that was useful. They descended the steps in silence, past the knot of spectators on the sidewalk who murmured among themselves when they recognized Acton. The spring weather had turned and it was a fine day.

"Where are you parked?"

"I came on the tube, sir."

He was angry suddenly—she could feel it. The only outward indication was that his words became clipped as he strode along. "Why does your supervisor have you travel to a crime scene on the tube?"

Afraid poor Habib would suffer Acton's wrath, Doyle protested. "No—it was my own choice, sir." To tease him out of his temper, she smiled up at him. "It's a wretched driver I am, and two of our poor unmarkeds have suffered at my hands in the past year alone."

The anger was gone and his mouth relaxed. "I had no idea you were so dangerous."

"You live and you learn, sir," she replied piously.

She thought for a moment that he was actually going to laugh; he contained himself, however, and was back to business. "Send me an email tonight at close and let me know where we are. If you learn anything particularly startling, call or text my mobile."

"Yes, sir."

"I'll give you a lift," he said firmly.

"Lead on," she said agreeably.

He was on his mobile on the drive back to the Met, requesting that Danny Capper be brought in for questioning. He returned a message from the detective chief superintendent and then was discussing available conference time with someone when he turned to Doyle, who hadn't been paying attention. "Are you available to conference day after next at four? We should have forensics by then."

She found herself blushing again and stammered, "No—I mean yes, if necessary."

He turned back to watch the traffic and continue his conversation. "Not good. How about tomorrow? We'll expedite the autopsy and toxics won't be important." He raised his eyebrows in question at Doyle, and she nodded to show she was available.

"Good." He disconnected and addressed Doyle. "We'll conference with Research and Forensics then. DCI Drake's team will attend."

"Grand." She had never been invited to a conference before, being as they were not intended for the lowly likes of her but only for those with dispositive authority. Acton was mentoring her again, bless him. She'd best study up.

He drove in silence for a moment or two and then asked in a neutral tone, "What's happening day after next?"

"Oh no," she protested, laughing. "Thus far today I've had to confess I'm pockets-to-let and I'm a wretched driver, and it's still morning. I'll suffer no more humiliations, if you please—it's more than a body can bear."

"Suit yourself," he said with a smile.

CHAPTER 4

*H*E DISCOVERED WHAT SHE WAS ATTENDING TWO EVENINGS HENCE *and it was a cause for concern. There was the financial problem to be addressed, also. He considered concocting an inheritance or perhaps a long-lost pension from her mother's employer, but he felt certain she would guess. She was no fool.*

The remainder of the day was spent slogging away in the field, reviewing surveillance tape and interviewing secondary witnesses who had been neighbors or workmates of the two victims, and at the end of it Doyle had nothing of interest to text to Acton. It was a very strange sort of case, she thought, gazing with furrowed brow at her screen. The forensics pointed to a professional killer, but the victims didn't point to a professional killer; there was no indication that either the trainer or Giselle had come a cropper with the sort of people who would hire a professional to finish them off. It was almost as though the killer was practicing, or showing off, or something. Or perhaps he'd gotten his assignments mixed—nothing worse than a mixed-up assassin, one would think—but no; Giselle had let him into her rooms, so she must have known him. Very strange, it was.

After carefully assembling what little information she had gathered, Doyle went in to work uncharacteristically early the next morning to prepare herself for the conference—it was not clear if she would be called upon to report and so she wanted to be up to speed on every detail. She had never been very good at detail—tending instead to instinctively jump to the heart of matters—but in this line of work the tedious details could not be overlooked, particularly in a case of this nature where a nice, juicy clue was needful. It would be so very fine if she could impress Acton with a case-breaker, but it seemed unlikely, given what they knew.

With steely determination, she resolved to go over everything yet again once she was at her desk and was aided in her endeavors by a latte, exactly to her specifications and delivered to her desk by a messenger. She stared at it for a full twenty seconds, wrestling with her conscience. Her conscience didn't win, and she briefly considered thanking Acton with a text but decided he would not want her to thank him—she knew him that well, at least. "*Sláinte,*" she said aloud, and drank it down.

Inter-team conferences were set on a regular basis as a means to cross-check for ideas within a basic command unit when cases became tough to crack or—as in this case—when different homicides appeared to be related, raising concerns of a serial killer. At least two DCIs would participate, along with pertinent staff to brainstorm ideas and information with the aim of encouraging fresh insights. The conferences were developed as a remedy for past problems when detectives, competing for attention and promotions, had become territorial and secretive about their cases to the extent that information acquired that might have been helpful to another case was instead withheld.

The practice was a good one—setting aside for a moment the fact that a first-year DC such as her fair self would almost never be involved. She double- and triple-checked her information and then decided to wear lip gloss to appear older than she was; as she did not usually wear makeup, it was a telling measure of her state of mind.

Armed with her lip gloss, she decided to ask Habib for suggestions. It would be diplomatic to defer to him since he could theoretically control her assignments, although there was no question he would, in turn, defer to Acton. On a practical level, Doyle was aware that her days as Acton's helpmeet could be numbered, and so she was careful to burn no bridges—someday she may need to come crawling back to her supervisor and beg for decent assignments. Besides, Habib seemed a knowing one, and she wanted to hear his opinion.

After she sought him out, he listened to her synopsis of the case thoughtfully, sitting up very straight in his chair with his arms crossed before him and his feet flat on the floor. "It seems apparent the two murders are by the same killer," she concluded. "A professional, we think, given that the scenes were wiped clean."

He bent his head once in acknowledgment. "Yes. Although there is much more emotion in the execution of Giselle."

Doyle thought it over. "Because he shot off her face."

The Pakistani man nodded with a quick movement of his chin. "Yes. It takes a great deal of anger to do such a thing to a woman."

Knitting her brow, Doyle was not certain she agreed. "He used a large-caliber weapon so as to retrieve the bullet, we think."

"There are much easier ways to kill if that was the concern—and professionals normally do not face their victims."

This made sense, and Doyle could only agree. "So he was angry at Giselle—it was personal."

"Perhaps." Habib, ever cautious, was not going to commit.

Doyle bit her fingernail. "But the anger was not obvious to her, not enough to make her try to get away from him. There were no signs of forced entry or a struggle; she allowed him to approach her."

"That is true," he agreed with another quick nod. "His anger was not overt."

An excellent word; Doyle made a mental note to use it.

Habib continued, his demeanor thoughtful. "There is a strong emotion beneath the anger. It may be sexual in nature."

Doyle was impressed; sometimes Habib sounded a lot like

Acton. "Acton and I don't think it's the boyfriend, though, because we don't think he killed the trainer and one would think the same man did both—it's someone who knows his forensics."

"Then look for other suspects," Habib suggested, "—others who would be enraged at this woman."

Doyle had rather thought the killing was to keep Giselle from talking to the authorities, but what Habib said made sense; this killer, so meticulous, shouldn't have been so vindictive—not if he was merely eliminating a perceived leaker of information. If there was a sexual aspect, it would mean the investigation had to cast a much wider net, given Giselle's proclivities. "A rival for her affections, jealous of the boyfriend? Or perhaps the other way 'round—Giselle had a rival who wanted Capper and so she was eliminated."

"Not a woman," Habib pronounced with certainty. "It was not a woman's crime."

Doyle decided she wouldn't challenge this assumption, which seemed a little simplistic—she hadn't been doing this very long, but she'd seen some first-rate nasty women capable of doing some first-rate nasty things. "But by all accounts this is not the standard love triangle—it started with the trainer's execution, perhaps in connection with a money-launderin' scheme, although we haven't found anything definite. It seems odd to suggest there may be a sexual aspect to it."

Habib bent his head in acknowledgment. "Perhaps, perhaps not—but there must be a commonality; we have only to understand why the woman was murdered so brutally compared to the other."

Doyle nodded, thinking such an understanding a tall order, given there was so little to go on.

As if reading her mind, Habib suggested kindly, "You would do well to ask the chief inspector for his opinion, or DC Williams, who also may have good suggestions."

With a nod, Doyle took the implied vote-of-no-confidence in stride; Habib was very capable and fair to those under his supervision, but Doyle knew he felt—a cultural thing, to be sure—that women had no place in this type of police work, where grubbing about with the bottom-dwellers was not for the faint of heart. As for Habib, he was single, appeared to have a nonexistent social life, and was intensely dedicated to his job. Pausing in reflection, Doyle realized that she fit the same description and so perhaps shouldn't be so judgmental. "Thank you for your help," she said in her best I-should-really-be-cooking-something tone of voice.

"You are welcome," Habib said gravely. "It is an interesting case."

CHAPTER 5

*H*E MONITORED HER LAPTOP AS SHE WORKED; HE LIKED TO SEE HER *thought processes.*

Doyle was the first to arrive at the meeting room on the fifth floor and slid into a chair toward the far end of the conference table. After setting up her laptop, she leaned down to check her teeth in the reflection on the screen, hoping against hope that she appeared competent and professional and humbly asking any available saints or holy angels to see to it that she didn't make any obvious mistakes that would make Acton look foolish for having recruited her. It was true the two of them had an exemplary record of solving cases thus far, but it was also true she was a first-year and they were an odd pairing. He had taken a professional risk by enlisting her to work on his cases, and she did not want to let him down; his approval meant a great deal to her.

The second person to appear was a slightly plump, cheerful woman wearing a white coat over her clothes who smiled upon Doyle as she breezed into the room. Carrying a file in one arm and a doughnut in the other, she paused to offer her hand, temporarily holding the doughnut in her mouth. "Forensics," she mumbled as rainbow sprinkles were dislodged. "Fiona from Forensics—Morgue."

Doyle shook hands and introduced herself, feeling self-conscious.

"Are you working with DCI Drake?" Fiona's eyes held a gleam of speculation.

"DCI Acton, instead."

"Ah." The gleam was quickly extinguished. Fiona took a seat and they were joined by a research assistant named Sid who also shook hands all around. He was about Doyle's age and the type of man who spent a lot of time in clubs. He sat next to her and began chatting her up, as she was female and it was second nature to him.

Acton then entered, already in conversation with his counterpart, DCI Drake. Drake was about Acton's age, tanned, and had a luxurious head of hair that was apparently a source of some pride. He also had a reputation for being overly friendly with female subordinates, which had landed him in the soup on more than one occasion. Technically, the racecourse murder had occurred in his territory, and so he was the other presiding officer for the meeting—he had been out of town at a sex-trafficking conference, and Acton had been called in to handle it instead.

They sat and Acton began by thanking Fiona for expediting Giselle's autopsy.

"Nothing to it," the woman demurred, wiping her hands with a napkinette. "Opened her up over lunch yesterday."

"Same shooter?"

"Hard to say. I can offer something, though. The bullet was not a through-and-through on the trainer. Instead it was removed with a delicate instrument; I'm guessing a surgeon's probe. The bullet lodged near the nape of the neck, an inch off the spine. It wouldn't have been too difficult to remove with the right tool."

This pronouncement was met with the surprised silence it deserved. Faith, thought Doyle; here's a wrinkle.

"Residue?" asked Action.

"None on either. My guess it was wiped away with alcohol or something that evaporated with no trace."

"Caliber?"

"Large for her; not so large for him."

"So not the same weapon," mused Drake.

Acton offered, "He may have wanted the bullet to exit her head to retrieve it more easily, after having to operate on the trainer."

Doyle decided there was no time like the present to put forth Habib's theory. "Or it may have been a crime of rage."

The others turned to look at her. She decided they couldn't have been more surprised if her laptop had spoken.

"How so?" asked Drake, intrigued.

"It was a vicious way to be killin' a woman, face-to-face—and there are less messy ways to leave no evidence."

"Good point." Drake eyed her with renewed interest. "The boyfriend, then? He was present at both scenes and they had a falling-out."

Doyle could not very well point out that her instinct had told her that Giselle had been lying about the falling-out, so instead she offered, "The crime scene did not lend itself to a crime of rage, though—no forced entry and no sign of a struggle." She realized she had not used the word "overt," and mentally chastised herself. "And the trainer's death seems to be a different pathology altogether."

Acton steepled his long fingers, his eyes hooded. "I didn't think it was Capper on the trainer; the work is professional. But he was present at one scene, directly connected to the other, and is behaving like a prime suspect."

To Drake this seemed to be what mattered most. "Better find him. Any leads?"

"Not as yet." Acton said to Fiona, "Anything else?"

Fiona brushed the crumbs off her report and went down the checklist. "Not pregnant, some alcohol. Smoked a lot. No defensive wounds—but you already know that. Hair and fibers are in the lab and will take another day or so. Nothing startling that I could see; just routine. We should have tox screen results in a few more days."

"Thank you," said Acton.

"Always a pleasure." Fiona smiled her cheerful smile at him and stood to re-gather her file. "Nice to meet you," she nodded to Doyle as she left. Interestingly enough, this last was not true, and Doyle watched her exit with some surprise. She had the brief impression the woman was sad for some reason, despite her pervasive cheerfulness.

Drake leaned back in his chair and contemplated the ceiling. "So if the boyfriend is not shooting her in the face, who is? And doesn't that make it seem it may have been two different shooters?"

Acton shook his head slightly. "She was killed just after we interviewed her—we had the impression she was getting ready to grass. And the clean forensics seems too much of a coincidence."

"Maybe he was only trying to obscure identification by shooting off her face," suggested Sid, who had not contributed to this point.

Doyle could see that Sid had a drug problem, couldn't concentrate, and was trying to cover it up. "Perhaps," she responded diplomatically. "Although the shootin' did occur in her own apartment."

The participants sat in silence for a moment, each trying to concoct a scenario with little success. Drake asked, "Any drugs around? Personal items missing?"

"No—no drugs and her purse held nothing unusual." Doyle paused, suddenly struck, and turned to Acton. "I didn't see the card you gave her in inventory, sir."

Acton drew his brows together, considering. "It should have been in her purse—in the outside sleeve."

"Yes," Doyle agreed. "I remember that's where she put it."

"The killer took it?" With a small smile, Drake shook his head in bemusement. "Maybe he's planning on giving you a call."

"I wish he would," said Acton, and it was the truth, which only reminded Doyle that Acton was not your ordinary hail-fellow-well-met.

"It was a good thing I was away," joked Drake. "I could have been the lead on both of these."

"Let's look at the participants. What did you find on background, Constable?" Acton turned to Doyle.

On cue, she recited what she had learned, trying not to speak too fast, which is what she normally did when she was nervous. "The shooter covered the surveillance camera in the lobby of the building with tape; he must have known it was not a live feed. There was a camera on the street, but there was nothing useful. He knew how to avoid it. Giselle had no priors; neither did Rourke, the pub owner. Danny Capper did two years for larceny and was barred from workin' at the track by the racing association, which may explain why he took off when we were knockin' about. Smythe, the barkeeper, has no priors but is a known associate of the dead trainer, who was on the Counterterrorism Watch List."

Drake whistled softly. "Where was the trainer from?"

"Ireland." Doyle tried not to look self-conscious but knew she failed miserably.

Drake spread his hands and made an exasperated sound. "Oh, well—practically everyone from Ireland is on the Watch List. That doesn't mean much." He smiled at Doyle. "No offense, Constable."

"None taken, sir." You will never make chief inspector, my girl, she thought with resignation. Not wi' this accent.

"Any working theories?" asked Drake, speaking to Acton. "Everything suggests a professional except when it comes to the way Giselle was killed; was he trying to send a message to someone, perhaps?"

"Perhaps," Acton agreed slowly. "Perhaps the manner of death was a warning of some kind. I don't think its Capper, however; plus I'm not convinced he'd be foolish enough to shoot his girlfriend in her own apartment."

"No hint of violence in his record," added Doyle, who was aware that Acton's unease stemmed in large part from her truth-detecting abilities, which could not be cited before present company.

"If it was a surgeon's probe, the killer might have been a medico connected with the track," suggested Sid.

Good one, Sid, thought Doyle; I hope you clean yourself up and keep your job.

Acton nodded at him and said to Doyle, "Cross-check medical and veterinarian personnel who worked at the track for criminal record or known associates involved in doping or money laundering. Follow up on the men in Giselle's life in the event it is something unrelated."

"Should we start with the presumption the two murders are connected, then?" asked Drake.

"Until we can definitively say otherwise." Acton's dark brows were drawn together. "I don't believe in coincidences."

And I don't believe I made any mistakes, Doyle thought with satisfaction, snapping her laptop closed. Good one.

CHAPTER 6

SHE WAS NOT WITHOUT ADMIRERS, AND IT GAVE HIM PAUSE. HE KNEW her; someone would penetrate her defenses and she would be forever loyal to him—it was her nature. He did not know if he could accept a secondary role.

After the meeting adjourned, Doyle watched Acton walk over to the windows to stand with his arms crossed, gazing down toward the street below. She had declined Sid's lunch invitation, recognizing it was made only as a matter of form. A bucko, he was; she had a fine-tuned radar when it came to men of that stripe.

With an eye on Acton, she gathered up her things—she could see that something was troubling him about his business.

"I should have listened to you. It was good advice."

She paused, and as there was no one left in the room, she concluded he must be speaking to her. "Which good advice was that, sir?"

"Giselle."

"Ah. You were not to know she would be killed, after all." Apparently Acton suffered from the same sort of remorse she did; it was a hard thing to feel one should have known, somehow.

He glanced over his shoulder at her. "She was ready to talk, with a little coaxing."

"We'll find someone who knows somethin', sir. No point in second-guessin'." It was interesting that he dwelt on it; he did not seem a dweller to her.

He turned and approached to stand beside her, still deep in thought. "This case has too many variables and no governing theme. Did you discover anything of interest from the neighbors?"

"She wasn't a favorite. Not very friendly; a lot of men in and out and complaints about noise. She had an ex-husband but by all reports was on good terms."

Acton lifted his head. "Did he owe her back support?"

Here was a motive, she supposed. "I will check, sir."

"Phone records?"

"I'm going through them, but there was nothing after ten o'clock that night."

He dropped his gaze to the floor, thinking. "Who called in the report?"

Doyle realized this was a good question; the call had come in so early the next morning that presumably Giselle hadn't yet been missed at work. "I will check," she said again, and wished she had thought of this herself.

He must have sensed she was feeling inadequate because he lifted his eyes to hers and said with sincerity, "You made a good report. It was very helpful."

She smiled, pleased because it was the truth. "Thank you, sir."

He made a gesture indicating they should leave. "Can you come to the canteen? I'd like to pick up something to eat and reassess our working theory."

She wasn't certain they had a working theory as yet, but she was not one to demur. "Yes, sir."

They descended in the lift to the third floor and didn't speak on the journey; Doyle felt it was one of the reasons they were so compatible—neither felt a need to fill up the silences that fell between them. They emerged into the canteen and were met with the familiar faint smell of curry mixed with fish and wet umbrellas, then made their way toward the display cases to survey the offerings. The usual crowd at the canteen was thin at this hour, but there were enough glances thrown their way that Doyle felt her color rise; Acton sightings were rare.

After picking up sandwiches, they stood in line at the cashier, and as he pulled his billfold from an inner jacket pocket, Acton said to her, "My treat, Constable."

She raised her eyes to meet his and knew that the only reason he had deigned to mingle with the *hoi polloi* was because he was determined to pay for her lunch. He met her gaze and she knew that he knew she knew. They regarded one another.

"I see, sir, that it was a mistake to tell you about my financial plans." With a show of defiance, she pulled a bill from her own wallet. "You would do well to be more careful with your money, if I may say so. If you're to be throwin' it after every DC who wrings your heart with a hard-luck story, you'll soon have nothin' left."

He gave her his half-smile and did not move. They were holding up the line. "Just this once," he said in a mild tone. "Indulge me."

But she stood firm, knowing it was a slippery slope. "No. It's for your own good, it is. Have done, please." She dared to scold him and he conceded, amused. As she paid, however, she ruined the effect by adding in an aside, "Except for the lattes, which are very much appreciated." Pride was a sin, after all.

As she followed him to a table, she speculated on what it would take to make him laugh, or at least unbend enough to chuckle. He had come very close several times—she could feel it. It would be a new project for her—to loosen him up a bit. With an exhilarating sense of well-being, she decided that something had shifted between them, starting from his offer to loan her money. Proprietary, is what he was. She was pleased; it was a vocabulary word.

Doyle could feel the interested gaze of passers-by upon them as they ate the sandwiches, and she tried not to look self-conscious— usually her role as Acton's surprising protégé was not so public. Out of the corner of her eye, she saw DC Izzy Munoz hovering nearby whilst pretending to buy a soda from the machine, her ears on the stretch. Fortunately, there was as yet nothing to overhear. Move along, Munoz, thought Doyle, annoyed; nothing to see here.

"It is as though there are false trails being laid."

Doyle refocused her attention on her commanding officer and realized she was at sea. "I'm not sure what you mean, sir."

Acton rested his thoughtful gaze upon her. "As you aptly pointed out, Giselle's death was not an execution; it was an act of rage and probably pathological. But there is no indication she was aware of her danger."

"It was not overt." Good one, Doyle.

"No. On the other hand, the methods are those of a professional. Looking at the motivation for the murders, the two deaths should not be connected, but the removal of the evidence and the fact Giselle was killed immediately after we spoke to her about the first one is just too coincidental."

"The case should fit two different profiles, but it doesn't," agreed Doyle. "It's almost as though he's tryin' to throw us off." They thought about it for a moment, mulling over this odd combination of events. "Was there any evidence that the trainer acted defensively?" She wouldn't know, having been locked in the tack room like a dosser.

"No. He didn't see it coming, either."

"So the killer is innocutous."

There was a small pause. Oh-oh, she thought; got that one wrong.

"Apparently," he agreed.

She realized she was biting her fingernail and desisted. She should really try to grow her nails out; Munoz had long and well-tended nails that Doyle secretly envied. With an effort, she refocused her thoughts. "So it's either someone they know or someone who does not appear threatening."

"Or both," Acton noted.

"Or both," she agreed. "And perhaps the murder of Giselle was so brutal so as to send a message to any other potential grassers."

"Perhaps. But remember she had not yet grassed and as you pointed out, there are cleaner ways to silence someone. I think it is a good working theory; I think he wanted to punish her for his own satisfaction."

She remembered what Habib had said. "A crime of rage that was perhaps sexual in nature."

He met her eyes dispassionately. "Something along those lines."

She nodded, wondering if she had the wherewithal to discuss crimes of sexual rage with Acton. Coward, she thought— it's strictly business; take hold of your foolish self.

Apparently she was indeed a coward because she changed the subject. "Perhaps Sid's idea is a good one, then; it may have been a medico at the track."

Acton's gaze was suddenly sharp upon hers. "Never say you found Sid persuasive."

His tone held an edge of derision, which surprised her—although perhaps Acton had noticed it, too. She said carefully, "I think Sid may need some help; some sort of intervention."

He nodded and then seemed to be deep in thought, which happened on occasion and which usually resulted in some extraordinarily shrewd insights, so she respected the process by keeping her own mouth shut as they finished their lunch in silence. Doyle noted that Munoz was now seated strategically nearby, lingering over her soda and awaiting her moment with all the strategy of a field marshal. There is nothing for it, thought Doyle with resignation; Munoz was not going to let the opportunity pass, but on the other hand, Acton was not one to tolerate toad-eating and the best that could be hoped for was there would be no blood spilt.

"Should I interview the medical personnel at the track, then?" Doyle craved a better field assignment than the one she had been relegated to thus far.

"No," he said immediately. "I will put a DS on it."

She didn't want to challenge him, but it appeared he was forgetting her one—and rather formidable—talent. "I may be of more use, sir."

His gaze met hers, and she could see he debated what to say. "I'd rather not. I don't like this killer; I don't understand him."

She assimilated this comment in surprised silence. It appeared he thought it too dangerous for her to interview suspects even though she would know if lies were being told. She wasn't sure how to respond—it was her job and she was good at it.

He offered, "If we bring someone in, you can watch from the gallery." The gallery was adjacent to the interrogation room where the suspect could be observed unseen through one-way windows. Acton was throwing her a bone.

"Grand," she replied, trying without much success to hide her annoyance.

"Are you reading Trendelberg?"

It was a deft change of subject, and forced her to abandon her inclination to sulk. He had seen the book, then, when she was packing up her rucksack in the meeting room—she had forgotten it was there and hoped he hadn't noticed; a faint hope. Acton noticed everything. "Not exactly," she admitted in a dry tone. "It's somethin' I picked up for your birthday. Since you've spoiled your own surprise, you may have it now instead of next week."

She pulled it out of the bag to hand it to him, and he said nothing—only held the book as though he had no idea what to do with it. His reaction was such that she feared for one horrifying moment she had overstepped. It was a new book by the physicist Acton had mentioned once whilst trying to explain probabilities to her. At the time, she had no idea what he was talking about and she still didn't—she was thick as a plank when it came to such things, which was a regrettable handicap in this business. The book had been on display at a bookstore she passed on the street, and she remembered the author's name.

The silence stretched out and she fought an almost overwhelming inclination to squirm. "Do you have it already, sir? You can exchange it, you know."

"No," he said. "I don't."

He was lying, which was rather sweet, and she hid a smile. He handed it to her. "Will you inscribe it?"

Now it was her turn to stare at it. A crackin' minefield, this was—what should she call him? Sir? Chief? Not Holmes, which is what the young detectives called him behind his back. She wrote on the flyleaf, *To Acton: Many happy returns. Doyle.* He watched her hands as she wrote.

She handed it to him and he reviewed what she had written. "How did you know it was my birthday next week?"

"Oh, I have my ways of obtainin' secret information, sir—recall that I am a detective."

He was very much amused for some reason and met her eyes. "I see that I will have to guard my secrets, then."

Munoz could stand it no longer and at this juncture approached the table in an obvious bid for Acton's attention. "Hallo, Doyle." The girl waited for an introduction, smoothing back her long black hair with a graceful gesture that inspired Doyle to decide she should practice it later in front of a mirror.

Resigned, Doyle made the introduction and hoped she wouldn't regret it. "DCI Acton, may I present DC Munoz?"

Acton stood and briefly took Munoz's hand. "A pleasure to meet you, Detective Constable." He then nodded to Doyle and took his leave with no further ado, Doyle's book in his hand. It was smoothly done and Doyle was all admiration; how useful to have the ability to issue a snub and remain so polite—it was in the breeding, it was.

Munoz watched him go and then sank down beside Doyle, who wished for a moment that she had Acton's resolve. "What were you talking about?" Munoz was fascinated by Acton; she was beautiful and tempestuous and specialized in dating well-connected men. Acton fit the bill.

Doyle blew out a breath. "A case. A case that doesn't make much sense."

"I'd be happy to work his case." Munoz pursed her full lips in appreciation as she watched his figure in retreat.

Openly annoyed, Doyle chided the other girl. "Whist, Munoz—you'll not stay in CID for long if you start makin' eyes at him, I promise you."

Acton having left the room, Munoz reluctantly turned back to Doyle. "He's never married. Do you think he is gay?"

No, thought Doyle immediately, not knowing how she knew with such certainty. She equivocated, "I don't know. The subject has not come up."

Munoz smiled the slow smile that had enslaved many a man. "Normally I don't go for the unattainable type, but they say still waters run deep—I may give it a touch."

"You'd be a fool," Doyle continued, annoyed.

Munoz raised her brows. "Why? Are you having sex with him?"

Doyle was horrified. "Munoz, lower your voice, for heaven's sake—he's my CO."

The other girl smirked. "Turned you down, did he?"

Doyle counted to ten.

At the other's reaction, Munoz laughed. "Oh, give over, Doyle—you can't take a joke. No one thinks that's what it is, but there must be some reason you're in his pocket and it's a mystery, believe me."

Doyle tried to sooth away the other girl's resentment; Munoz was a good detective and ambitious—she didn't like the thought that Doyle had an advantage. "We work well together, is all. We've cracked some thorny cases."

"Habib won't take me off misdemeanor thefts." Munoz tossed back her long black hair in chagrin. "It's not fair."

"No," Doyle agreed. "It's not."

Mollified, Munoz offered to buy Doyle a cup of coffee, but Doyle declined; she was certain that she would not be reduced to plain coffee ever again but decided this was a piece of information Munoz needn't know.

CHAPTER 7

He was on a precipice, painful and pleasurable. He could sense she was not indifferent; he had only to risk it.

Doyle was back at her cubicle researching Giselle's ex-husband and how the call came in about her murder. The ex-husband ran a pawnshop in Southwark and had a record of misdemeanor pleas and convictions, which was rather a surprise, as the licensing authority looked with disfavor upon criminals who ran pawnshops—may as well issue an open invitation for trouble. She could find no order for support stemming from the divorce, so it would appear that money was not an issue of contention between them. The phone records showed they spoke occasionally, and Giselle had called him the day before she died; it may be helpful to discover what they spoke of.

Dispatch showed that the call reporting Giselle missing was from a man who did not leave his name but said he was worried about her. It was made at 0600 hours, which did seem an odd time to be making such a call. Upon discovery of the body, Acton's office was contacted just before 0700 hours because the victim was already in the database as a witness for one of his cases. Acton arrived at the scene shortly thereafter, presumably after ascertaining that Doyle still walked the earth and coming by to leave his note with Habib. There was no indication the caller had ever come forward.

She rested her elbows on the desk and thought about it, staring at the screen. Acton arrived at work early; mental note. She may have to start coming in earlier in the event something came up first thing, like this one—all it needed was for Munoz to be Johnny-on-the-spot one day and take her place. Pigs would fly.

Other than that, there was something not right about the caller. It was too early for Giselle to have been missed by coworkers, and if the man had been a nonwork friend, he would have waited to see if she showed up at work before calling in. In addition, there was no record of a worried friend calling back to check on what had transpired.

Doyle's scalp tingled. The caller was probably the killer—the forensic psychology people would say some killers enjoy standing among the spectators, seeing the results of their handiwork. Doyle may even have interviewed him, which was a chilling thought, but she did not recall speaking to anyone who was trying to suppress the exaltation the killer must have been feeling. She paused, struck. Again, it made no sense; if it was a professional killer—and by all accounts it was—why would he report the murder? A professional would not have hung around to watch them process the scene. On the other hand, the ex-husband may have killed her and been remorseful enough to want her found before she lay in a congealing pool of blood and brain matter for another day.

She was just starting on an email to Acton when her mobile buzzed—he always seemed to ring her when she was ready to report, which was useful, as it saved her from typing up an email.

"Sir, I was just goin' to write you. The report was by an unidentified male caller at oh-six-hundred, which is mighty early to be reportin' a murder. He has not come forward."

"Do you think it was our suspect?"

"Perhaps. Or the husband, feelin' sorry for his misdeed."

"Let's check the CCTV during the time when the scene was

processed for faces in the crowd. And see if Dispatch remembers anything about the call."

"I did, sir." She was pleased to have anticipated him this time. "Nothin' stands out on CCTV; we'll have to do a face-recognition review. Dispatch remembers she had trouble hearin' him. There was a lot of noise in the background, as though it was a public phone."

There was a pause while he was thinking. "I'd like to eliminate the ex-husband; is he at hand?"

"Yes, sir. He runs a pawnshop at Fremont."

"I'll meet you at the parking garage, then."

She rang off, and as she was gathering her things, her mobile buzzed; it was a text from Williams: "RU busy?"

She texted back: "Yes; sorry," then headed toward the lift. Williams was another DC who worked on Acton's cases, although he didn't interact with the chief inspector to the same extent that she did. He had been first in their class at the Crime Academy and was the current favorite of the powers-that-be, including Habib. Williams was reserved to the point where many thought him arrogant, but Doyle knew better; he had offered to help her pass ballistics when she had despaired of it, and she considered him a good friend. Munoz saw him as her chief competition for advancement in the ranks but couldn't despise him because he was tall and athletically handsome and therefore her natural prey. Doyle didn't have time to wonder what he wanted; she was at the parking garage and Acton was waiting by the unmarked to open the door for her.

She smiled and slid in, reading out the address. He would listen to her report on the way over, and she would then take notes on his thoughts or suggestions. We are like an old married couple, she thought; we know our routine. "He is William Blakney and presently on parole. His last run-in was larceny by trick; cheating pensioners—charmin' fellow. There was a call to him from Giselle the afternoon before her death."

Acton thought about this. "How often did she call him?"

"Not very often." She watched him for a moment as he drove and ventured, "If he's the killer, then it does not appear that the two murders are connected. It seems unlikely that a professional would have called it in to Dispatch and then hung 'round to watch the show."

"You are forgetting the scene was cleaned."

She leaned her head back against the seat in frustration; stymied again, and just when she had hold of a semi-coherent working theory. Giselle's murderer knew his forensics; he was a professional. A professional who had called it in, apparently. "Why would he call it in, then?"

"He wanted the murder discovered, and sooner rather than later."

This seemed obvious, but sometimes the obvious was overlooked and needed to be said. She knit her brow. "I wonder why?"

Acton, apparently, had already puzzled it out. "The murder must have been a message, or a warning of some kind. The killer wanted another player to know of it."

"So it is probably not the end," Doyle concluded soberly.

"No," he agreed. "The timing is of interest. There is a reason he wanted her discovered that morning rather than a day or two later. I will check to see if anything of interest was going forward on that particular day."

Doyle debated but decided she was not going to ask how Acton would find out when underworld doings were scheduled. "It is a rare shame that DCI Drake managed to avoid these two cases; they should be his by all rights."

"It evens out," Acton replied philosophically as they waited at a light. "What was Giselle's relationship with the dead trainer, if any?"

"Oh." Here was a wrinkle; perhaps there was indeed a love triangle going on, and the jilted lover was coincidentally a professional killer. "I'll check on it."

They were almost to Fremont and he glanced at her. "Blakney may be dangerous; have a care."

Still smarting from his refusal to let her interview the medical personnel at the racecourse, she retorted, "Perhaps I should just stay in the car, then." The moment the words came out of her mouth, she was horrified and desperately tried to backtrack. "I didn't mean that the way it sounded—I'm that sorry, sir." Her wretched, wretched tongue.

With a quick movement, he pulled over and parked the car, then shifted in his seat to face her. Holy Mother of God, she thought; I am getting the sack.

He ducked his head, gathering his thoughts, and then met her eyes. "You are very competent, but you have not the seasoning you need to help you judge when a situation is dangerous. Sometimes you are impetuous."

She listened and repented. "Yes, sir."

"The tack room."

She nodded. Excellent case in point.

"You learn in this business that anyone is capable of anything. I don't want you to be hurt."

This last was true, and she nodded again, ashamed of herself.

He watched her for a moment. "Do you understand?"

"Yes, sir. I am so sorry."

He turned to restart the car, irritated. "I wish you would stop apologizing to me."

"Well then; I won't anymore." Apparently, her wayward tendencies had not been curbed by the lecture.

A smile tugged at his mouth and the tension was broken. Almost a chuckle, she thought, relieved. But I am still too flippant by half.

The pawnshop was typical of its genre—a small and overcrowded establishment with iron bars protecting the windows. A variety of items were displayed on shelves with the more expensive items, such as jewelry, in locked glass cases. The proprietor watched them come in with a sullen expression, drawing on a cigarette. Another smoker, thought Doyle with an inward sigh; I'm to wash my sweater yet again.

"William Blakney?" asked Acton, showing his warrant card.

The man nodded. "This about Giselle?"

Acton leaned against the counter, glancing over the merchandise. "Can you tell us when you last spoke?"

"She called me the night before. Do you know who did it?"

"What did you speak of?" Acton never let the witness run the interrogation.

Blakney crossed his arms on the counter, a movement that displayed his impressive tattoos to advantage. "She was shook up about the murder at the track—they were all of them shook up, I guess. She wanted to know if I heard any rumors."

"Who is 'all of them'?"

He was wary, suddenly. "Her friends. The ones at the Laughing Cat."

Doyle saw Acton glance at her to check for veracity, but this was true.

"What sort of rumors?"

Blakney was weighing what to say. "Whether I'd heard about who did it, and why."

"Why would they think you would know?"

He shrugged. "I hear things, sometimes, in this business."

Doyle thought this an interesting piece of information; one would think a pawnbroker may know of thievery, but little else. Perhaps this man, like Acton, had his finger on the pulse of underworld doings. As Acton had said, anyone was capable of anything.

"And had you heard anything?"

"No."

Acton watched him for a moment. "Do you know any Russian nationals?"

Doyle blinked, as this seemed off-topic.

Blakney didn't like this question and shrugged in a deprecatory fashion. "You meet a lot of people in this business."

The two men looked at each other. Doyle had the impression Acton had more to say but was constrained by her presence. "Did you and Giselle quarrel?"

"Not lately. We used to."

"Why did you break up?"

"She liked men."

Yes, thought Doyle. That was evident; but some man didn't like her.

"Did you kill her?"

"No; if I was going to kill her, I would have done it a long time ago."

Acton was asking the questions out of routine; he didn't think Blakney killed Giselle and neither did Doyle.

"What do you know about Capper?"

He spread his hands. "The latest boyfriend."

"Were they quarreling?"

"I wouldn't know."

"Have you seen him in the past few days?"

He was surprised at the question. "No. I never met him."

Acton glanced at Doyle to verify, but thus far the man had not equivocated in the least. An honest pawnbroker, she thought; give the man a prize.

"Did she have a relationship with the trainer?"

He looked at them, amused. "I doubt it. He wasn't exactly heterosexual."

Oh, thought Doyle; there goes the love triangle angle.

"Were they friends?"

Blakney considered. "She would mention him; I think they were friendly. She wasn't happy he was killed."

Doyle took down Blakney's information and he agreed to call if he heard anything further. The man watched Acton warily as they left, not having moved from his stance at the counter. It was the comment about the Russians, thought Doyle—I wonder what that was all about.

Acton was quiet in the car, and Doyle respected his mood as long as she was able. "Do we have a workin' theory, sir?"

He stared straight ahead and said absently, "Not as yet. I would very much like to speak to Capper, with you to listen in."

"Any leads on him?"

"There are too many—that's the problem. He could have gone to ground any number of places. "

She ventured, "The case is a ball of snakes, it seems—impenetrable." She glanced at him sidelong. Now there was a ten-pound word.

He pulled himself from his abstraction and glanced her way. "I hope my lecture on the way over didn't terrify you. You were cowed, I think."

"Never," she replied with spirit. "I am uncowable."

"What did you think of him?"

She ventured carefully, "I didn't think he was hidin' anything and he didn't seem very concerned. That is, until you scared him, speakin' of Russians."

Acton glanced at her. "He is running illegal weapons. It's common in a shop like that."

She was left to assume it was Russians who were doing the aforesaid gunrunning. "Oh. Will you report him?"

This question threw him for a moment. Interestingly enough, he had to think about how to answer. "It depends."

Doyle's scalp tingled. She bent to fish around in her rucksack, sheathing her occurrence book as she added casually, "I imagine runnin' guns must be lucrative, to take such a risk."

There was another pause. "I imagine so."

Mother a' mercy, she thought. Mother a' mother a' mercy.

He changed the subject. "Let me buy you dinner."

With a mighty effort, she pulled herself together and smiled at him. "Are we to arm wrestle about this again? I may be poor but I am prideful."

He bestowed a rather warm look upon her. "I promise I won't lecture you."

"As much as I enjoy your lectures, I am off to church tonight." She paused. "You are welcome to come along."

He teased her. "What would you do if I accepted?"

She laughed aloud at the picture thus presented. "Why, I'd parade you through St. Michael's like a holy conquest."

He chuckled.

There it was—an honest laugh, she thought with satisfaction. Good one, Doyle; on to the next project, which may necessarily involve trying to keep the exalted chief inspector out of prison.

CHAPTER 8

*H*E *SAT AT HIS DESK, DRINKING SCOTCH AND DECIDING THAT HE* *really had no choice; he could not go on as he was. He ran his hand over the book she had given him; back and forth, repeatedly. He would couch it in terms that were least threatening to her and work from there.*

The next evening Doyle received a call from Acton just as she was finishing up. She hadn't heard from him at all during the day, which was unusual—he must be hip-deep in trying to make some sense out of this nonsensical killer before the wretched man haled off and did it again; she had certainly drawn a blank. Her best theory could not withstand the light of day—she wondered if perhaps the killer was indeed a professional but called to report the crime so as to watch as the scene was processed—to see how CID handled it. Quality control, so to speak; perhaps he thought it would help him determine how to evade identification. She didn't know if she could broach said theory to Acton—he may humor her, and she hated it when he humored her.

Taking the opportunity to catch up on her other cases, she tried to organize the assignments on her desk. She was not very organized; on the other hand, she suspected that Acton was OCD. We amalgamate, she thought with satisfaction—now, there's a good word. Of course, there was the little problem of illegal gunrunning, but the more she thought about it the more she thought she must have crossed her wires and misunderstood. It happened sometimes—she'd leap to a conclusion that wasn't warranted. That little run-in with the dry cleaners came to mind. And it was ludicrous to think that a chief inspector at New Scotland Yard was some sort of underworld figure; ludicrous. She paused for a moment, trying to remember if ludicrous meant what she thought it meant, but then decided she wasn't going to think about it just now, she was going to think about this wretched case that made no sense.

Her best working theory was so lame as not to count, and she knew that when Acton couldn't come up with a theory, he simply processed the evidence without the distraction of a theory. In this case, since there was so little hard evidence, it meant questioning witness after witness and running backgrounds, hoping to notice something of interest. Therefore, when Acton buzzed her at the end of the day it was a welcome respite.

He sounded a bit weary himself. "I may have a tip that Capper will make an appearance at a friend's house. I think I'll stake it for a while."

This was encouraging. Doyle had begun to think perhaps Capper had been killed as well. If he was still alive, his going to ground would indicate he was trying to avoid questioning. While they didn't think he was their killer, he must know something or he wouldn't be playing least-in-sight.

"Where is it, sir?"

"An address on Grantham Street. It's possible he'll show up there tonight—are you free?"

"Yes, sir." Of course she was free; it was her job. He only asked as a matter of form, but she didn't mind; it had occurred to her that after the pawnshop visit, they had been bantering in the car. Who would have thought Acton could banter? The stakeout could be interesting instead of mindlessly boring. It must be a good tip; stakeouts were usually left to lesser beings such as herself—he must truly think Capper would show up.

"I'm in an unmarked. I'll swing by and pick you up in front."

She was packing up her rucksack when Williams leaned into her cubicle entryway, his broad shoulders filling it up. "Doyle."

"Williams; I wish you were on this wretched case."

Williams had a lopsided smile that was rather charming, all the more because he didn't bestow it often. "Shall we brainstorm? We can get something to eat." He was wearing a steel-blue sweater that brought out the blue in his eyes, and she breathed in the faint scent of cologne.

"Sorry. I'm due on a stakeout and I'm on my way out—next time; I promise."

"I'll go with you, Williams." Munoz had overheard from the next cubicle and appeared beneath Williams's arm, giving him her brilliant smile. "Where shall we go?"

Williams, poor soul; you don't stand a chance, thought Doyle. She met his eyes for the briefest moment and saw an answering gleam of amusement before he followed Munoz out. Ah; I stand corrected—Williams is nobody's fool.

Doyle took the lift up from the basement and walked through the lobby and past the security desk to the front of the building. Hopefully the stakeout would not last too long; this case was making some serious inroads into her sleep. And for some reason she didn't feel optimistic about finding Capper tonight; something in Acton's voice—

Acton was pulling up to the curb just as she walked out, and she hurried over to get in so that he wouldn't have to explain to the patrolman in front that he was waiting for her. Good timing, she thought; he must have been close by.

She slid into the unmarked as he took her rucksack and placed it in the back seat; then they drove away into the miserable Westminster evening traffic. With some surprise, she was immediately aware that he had been drinking, although there were no discernable signs. He said nothing and she said nothing, but she covertly observed him, wishing she knew the protocol for a DC to tell a DCI that he shouldn't be driving. Of course, there was the very real potential that it would be just as dangerous for her to attempt to drive, and so she held her peace and hoped for the best. After a few moments she relaxed; he seemed competent to drive, and truly, there was no indication other than her sure knowledge. He may have come by the tip at a pub; he did not offer to tell her and she did not ask. No bantering tonight, she thought with a pang of disappointment; he seemed preoccupied.

They arrived at the Grantham Street address just as darkness fell and sat in the unmarked watching the house from across the street. Occasionally a car would drive by, but there was no sign of activity at the house. It was a very quiet neighborhood.

He said little for nearly an hour and seemed disinclined to talk, and as she had little new to report, she respected his mood and stayed quiet. It was the longest he had ever gone without taking a call, and she wondered if he had turned off his mobile. She finally shifted her position and ventured, "Not a lot to see, so far, and it's dinner hour. Was it a reliable tip, d'you think?"

"No more or less reliable than the usual," was his rather equivocal answer. He tapped his thumbs on the steering wheel. "I hope it isn't a wild-goose chase."

She didn't want him to feel badly if it was a false alarm and assured him, "It is well worth the possibility of takin' in the duplicitous Mr. Capper, sir." Now, there was an excellent vocabulary word, and deftly used. She hoped for an opportunity to use "innocuous" again, now that she had straightened it out.

"What would you ask him?"

She smiled. "Before or after I beat him with a nightstick?"

He considered. "After."

So; perhaps there was to be bantering after all. "I'd ask him if he killed Giselle. Then I'd want to know who he is afraid of, and why he didn't want to ring her up that night but wanted to meet in person, even though he knew the coppers were after him."

"Good questions." He nodded with approval.

"You, sir?" She glanced over at him. The light from a street-light slanted across his face so that his eyes were illuminated.

"I'd ask what was so important that he risked arrest to go speak to a man at the track he didn't know who could get him in a lot of trouble—and then why he stayed to wait for the police."

Doyle hadn't even thought of this. "Your questions are better," she conceded.

"Yours were just as good."

"Please don't humor me," she pleaded, half joking and half serious. "I hate it."

There was a pause. "Fair enough," he said, and meant it.

She felt a little foolish, and subsided. He spoke into the silence, "If nothing occurs within the hour, I will call for relief."

"I am fine for as long as you need me." She was trying to make up for her fit of the sulks.

But Acton was not to be outdone. "No; I have imposed upon you. I hope you didn't have to scuttle any plans."

"Free as a bird, sir." Although there was an instant meal in her freezer that was calling her name—she hoped her stomach didn't start growling.

"My mistake; its tomorrow that you're booked. A seminar, I believe."

She blinked, wondering how on earth he knew of this; she would not have confessed to it under torture. As they were being overly kind to each other, she admitted, "I wouldn't mind missin' it, truth to tell—do your best to get hold of another tip for tomorrow, if you will."

He leaned an arm on the back of the seat and turned to her, intrigued. "You attend under duress? What is the topic?"

She made a wry face and glanced again at the dark house, trying to decide whether it was too embarrassing to tell him. He did ask, though, and she didn't like to lie. "It's a singles mixer, disguised as a self-help seminar so as to preserve our dignity."

"Ah—I see. What is the protocol?"

She appreciated his making light of it, and unbent. "It's a shameful process, truly. We are given a profile of all persons attendin' so that we can discreetly eye the possibilities whilst pretendin' to listen to a speaker. Then we're supposed to assess our 'shape' and create a 'rubric of our potential compatibility' with the other poor souls. As a reward for survivin' the ordeal, there is punch and cake afterwards. It sounds horrifyin' and I may lose my nerve—it is a wretched, wretched pity at times like this that I don't drink."

There was a pause while he ducked his chin, considering. "What is wrong with the men of London that you must resort to this?"

It was a sweet compliment, and much appreciated. She smiled and disclaimed, "Faith, I suppose it's not a bad idea. In the first ten minutes of a blind date you know whether it's hopeless, but by then you've committed to the whole evenin'. This saves you a great deal of time and trouble." She paused. "And I know for a fact they're going to serve plum cake, which is an added incentive, as I couldn't possibly date anyone who likes plum cake."

"Are you seeking a companion?"

She was startled by the tenor of the question, but his interest seemed genuine and she didn't want to embarrass him by being embarrassed. Choosing her words, she replied, "I feel obligated to make a push, I suppose. It's a bit difficult for me to mix with people—" she halted abruptly, wishing she could take the words back. Doyle, she warned herself in horror, you *knocker*, don't speak of it—

But he said with much sympathy, "Yes, I imagine it is."

For some reason, she felt the sting of tears and had to compose herself for a moment; she was a solitary soul for all the obvious reasons and she was touched that he understood. Of course, he was an oddity himself—they were kindred spirits, in a way. With an effort, she pulled herself together and said lightly, "I'd invite you to come along, but it's through the Holy

Mother Church and you'd throw a rare wrench into the works."

He tilted his head forward and contemplated the house for a moment. "I have a different sort of problem, meeting someone."

This was unexpected. Why, I believe we are having a personal conversation, she thought in surprise. "You astonish me—is it the title or your handsome face?" Acton held a barony that went back generations; it was probably awarded for beating down the pesky Irish.

He reacted to her teasing with a small smile but continued, "You would be amazed how many insincere women are very good at pretending to be sincere."

"I believe it," she said readily. "We meet a good many of them."

He nodded. "Yes, we do. But I am also expected to make a push."

Doyle shook her head in sympathy. "Poor us. It is a truth universally acknowledged, sir."

As he turned to face her again, she noted that all thought of watching the house had been abandoned in favor of discussing the moribund state of their respective love lives—Jack the flippin' Ripper could emerge from the Grantham address and she would bet her teeth that the illustrious chief inspector would not notice.

"I think the solution to our mutual problem is to marry each other." His dark eyes met hers.

There was a moment of stunned silence whilst she could feel her heartbeat in her throat. Holy Mother of God; he was dead serious, and he knew she knew he was dead serious. Tamping down panic, she bit her fingernail and pretended to consider it. "I wouldn't have to worry about makin' detective sergeant."

"We are compatible," he continued as though she hadn't spoken. "We spend a great deal of time together already; our lives would not change very much."

For once, she could think of nothing to say, flippant or otherwise. She had never noticed how long his eyelashes were.

"I think it a very sound idea." They regarded each other in silence, and Doyle wondered if anyone had ever died from excessive blushing. When she did not respond, he reached over and put his hand on her arm, briefly. "I'll not press you; think on it, please."

"All right." She added as an afterthought, "sir."

As he pulled the car out, he glanced over at her. "You look as though you have been put to the stake."

She rallied. "No; my feet are too cold."

He smiled. "Better."

With a monumental effort, she calmed herself. "It's not—not that I don't appreciate the offer; I am surprised, is all."

"Understood. I'll drop you home."

He did drop her home—he knew where she lived. He walked her to the security gate, and she wondered for a panicked moment if he was going to try to kiss her. He didn't, which was a little annoying in its own way—marriage proposals usually involved kissing, one would think. Perhaps it wouldn't be that kind of marriage.

"I'll see you tomorrow," he said, and watched her walk in.

Later, she thought about it as she stood over her kitchen sink as if in a trance and let the tap water run unabated down the drain. She had already come to the conclusion there had never been a tip in the first place; his sole aim had been to propose marriage. Out of the clear blue, Acton had said he wanted to marry her, and he meant it.

With a brisk movement, she turned off the running water and decided she could not possibly eat. She had work to do but found she couldn't concentrate. Instead, she made ready for bed and crawled beneath the covers to stare into the darkness, listening to the silence. He couldn't be serious, someone like him marrying someone like her—generations of Actons would rise from their graves in protest. Faith, generations of Doyles would, too. Despite everything, class demarcations continued to exist, and she would feel like a freak in the circus.

Sleep eluded her. After another hour she repositioned her pillow and reenacted the conversation yet again. She had sensed that he was vulnerable, despite his light tone. She didn't like to think that she made him feel vulnerable—made him feel he had to imbibe some Dutch courage to speak thus to her. If she was honest, she would admit she was aware that he had a—fondness was perhaps the right word—for her fair self. She often caught his unreadable gaze resting on her. There was his surprising offer to loan her money. He had been protective about her attendance at the unit party until she had assured him she did not drink and would be leaving the festivities in short order. There were the lattes, too. But this? Should she have seen this coming? No, she thought in bewilderment; I stand acquitted of leading him on.

He was not like normal men. Not that he was abnormal, of course—well; not truly. But he struggled with it sometimes. He hid his true self. Tonight he was hiding his true self; he was humoring her. Again, she hated to think she made him feel vulnerable. He can trust me, she thought, he should know that by now.

Looking yet again at the clock, she wished she could read him better, and she wondered what he was thinking right now. For that matter, she wished she knew what she was thinking, even thinking about it—the whole thing was a pint full o' ridiculous, as her mother used to say. She hardly knew him and people didn't marry when they hardly knew each other—this wasn't the Middle Ages. He had no business making it sound so reasonable or meeting her eyes in a way that took her breath away.

There was always the possibility that he had been drunk; with the strong and silent type sometimes it was hard to tell. He hadn't *seemed* drunk, but she could not be certain. Perhaps he would be embarrassed by his lapse of decorum and would never mention the subject again. Only he had, and she had caught herself entertaining the idea for a mad, mad matter of moments; how easy it would be to simply agree. Even if he never mentioned it again, it would change everything between them; if she knew nothing else, she at least knew that—*stupid* Acton and his *stupid* proposal.

She finally decided that she had no option but to await events; she'd best get some sleep and gird her loins for whatever tomorrow brought—if she botched her job, she'd be left with no other choice but to marry out of her class.

CHAPTER 9

*H*E STAYED PARKED OUTSIDE HER FLAT WATCHING THE LIGHTS GO ON *and then, after a small space of time, go off. He used his binoculars but didn't glimpse any movement. It had gone as well as could be hoped; the idea was not repugnant, he could see it in her eyes. He doubted he would sleep.*

The next morning Doyle planned to avoid dwelling on the one subject that must not be dwelt upon by spending several mindless hours cross-referencing the two murders in an attempt to find a new lead. It was a good plan, but before she had gotten under way, Acton himself appeared at her cubicle—think o' the devil and up he pops.

She could feel herself blush to the roots of her hair. "Good mornin', sir."

"Good morning, Constable." Yes, there was a definite awareness in his eyes—so much for the theory that he had been insensibly drunk. "Possible homicide in Somers Town; let's go."

Grabbing her rucksack, she kept pace with him down the hallway and into the lift while he nodded to the respectful underlings they met along the way. He usually avoided such by meeting her at in the utility garage, but this morning he had come to get her rather than call—probably because he didn't want to give her the opportunity to duck him. As if she would—she was made of sterner stuff and therefore made a point of smiling at him in the lift to show she wasn't thrown. She then ruined the effect by pressing for the wrong floor, but he returned her smile as he corrected her mistake and so she felt the ice was broken. He said nothing and she said nothing. She longed to look at him from the corner of her eye but resisted the urge; she was a professional and should be able to maintain a certain decorum, after all. He gave no hint that he was thinking of their conversation last evening, and she would take her cue from him; if nothing was said, well, then—that was that. He is very tall, she thought, and gauged that she came up to his shoulder—she hadn't tried to gauge it before.

Acton gave her a briefing in the car as she jotted down almost indecipherable notes and wondered if he had noticed that she had decided to wear perfume today—or eau de cologne, more appropriately, as she couldn't afford real perfume. He gave no indication that he was at all distracted by this unusual occurrence, however, and recited the facts with his usual brevity. "Man and wife in Somers Town—both dead. Looks to be a murder-suicide but the duty PC is suspicious enough to call us in."

"You should give it to DCI Drake, sir; tit for tat," she replied, then fervently wished she hadn't said "tit."

"I was requested, apparently. A reference to bloodstains." Acton was the grand master of bloodstains.

So; the scene was another bloody one. Despite the awkward circumstances, Doyle felt the avid interest she always felt when there was a call to sort out humanity's carnage. She loved this job; no need to get all doe-eyed over a handsome man. And she meant handsome in a dispassionate sort of way, of course.

They drove the remainder of the way in their usual silence. In the cold, sober light of day Acton had apparently decided to overlook their conversation of the night before, and it was just as well, she reminded herself. She should heed the advice she gave Munoz—no good would come of getting too personal with him, being who he was and all. The sleepless night of wondering "what ifs" was best forgotten.

Their destination was a war-era building located off St. Pancras in Somers Town, a less affluent area that saw more than its share of criminal behavior. Two PCs awaited their arrival at the front entrance; a sergeant was upstairs securing the scene.

"Have the SOCOs been called?" asked Acton of the female PC.

"No, sir, we await your opinion," she responded with a great deal of respect.

"Who called for me?"

"I—I did, sir," stammered the other as he looked upon Acton with a mixture of awe and fear.

I imagine I looked the same that first morning I met Acton, thought Doyle, and smiled at him to put him at ease. His name tag said OWENS, and he seemed young, even to Doyle. Owens was excited about the case, although he was trying to appear professional; it must have been his first murder. Blackburn, his counterpart, was by contrast not excited. She doesn't feel well, Doyle knew; a bit green around the gills, poor thing.

"Come inside," said Acton, and Doyle followed while the patrolmen led the way.

The bodies were on the floor in the dining area of the shabby flat, the man's right hand clutching an illegal large-caliber handgun and the woman's face nearly blown away by a blast from the gun. Another woman shot in the face, thought Doyle with interest—must be the new style. There was a bright spray of blood spatter on the wall and on the floor near her body.

The man's head showed an entry wound on the right temple, with obvious residue marking the wound as close range. As was always the case with large-caliber, the exit wound was a mangled mess above the left temple, and brain matter and blood were spattered on one wall. There was little blood on the floor near the man, which was usually the case with a standing suicide, as the heart had stopped beating before the body hit the floor. A sergeant was already on site, having followed proper protocol by cordoning off the area and securing the scene once the CID detectives had been called in.

"Nothing has been moved, sir."

Acton gave the sergeant a cursory glance and then surveyed

the scene while Doyle did the same. She noted that Blackburn, the female PC, looked everywhere in the room save the remains of the slain woman's face. Doesn't like this job, Doyle concluded with sympathy; will be putting in for a transfer very soon.

Doyle assessed the rigidity of the bodies and tried to take a guess at time of death. The scene had all the earmarks of a murder-suicide, certainly. Acton seemed to be deep in thought and said nothing for a few moments—she had the brief impression he was wary as he pulled on latex gloves. He had long hands and fingers; with dark hair on the backs of his hands. Breaking her gaze away, she pulled on her own gloves and awaited instruction.

Acton said, "By all appearances it's a straightforward murder-suicide. Why did you call us?"

"Well, sir," volunteered Owens, who was sounding a bit less nervous, "I thought there were some inconsistencies."

Acton lifted his gaze and regarded Owens for a long moment. Poor Owens, thought Doyle, but he was handling it well, by which she meant he had not been reduced to tears.

"Proceed," said Acton finally.

"Sir, I don't believe the man could have held on to such a large-caliber gun after shooting himself. The recoil would have flung it away from him."

"I see," said Acton, who had not taken his thoughtful eye from Owens. "Anything else?"

"The bloodstains, sir. The angle is slightly off for a right-handed man."

"What do you know of bloodstains, Constable?"

Owens appeared to be gaining confidence and revealed, "I have read Westin's tract on bloodstains, sir. The illustrations are very illustrative." He caught himself, realized this last sentence sounded inane, and tried to make a recovery. "I am interested in forensics, sir."

"Then I suggest you call in the SOCOs and have them made aware we believe there was a third-party killer—well done."

"Yes, sir," said Owens, and Doyle could feel the relief and pride emanating from the young officer as he moved off to contact the Evidence Recovery Unit.

Good one, she thought; it is a fine thing to feel you have out-smarted a killer.

Acton crouched and scrutinized the bodies, Doyle following suit by his side. She reviewed the kill site carefully, noting the brain matter spattered on the wall, the blood spray patterns, and the gun. It took a careful eye to notice the details, which turned a garden-variety murder-suicide into an unsolved mystery, and the young constable may have the makings of a good detective.

While she was assessing, Acton broke into her thoughts. "Have you been thinking about my offer?"

She met his eyes, startled; so—it wasn't off the table, after all. And how nettlesome that he brought it up now—did he really want to discuss this while knee-deep in brain matter, for heaven's sake? Off balance, she blurted out the truth; "I thought you were bosky, sir, and the subject wouldn't arise again."

Almost imperceptibility, he flinched. "Unkind."

She stared at him and felt her throat constrict with remorse.

Constable Blackburn re-entered to advise them that the forensic photographer and the SOCOs had arrived. She looked to Acton for instruction, but he had not taken his eyes off Doyle and did not respond, and Doyle could not respond either because she found to her great distress that she was going to cry. Knocker, she thought in horror—take *hold* of your ridiculous self. In a panic, she fixed her eyes on the floor so that she could blink away tears before the others saw.

"Constable, give us a moment, please." Acton took Doyle's arm, pulled her to a standing position beside him, and then swung her into the tiny kitchen and closed the door behind them.

Doyle stood numbly in the dim and dirty kitchen, wholly embarrassed and brushing away tears with the flats of her fingers. She hung her head, too ashamed to look at him as she struggled to get the words out, her voice thick. "I *am* unkind; you were not drunk. I am too flippant and I would say I'm sorry but you will not allow me." She gasped to suppress a sob. I am a complete knocker, she thought in extreme distress—it is a rare wonder this man wants me.

"No; I am sorry to distress you," he said very gently. "I'll not mention it again."

This, however, was unthinkable. She raised her head resolutely to meet his eyes and with a monumental effort, brought herself under control. "No, no—it's not you. I didn't sleep well last night." She drew a ragged breath and hated the thought that she was lacerating him again—he who hid his vulnerability so well. "I don't think it's a terrible idea, truly." She wasn't certain where this thought came from, but once she said it she knew it was true.

She watched him search her eyes with his dark ones—there were flecks of gold around his irises and his proximity was affecting her concentration. She swallowed. "Perhaps we should try havin' a date first or somethin'."

"Is that your answer?"

Bewildered by his insistence but finding, paradoxically, that it pleased her very much, she confessed, "I don't think I can give you an answer—someone once told me I was too impetuous."

"Don't listen to him."

She had to smile. "Who are you, and what have you done with the chief inspector?"

He bent his head and she could sense the vulnerability again—a wave of it, deep and unfathomable, so that she said without thinking, "You can trust me, you know. I would never use it against you or embarrass you—" She broke off, uncertain as to why she was offering him comfort.

But he went on, and she caught a glimpse of some emotion so intense it nearly suffocated her. "I have to tell you something."

Oh—it was bad, she could feel it. He is married, she thought in a panic. Or he has former girlfriends all buried in the basement—

"I am a Section Seven."

A silence followed the quiet words. They stood, their gazes locked whilst she tried to hide her astonishment. It was the pure truth, and it was a reference to the Stalking Act. Be very careful here, my girl, she thought; do not panic. "I see. Is it only me, or are there others?"

"Only you." The intensity began to dissipate, now that he had made his confession.

"Misdemeanor or felony?"

He thought about it for a moment. "Felony."

She raised her brows. "Oh. That *is* impressive."

He chuckled and she chuckled also, the tension broken and the goodwill flowing between them once again. The scent of decomposition wafted in from the next room to mix with her eau de cologne, and she tried to suppress a reckless feeling of euphoria. "Would we have sex?" She could have bitten her tongue; she hadn't known she would blurt out the question she had puzzled over in the wee hours.

"Yes. Definitely."

Almost without conscious volition, she pulled on his lapel, lifting her face for his kiss, and he obliged her.

She had wondered what it would be like to kiss him during her restless night—wondered whether there would be any chemistry between them. She discovered that indeed there was and that it was powerful in its intensity. The kiss rapidly evolved into a deep, openmouthed, clinging embrace that banged her with a soft bump against the wall; his hands—sheathed in the latex gloves—began liberally exploring her body, molding her against him. She broke away to gasp for breath and cradle his head in her hands as his mouth moved along her throat, the heat of his hands at her waist and penetrating to her skin. She had lost all sense of where they were until he pulled at her shirt and lifted his head. "Let me lock the door."

The quiet remark acted upon her like a bucket of cold water; this was not the time nor the place for a sexual initiation. She disengaged to pull away and they stared at each other, breathing heavily. She stammered, "We're—we're on duty."

Amused, he smoothed a tendril of hair back from her face and leaned in to kiss her one last time. "So we are."

While she attempted to tidy her hair, he refastened her buttons with his long fingers, then ran his gaze over her and nodded, assuring her that she was presentable before they stepped out into the crime scene again, Doyle hoping her face would not betray what they had been about.

She needn't have worried; the SOCOs were speaking in low voices with the two PCs and made a show of casually wandering over as though it was entirely normal for an investigation to be sidelined while the chief inspector was closeted with an underling. After several sympathetic glances were thrown her way, Doyle realized they thought she had been taken to task for breaking down like a newbie. Faith, she thought as she tried to settle down; it serves me right—cavorting with the brass.

After the photographs were taken, Acton gave the instructions necessary to process the crime scene and they left the team to finish up. As usual, Doyle was to review the surveillance tape, interview witnesses, and do the background checks. He asked the other officers to send him a report and gave Owens his card, speaking to him briefly.

As they walked out of the building, Doyle noticed that Acton was deep in thought and it appeared it was the crime scene itself that prompted this mood and not the torrid episode in the kitchen. By contrast, she felt as though every nerve was on end and attuned to him as they re-entered the car, only holding her tongue with an effort, which was just as well, considering its recent use. It wasn't until they were nearly back to headquarters that he finally asked, "Would you have noticed what Owens noticed?"

She thought about it. "I am not sure I would have noticed

the inconsistencies unless I was alerted that there was something unusual—it was very sharp work."

He nodded. A silence fell and it appeared he was not inclined to discuss what had passed between them. Never one to pour oil on troubled waters, she finally ventured, her accent very broad, "D'ye think we should have some sort o' discussion?"

"No," he said in a tone that brooked no argument. "No more discussions."

This was only to be expected; she felt herself lucky that he had given her a glimpse. The man is certifiable, she thought rather happily. And so am I for taking up with him.

CHAPTER 10

*I*T HAD GONE BETTER THAN HE COULD HAVE HOPED. HER NATURAL IN-
*clination was to come to his aid and as an added incentive it appeared
she was eager for him—surprisingly so, considering her shyness. There
was another mole just above her medial clavicle.*

That afternoon Doyle was ruthlessly concentrating on the
background search for the slain Somers Town couple—mainly
as a means to keep her from placing her forehead on the cool-
ness of the desk and just leaving it there for the foreseeable future. Anything to keep from stepping off the ledge and into a
future that hadn't even been on her radar screen two short
days ago.

She found plenty of useful information, which was to the
good, as the surveillance tape showed nothing and the neighbors weren't very helpful—although in that neighborhood,
withholding help from the police was an honorable pastime.
The couple had incited little interest and lived quietly, despite
the fact they didn't die quietly. Although no one had heard the
shots—and with that size weapon, it must have been quite a
crack; perhaps it was a commonplace in the building. There
had been no unusual visitors over the past several days. A report had been called in when Helen did not appear for work at
the local restaurant. They had no children.

At least at this scene there was forensic evidence in the form of bullets, although the gun was illegal and therefore unregistered. Even if there were ballistics, it may not prove much, as the mystery was not the weapon but who had fired it and then arranged the scene to appear as a murder-suicide. With a quick breath, Doyle blew a tendril that was tickling her forehead. The case appeared to be another long slog, requiring a lot of footwork by the fair Doyle, who was already being run ragged on the racecourse cases. Faith, she thought; what I wouldn't give for some DNA or a fingerprint or something—the villains were not making this easy.

Which is why she was relieved to see the voluminous background information, as unexpected as it was appreciated—perhaps some leads would develop. The surfeit of information had the added benefit of taking her mind off the one subject that should not be dwelt upon lest she completely lose her grip on reality.

In the next cubicle, Munoz had been pointedly rustling around for twenty minutes. When Doyle didn't rise to the bait, the other girl finally stood and peered over the partition, the fluorescent lights glinting off her raven hair. "Want to talk about it?"

"No," replied Doyle, not looking up.

"Will you be sacked, you think?"

"Hope not." Doyle wondered what Munoz's reaction would be if Doyle were to tell her that she was thinking about quitting so as to pursue a new career as Lady Acton.

"What happened, exactly?"

Doyle paused and considered. "What is everyone sayin'?"

"You were sick at a homicide scene this morning."

Doyle thought about this. "I think 'disconcerted' is more accurate; I needed a moment to recover." And as an added bonus, disconcerted was a vocabulary word.

Munoz was agog, as Doyle's imperturbability was legendary. "And Holmes was not happy," she concluded with ill-concealed relish.

"No," Doyle said truthfully. "Indeed he wasn't, and he took me aside."

Munoz crossed her arms on the top of the partition and made a small sound of intense admiration. "I wish he'd take me aside."

"That's not very professional, Munoz."

"Oh, I'd be professional, all right—he'd not look else-where."

Doyle decided the conversation was a little too ironic for her taste and turned the subject. "What are you workin' on?"

Munoz smirked. "Taking over your cases, since Holmes seems to find you lacking."

With an effort, Doyle held on to her temper. "It's blown over and there is no reason to take me off the cases."

"Tell Holmes I don't faint at the sight of blood."

Stung, Doyle insisted, "I wasn't faint—I just needed a mo-ment. The murders were with a large-caliber gun and it was a crackin' mess."

Munoz's envy was palpable. "I hate you, Doyle. What I wouldn't give for a homicide."

Doyle felt badly; Munoz did have grounds for complaint as it turned out Doyle indeed had an unfair advantage. "Speak to Habib," she suggested. "Tell him you'd like to be an extra hand when the next one is reported."

Munoz sulked, her mouth drawn down. "He'll just give it to Williams—it's a boys' club." She paused. "Except for you. Would you put in a good word for me with Holmes?"

Doyle was exasperated. "If you are civil to me, perhaps."

"Come on, Doyle; we girls have to look out for each other. When he throws you off the cases, mention to him that I'd do much better."

Doyle controlled herself only with an effort. "Leave off, Munoz, someone's coming."

The visitor turned out to be Acton himself. Doyle reflected that lately he spent more time in the cubicled basement of this building than at his fancy office in the other—you're quite the attraction, my girl, she thought, and hid a smile.

Munoz's chirpy "Good morning, sir," received a nod of acknowledgment before he halted in the entryway to Doyle's cubicle. "Constable; would you come with me to the review room?"

She met his eyes in speculation, but he gave no outward indication that he was inclined to maul her about again; therefore, she picked up her laptop and followed him down the hall to the review room. After closing the door, he asked, "Who was that?"

"That was DC Munoz. You met her the other day in the canteen." Poor Munoz, Doyle thought with no sympathy—serves her right for pushing herself forward. "She is castin' a proprietary eye on my cases because my job is in jeopardy, accordin' to the general consensus."

Surprised, he met her eyes, and she explained, "They think you were chewin' me out yesterday. Although to be fair, indeed you were—after a fashion. But I'd rather not explain to all and sundry exactly what's going on until I've had a chance to find my feet, so to speak—" With a mental yank on her wayward mind, she concluded, "I know I'm gabblin' and I beg your pardon. I'm nervous."

"Don't be." He touched her hand with his. "We'll take things slowly."

She eyed him in disbelief at this unmitigated falsehood but didn't call him out; best to think of how to proceed from here. "I know there's not to be any discussion, and I'll bear that in mind, but there are two things I would like to tell you and two things I would like to ask you." Good one, Doyle, she thought. When she had rehearsed this, she had not been sure she would have the courage to say it.

There was a silence. "If you don't mind," she added, her resolve collapsing under his unreadable gaze. Small wonder everyone confesses to him, she thought; I'd be terrified of him myself if it weren't for the fact he was kissin' on me something fierce just recently. She blushed.

"If you wish." He was wary; he didn't like the thought of having to answer questions. Small blame to him, what with the whole Section Seven thing going on.

"Surely there are some things you'd like to ask me," she countered.

"No," he replied with a small smile. "There are not."

Saints and angels, she thought, unable to resist smiling in return. The wretched man's completely nicked, to take the likes of me at face value.

"What have you discovered about the murders?"

Back to business, then; apparently there was to be no unbridled lovemaking in the review room—which is as it should be, she told herself firmly. They sat and she queued her laptop to bring up the criminal records of the slain couple and turned it so that he could view the screen alongside her.

"Not your ordinary mister and missus. His prints come up as Grady O'Brien, although there are several aka's—all Irish, I'm ashamed to say. He did time for drug traffickin' and money launderin'. He's been out for over five years—no recent record. She was known as Helen O'Brien but no evidence they had married. She did cons and skirted hard time with community service."

She paused and looked up, as he did not seem to be listening. He read the screen, frowning, then pulled the laptop closer and re-read the information. Recognizing that he was deep in thought, Doyle waited. After a few long moments of profound silence, she ventured, "No immediate leads on who would want them dead, but their records mean there's a wealth of possibilities—a blackmail victim or a fallin' out among thieves."

He lowered his eyes to the table, thinking, and she had a brief and startled impression that he was profoundly distracted. Puzzled, she was going to ask for his thoughts when he re-focused with an effort. "But whoever it was wanted to cover his tracks."

"Yes," she agreed. "It was disguised as a murder-suicide—a closed case."

"So not someone who wanted to send a message." He said it slowly, as if he was testing it out.

She was getting mixed signals from him and was confused. "No, it doesn't appear that a message was sent, so not a turf war. Not revenge." She paused for a moment. "Helen was shot in the face, like Giselle. Perhaps another crime of rage?" Doyle thought this was doubtful. After all, the woman was over forty and didn't look to be one to inspire passion.

At her words, Acton looked up at her, and she had the impression he was struck by something she had said. "Perhaps," he said in a neutral tone, the words at odds with the signals she was receiving. "However, you needn't worry about it. You have too much on your plate already. I'll see to it that the case is reassigned elsewhere."

She blinked in surprise. "Yes, sir." Her caseload was heavy at present, and if this one was reassigned, it would help relieve the grumblings about favoritism. Unfortunately, Munoz and the others would think he had taken her off the case in disgust after her behavior at the crime scene. It doesn't matter, she told herself firmly. I know better. She glanced at him sidelong as he almost absently closed her laptop, still deep in thought. Hard to believe he had been so enthralled by her fair self that he had lost all control; she had a faint bruise near the base of her throat to show for it. She hoped he would touch her hand again.

Rather abruptly, he stood to leave. "Send all the information you've gathered to me, if you please." He paused at the door, and her pulse quickened, despite herself.

But he was not to broach matters personal. "PC Owens has asked to be transferred in as a TDC, a trainee."

She was not surprised. "It is a good opportunity for him to put in for it, havin' met you and done well. He can't be blamed for puttin' it to the touch." She paused, stricken with embarrassment by her choice of words, but he only smiled in acknowledgment. She realized that she had seen him smile more in the past two days than the entire three months she had worked with him.

"I'd be interested in what you think of him," he continued, as though there hadn't been an awkward pause. "See if you can draw him out."

"All right." Here was a wrinkle; Acton must be keen on him, then.

"Shall we have our discussion over dinner?"

"Oh—yes, of course; if you would like," she stammered, unnerved by the switch in topic.

He regarded her with no little tenderness. "Kathleen, there is no shame in our having dinner together."

With a massive effort she calmed down. "I know, sir; I'm afraid it's goin' to take some gettin' used to is all."

He teased her, "You needn't call me 'sir' when we are alone, you know."

"Yes—I do know—" She bit back another sir just in time and then shared another smile with him over it.

"China Flower?" he asked.

"Done." She was very fond of Chinese food.

CHAPTER 1 1

*I*T WAS AN EXTRAORDINARY COINCIDENCE AND HE DID NOT BELIEVE IN *coincidences. Just when everything had gone so well—now all he could feel was a grave uneasiness. It was all the more difficult because he was not yet certain that it wasn't, after all, an extraordinary coincidence. If it wasn't, there was a message here but damned if he knew what it was.*

After work Doyle walked over to Acton's building and then waited for him at the lift in the lobby. He was a few minutes late and apologized, which in itself was a sign of the change in their relationship. "I had to push back a meeting; something unexpected has come up."

"Whist," she said easily. "No need to explain." She was careful not to call him "sir."

They descended the lift to the premium garage, and she was almost amused to discover that any constraint she had felt in his presence had completely disappeared. All prior uncertainties had arisen because he was one of the few people she was unable to read, but now she had a very good guess at exactly what he was thinking and apparently there was little she could do to fall from grace. She ducked her head to hide a smile and was aware that she was very, very happy. She would have touched his arm, but she still felt a little shy around him and besides, there were security cameras in the lifts and the security personnel were not known for their discretion.

Acton drove a new model Range Rover, and as they made their way in the evening traffic to the West End, she admired its finer points. "You'd be ill-advised to let me drive it, though," she confessed with some regret. "It's a hazard, I am."

"You need practice, is all. We'll go out of the city sometime and find a quiet road."

"I would be much obliged." Although men were particular about their cars and there was perhaps no faster way to take the bloom off the rose—not to mention it was hard to imagine Acton off the clock. But in the same way she was consciously trying to be at ease with him, she was trying to imagine how this new and unrehearsed relationship would work. She tested it out in her mind—we are like any other couple, and we will do things together and go places that do not feature mangled corpses. The picture thus presented was so utterly fantastic she decided to think about something else.

Apparently Acton's thoughts were running along similar lines as he threaded his way through Piccadilly. "Have you spoken to anyone about us?"

Here was a question that, coming from him, generated equal parts surprise and alarm. "No one."

He turned to her for a moment, searching her face. "No mention to anyone? No hints given?"

Doyle shook her head. "Not a soul, my friend. Is rumor control a concern?"

He turned back to face the traffic. "I only wondered."

She teased him, "Little risk there, no one would believe me in the first place."

He glanced at her again and she suddenly felt a little warm. "They will."

Here was a thought that made her uneasy—when she was with him, she felt they were well-suited; she was gaining confidence with each passing minute, and she could easily imagine going somewhere quiet together to practice her driving. However, a cold knot of dread formed in the region of her midsection when she contemplated the reaction of the public at large to this monumental mismatch. Not to mention his mother, the dowager. He had mentioned his mother only once, and Doyle had sensed he held her in great dislike; she didn't sound like one who would embrace the fair Doyle to her aristocratic bosom.

"Has anyone guessed, do you think?" he persisted.

With some surprise, she intercepted a glimpse of unhappiness—no, more like uneasiness—emanating from him, startling in that it seemed so out of place and of a tenor that did not gibe with mere concerns about office gossip. "Acton," she said gently. "Tell me what is afoot."

He paused. "I'd rather not, I'm afraid. But I would like an answer."

It was a measure of her respect for him that she did not pursue it; whatever rumor he was trying to quash she was apparently better off not knowing—although she was well-aware there was rife speculation about their association. She thought for a moment. "Perhaps Habib."

"Your supervisor?" He raised his brows in surprise.

"He's very sharp, is Habib. He saw you on the mornin' of Giselle's murder when you were searchin' for me."

Acton frowned. "He doesn't strike me as a gossip."

"Definitely not," Doyle agreed.

Acton mulled it over. "The woman who is your friend from church?"

Doyle blinked. "Nellie? No. She knows who you are, but she doesn't know about us." She didn't mention that there had hardly been enough time to know about "us" herself, let alone tell anyone else.

"How about the dark-haired DC?"

Very pleased that he couldn't seem to remember her name, Doyle said, "Munoz? I don't think she has guessed unless she is trying to spread a false rumor to get me in trouble not knowin' it is, in fact, the truth. Do you understand what I'm sayin'?"

He gave her a look. "She sounds charming."

Doyle chuckled. "Oh, we're cutthroat at the bottom and no love lost, I assure you."

He reached to touch her hand. "You needn't work there any longer, if you'd rather not."

"We're gettin' ahead of ourselves," Doyle replied in a fluster. "Work is one of my two questions."

"I beg your pardon," he said gravely. "I withdraw the comment."

She smiled out the window at the city lights—definite sightings of a sense of humor. This was not so difficult after all. In fact, it was rather fun, except that he was worried that someone knew about their relationship, which seemed a bit odd, as he had not indicated he wanted to keep it a clandestine type of thing. She wondered what he had heard and then decided that whatever it was, it couldn't hold a candle to the truth.

When they arrived at the upscale restaurant, she realized it was a good choice for a private discussion. The back wall of the China Flower was lined with semi-enclosed wooden booths, and it was to one of these they were escorted by a deferential host. As was his custom, Acton sat where he could watch the restaurant and Doyle sat facing him. They ordered, and he opened the conversation by saying without preamble, "I'd like you to start wearing a weapon."

So much for romance, she thought—all in all, this is a very odd sort of date. "I am not authorized to wear a weapon, Acton." The protocol required six weeks of weapons training before a concealed weapon could be carried by a detective.

He contemplated her. "Nevertheless."

She contemplated him right back. "So I'm to ignore the protocol?"

His eyes didn't waver. "Yes."

She considered this. "I suppose I should not be surprised,

comin' as it is from the man who wanted to have his way wi' me in the midst of a sequestered crime scene."

He smiled that rare and wonderful smile. Proud of it, he is, she thought—men; honestly.

"I'd like you to start tonight."

She remembered his questions on the ride over and could not suppress a twinge of alarm. "Is there a particular reason that I should be concerned about my safety?"

He paused, deciding what to say. "Nothing specific. It is a precaution, and your safety is important to me."

This was true, which was a relief. She decided there was no harm in it—at least if she didn't get caught. The fact that she could be sacked and arrested—and not necessarily in that order—did not seem to enter into the equation. Come to think of it, this request was very much in keeping with their conversation after the pawnshop visit, when Acton had been trying to avoid a direct statement that would reveal he was involved in selling illegal weapons. A rare brumble, this was—a DCI selling black market; and here she was worrying about such trivialities as departmental policy. "All right, then. And where am I to get a weapon?" She listened for his answer with veiled interest; obtaining a legal gun in England was the equivalent of pulling hen's teeth.

But as could be expected, he was not going to give specifics. "I have it in the car—it's an ankle holster and shouldn't weigh you down much. I'll show you how to wear it."

Nodding as though this were an ordinary conversation, she privately thought that she'd best look lively and get to weapons training to keep them both out of trouble. She knew how to fire a gun—they had been taught at the Academy—but she hadn't practiced in a while. No question he was concerned about something tonight. Or he might be suffering from a general paranoia; he was a Section Seven, after all.

Their food was served and they began to eat, sharing between them. Despite it being a first date, he showed little curiosity about her past—apparently because he already knew everything. Aware on some level that she should probably be uneasy about this situation, she realized she was not; she trusted him. She knew—the way she knew the things she knew—that he would never harm her. And she knew she made him vulnerable—perhaps was the only thing in the world that made him vulnerable—which in turn made her fiercely long to protect him.

Any attempts to draw him out about his own background were deftly turned aside, giving her a very good guess he didn't want her to have a clear picture of how disparate their lives were. I am a coward, she thought, and I'd rather not know—not yet, anyway. Much of the meal was spent in companionable silence, which was one thing that had not changed between them; neither was inclined to idle conversation.

Nothin' for it, she thought. "I need to tell you two things."

He waited, watching her. Doesn't like this whole discussion business, she thought; but there's no bunkin' it. With a steadying breath, she began her recitation. "My parents didn't have much; my mother met my father at a dance and I made my appearance in short order. My da left us before I was two, so I don't have any memory of him. My mother died of cancer two years ago." She paused, because here it was and no putting it off. "I am not sure that my parents ever married—my mother never spoke of it to me."

"Yes," he said. "There is a record of it."

She stared at him in surprise. "There is?"

He leaned back, his manner matter-of-fact. "You've been vetted, of course, and because you are Irish, it's been very thorough. Their history is in your personal file and it shows they were married at St. Bridget's Church outside of Dublin. It notes you were born six months later." He showed a glint of humor. "I can show you the record, if you'd like, even though it would be against protocol."

"No," she replied, lowering her eyes. "That won't be necessary. Well, that is a relief—I was worried about stainin' the Acton escutcheon." She glanced at him to see if he appreciated the ten-pound word.

"It wouldn't matter to me in any event."

Doyle smiled at him, as it was the truth. "No, I suppose not." There was no question, of course, that a review of the parish records of St. Bridget's would show her parents' wedding. The real question was whether it had actually taken place, and she very much doubted it had. It didn't matter; she would not pursue it in deference to him—she had duly noted that he had couched his words so that she could not spot the lie. He was a wily one, he was.

One tangle patch down, one more to go. She soldiered on, "The other thing I have to tell you is about sex." Ah, this caught his full attention. "Truth to tell, I haven't much experience."

He met her gaze thoughtfully. "That is not a qualification."

She smothered a smile and explained, "And by not much, I mean none."

There was a pause. "I see."

So here was something he didn't know. She tried valiantly not to color up but failed. "Just so you are aware."

"Yes. Thank you."

CHAPTER 12

*T*HEY HAD NOT BEEN FOLLOWED. *HE SAW NO SIGN THEY WERE BEING watched. It was almost disappointing; he didn't like the uncertainty. He didn't like Chinese food either, but he would have to develop a taste for it; she was well worth it. He was almost desperate to touch her.*

"You have two questions," Acton prompted.

"Yes," she agreed, "—and then I'll not be botherin' you with a discussion ever again."

"Work," he prompted. Apparently he did not want to linger over the meal, and this was exactly what she deserved for bringing up sex.

"Can we continue to work together?"

"There is no policy that would prevent it, although I would be precluded from recommending you for advancement." He crossed his arms on the table, clearly having already considered this. "And I imagine if we continue to have success—and if it is a mutual desire—it would not be a problem."

She smiled with relief. "That's grand, then. I wouldn't like to be choosin' between the professional and the personal." His eyes held hers for a moment and she immediately realized her error. "I didn't mean that the way it sounded, Acton; it's only that I do enjoy workin' with you."

The planes of his face softened. "I can't be offended. I know this has happened very quickly; you have every right to be cautious."

"No—that's the wrong tack." She struggled to articulate her half-formed thoughts from these tumultuous two days. "I don't want you to feel you have to be—careful—because of—everythin'." Faith, how did one put this delicately? "Please, I hate it."

He was watching her intently but did not respond.

"Do you understand what it is I'm sayin'"?

"Yes," he said.

He does not want to talk about this, she thought; he hates it just as much. "I'm not goin' to give it up," she assured him. "No matter what."

At his silence she dropped her gaze and fiddled with a chopstick. He was not going to let her in, probably for fear she would abandon ship. She shouldn't push him; he knew himself. Wishing she had paid closer attention in forensic psychology, she concluded, "So you can be yourself with me; or at least as much as you are able."

"All right," he replied, and she knew he was equivocating.

She was compelled to reach across the table and take his hand. As a result, she experienced a jolt of awareness from him that was unmistakable in its heat. Now I've done it, she thought; best hurry this along before he loses all patience and starts mauling me about with the Chinese waiter looking on.

"The second question is a wee bit deep," she admitted.

He seemed equal parts intrigued and relieved by the change in subject and leaned back, crossing his arms before him. "I am forewarned, then."

"Do you believe in God?"

He pondered the question for a long moment, seriously, his gaze moving around the room. "I am open to the suggestion."

This was true, and she decided that this response was better than the one she had anticipated.

"Particularly after recent events." His eyes met hers.

Faith, she thought with no small sense of righteousness—

I've no choice but to continue on with him—it's for the salva-
tion of souls, it is. And the man could kiss.

"I will take instruction if that is what you desire."

She blinked in surprise. "I don't know if they'll take you if
you don't truly feel the call, Acton—I have a suspicion that you
would take instruction in Hindu if that is what I wanted."

His mouth drew down in amusement. "I may draw that line."

"We'll talk about it some other time," she temporized.
"Enough discussion."

She was relieved, thinking she had brushed through it as
well as could be expected and had covered the important
points. She did not fool herself into thinking he would be sharing innermost thoughts with her; she was well-aware he was not
able. In her own way, she was equally reserved—perhaps they
would manage to deal well together. On the other hand, she
would have liked to know more about the details of his life thus
far. It wasn't important, she decided; hopefully he wasn't the
brides-in-the-bath sort.

He drank green tea, which she declined, thinking it a sorry
excuse for a decent cup of coffee. "I contacted Giselle's parents; they live in Yorkshire."

He tilted his head to the side and contemplated the tea. "I
wasn't going to talk shop tonight."

She was touched. "That is very sweet, Acton, but I think I've
held out as long as I can."

He lifted his gaze. "What did they say?" Apparently he was at
the same point.

"There was little contact; they are country people and disap-
proved of her lifestyle. They did say she was to make a visit very
soon, however." A bit sadly, she wondered if there were any re-
grets that they did not have the chance to reconcile or if they
were the type that felt their estrangement was vindicated by
her gruesome murder. "I wonder if Giselle is a dead end, so to
speak—there is nothin' in her background that would be an
indicator. Perhaps we should be delvin' into the trainer's
death—he's the one who started it all, as far as we know."

Acton nodded. "It seems evident he was executed. Usually that kind of murder is a result of double-crossing or self-dealing with the wrong sort of people."

"D'you know what he was involved in, why he was on the Watch List?" Her security clearance wasn't high enough to allow her to research it, and she wondered if Acton would tell her.

Acton did not hesitate, which was only to be expected—come to think of it—as he seemed to have little patience with protocols or even the law of the realm. "He had some unsavory 'known associates' and was believed to belong to a Sinn Féin splinter group that is under scrutiny for suspected arms stock-piling."

But this revelation was puzzling in its own right, and Doyle knit her brow. "I thought Sinn Féin laid down their weapons." She had always steered well clear of the violent political doings in her home country.

"Which is why it is a splinter group," he explained patiently. "It is believed they have turned to black market and are arm-ing some of the zealots who do not agree with the cease-fire."

With an inward sigh, she considered the sorry fact that many of her fellow citizens could not seem to gravitate toward peace—not for the life of them. Or the life of anyone else who hap-pened to be in the way, for that matter. "So—perhaps there's a motive; the Irish trainer was double-crossin' the Irish splinter group, skimmin' the money or somethin' instead of supportin' the cause."

He thought about it, his gaze resting on the party entering the restaurant as a matter of habit. "I do not have a working theory as yet. But it does seem likely the murder is connected in some way."

But Doyle was making her own connection with what she had learned from Acton at the pawnshop. "Or how about your Russians, my friend? Perhaps they're unhappy with this Irish splinter group, if they're runnin' guns also—they'd be com-petitors."

His reaction was to become guarded; his eyes hooded. "There is that."

She eyed him for a moment, but he volunteered nothing further. Interesting, she thought; another forbidden subject—life with this man is going to be a rare crack.

He continued smoothly, "There are other possibilities, of course, and I am looking into his dealings at the track."

This went without saying—there were a lot of temptations at a racecourse that may not be connected to terrorism. The trainer may have been throwing races in some way or taking illegal wagers. Laundering money. The only thing that was clear was the man had crossed the wrong people and had paid the ultimate price.

Recalling his comment about checking for significant underworld events, she asked, "Did you find out if there were any shipments or other goings-on that day?" She kept her tone neutral, not wanting him to know she had a very good guess as to how he came by his own knowledge of such things.

"No, nothing significant."

"Other than Drake was out of town, wretched man; bad luck for us; bad luck for Giselle. Drake would have probably taken her home with no further ado."

"It is a puzzling case," Acton agreed. "Not your ordinary assassin."

Which seemed to be the theme lately among the villains of London, and she reminded him, "Nor were the murders today— the O'Briens were executed, but whoever they crossed didn't want it to appear as an execution, which seems strange; executions also serve as a warnin' to others."

Apparently, however, he was done talking shop. "We'll sort it out later. Shall we go?"

As they walked to his car, he was quiet and she could feel the tension emanating from him, although he was trying to hide it. The moment of truth is coming up, she thought; nothin' for it.

They drove to her building in the rather ragged Chelsea district and pulled up to the curb in front. He then reached beneath his seat to pull out a small black bag. "Here is your weapon." He withdrew a .38-caliber pistol, along with a nylon and Velcro holster and turning on the interior light, he leaned toward her to demonstrate how the safety was released and how to load a cartridge of ammunition in the grip. Doyle watched carefully; she wanted him to have confidence that she could protect herself from whatever it was that was worrying him.

"You may want to go up on the heath and practice shooting into a log or a tree—if you go to the range, they might ask questions."

"Right, then." No question it might raise some eyebrows if she were to show up at the New Scotland Yard shooting range with a black market weapon.

He glanced at her sideways. "Your target scores at the Academy were not the best."

Nettled, she retorted, "I would for once like to know somethin' that you don't do well."

With a gesture, he indicated the two of them. "I don't do this well." She understood that he meant their relationship. "But I want to."

"Well, then; thank God it's only me."

"Yes," he agreed. "Thank God."

She shot him a suspicious glance but could not read his expression in the dimly-lit interior.

"Let me show you how to wear it." He gestured toward her legs.

She debated with a knit brow. "Which one?"

"Whatever feels most natural. As you are left-handed, you may want to wear it on the inside of your right leg or the outside of your left."

She thought it over. "The left, I guess." She lifted her left leg and placed it across his lap, pulling up the trouser leg.

"Practice releasing the safety as you draw. In an emergency you may not have much time." He demonstrated clicking the safety off and on with his thumb as she nodded.

Adjusting the straps, he fastened the holster on her calf while explaining that it should be well-hidden but easily accessible. It was lightweight, and she imagined as long as her pant legs weren't too tight no one would notice—she hadn't worn a dress since confirmation, after all—but she couldn't help but be a bit concerned. "What if someone sees it and I am asked questions?"

He continued his adjustments with deft fingers. "Direct all questions to me." Pausing, he looked up at her. "That should always be your default; in the event you are asked any questions you'd rather not answer."

She nodded, wondering to what he referred and deciding it was just as well that she didn't know. I am indeed too impetuous, she thought, studying his averted profile, but I can't seem to help myself. "It's not very heavy."

"No. Try to wear it at all times." He was finished, and she practiced releasing the gun and taking it out of the holster, her leg still on his lap. He ran his hands along her leg and met her eyes, which had the electric effect of stilling all movements.

A classic moment, she thought; two peelers, a gun, and sex hangin' heavy in the air. Finding her voice, she whispered, "Would you like to come up?"

"Yes. If you would like."

"Yes." She would like. After all, she had bought new linens yesterday in anticipation of this moment.

They rode up the lift in silence; she noted he already knew her floor and her room number. Perhaps burglary was the Section Seven felony—she hoped the place was halfway tidy at the time.

She unlocked her door and then once they were inside, turned to lock it behind them. As she did so, he rested his hands on her shoulders from behind and then ran them slowly down her arms, raising gooseflesh. He kissed the nape of her neck and wrapped his arms around her, cradling her to him. As she leaned back into him with a sigh, his mouth moved along her shoulder and she decided he was probably not interested in a tour of the place. He turned her around to bestow languorous kisses along her throat, and she lifted her chin to accommodate him, listening to her own ragged breathing in the stillness and stroking his torso under his suit coat. He raised his head and began kissing her mouth with increasing urgency, and she could feel him unfastening her buttons as she ran her hands up his back, caressing the lean muscle beneath his shirt.

"Should I turn on the light?" she whispered. She rather wanted to have a good look at him.

He said nothing but seemed very intent on moving his mouth across her cheekbones; the sensation of his face against hers, the stubble of his beard brushing her sensitive skin was almost overpowering in its intensity and she would have crawled inside him if she could. Instead she gasped for breath and pressed against him while his hands moved on her skin, sliding off her shirt. She hoped he noticed she was wearing a much prettier bra than at the crime scene.

"Am I to take off the holster?" she teased breathlessly into his ear, exultant.

He kissed her bare shoulder and brushed his fingers along her arm. "No. I will."

He began to steer her toward the bedroom, and she suddenly felt the need for some instruction. "Acton," she whispered, "should I—"

"Hush," he said quietly, lifting her palm and kissing it. "Less talk."

"I talk too much when I'm nervous."

"I know." He caught her mouth with his.

He wins, she thought. Snabble it, Doyle.

CHAPTER 13

HE FELT AS THOUGH HE HAD BEEN LIVING UNDERWATER AND HAD finally burst through to the surface. He clipped a strand of her hair while she slept and then lay with her, his fingers resting on her sternum, feeling the pulse of her heart.

The following day Doyle arrived at work bright and early, absurdly cheerful—it was amazing what a clandestine relationship could do for one's spirits. No worry of being bored, that was for certain. Almost immediately, Munoz appeared at the entry to her cubicle. You're not his type, Munoz, thought Doyle with satisfaction. I—on the other hand—am, as he made quite clear on multiple occasions last night.

"Drake was here looking for you this morning. What would he want with you?" Munoz was annoyed that another chief inspector was beating down Doyle's door.

"Haven't a clue," Doyle replied, curious herself. "What did he say?"

"He wants you to come by to see him. He said it wasn't urgent." She paused and then warned, "He's something of a letch."

As Munoz was an authority on all things promiscuous, Doyle did not doubt her. "Thanks—I'll be bringin' my hatpin, I will."

She made her way across the walkway and up to Drake's office; she had never been to Acton's office and was curious to see how the upper brass lived—she was rather disappointed to find ordinary offices, not quite as cluttered as those on the lower floors but with the same air of busy distraction. The office door was ajar and she knocked, seeing that Drake was inside and on the phone. He smiled and gestured her in.

At his invitation she sat in one of the chairs facing the desk, noting the array of awards displayed on his bookshelves; he was the type of man who would display all awards.

Drake finished his conversation, rang off, and walked around his desk to lean casually against it while he spoke to Doyle, and it was clear that he believed this pose showed him to advantage. He chatted for a few moments and was definitely friendlier than he should have been with a lowly DC from across the metaphorical tracks. Mother of God, she thought in amazement—another one down.

Flashing his even white teeth, he said, "I came by to tell you how much I appreciated your help at the conference on the racecourse murders. Acton is lucky—you do an excellent job."

I do believe he indicated as much last night, she thought wickedly, but said aloud, "Thank you, sir," in the manner of a lesser being who is humbly grateful. Faith, it was either feast or famine—she was nearly paralyzed with dread, contemplating what she should say if he asked her out on a date.

He then hung his head in a way she could see that he thought was endearing, "I hope that my remark about the Irish did not offend you."

Doyle wanted to laugh aloud. Here she was, thinking every man jack had a fatal attraction to her fair self, and instead he was worried about being written up for sensitivity training; it served her right for being such a vain knocker.

She told him with all sincerity, "Please do not think of it again, sir; I assure you I thought nothin' of it." She added for good measure, "It's a sad day when we all can't tease each other with impunity." She hoped he was impressed with the fancy word.

"Yes, well, Acton mentioned that I'd best be careful—you

never know who might be offended even though no offense was intended."

Of course he did, thought Doyle—the overprotective meddler. "Chief Inspector Acton was perhaps bein' too sensitive." Understatement of the century.

Drake smiled and relaxed. "It's a good trait, though. Between you and me, he mentioned that he thought Sid had a bit of a problem. I checked into it and he's agreed to go to rehab. Never would have guessed it, myself."

Good one, Sid, thought Doyle with satisfaction. And here's another subject Drake shouldn't be flapping his jaws about; he was one who didn't think of such things. "I hope it all works out for him; he had a good idea about the medical personnel at the course."

"Yes, Acton's put the new TDC in to help out in Sid's place, he seems very eager to learn."

"Owens? I met him at the Somers Town murders. Perhaps I'll give him my regards." Poor Owens, she thought—no doubt he would prefer to be learning field work, what with his treatise on bloodstains and all. As for herself, Doyle would rather be tortured than left to do research all day.

"Certainly," said Drake, who stood when Doyle did. "He's down in Research—I'm sure he'd appreciate a visitor."

Thoughtfully, Doyle considered Drake's tendency to give out state secrets and decided to take a cast. "It's a difficult case, sir."

Drake chuckled. "But not on my watch, thank God."

"Do you think it could be the Russians?"

He tilted his head, thinking about it. "Solonik, you mean? No—he'd never be such a show-off."

"Ah."

They shook hands and parted, Drake taking the opportunity to try to glance down her shirt. I don't think sensitivity training would succeed, she thought as she left. But he may respond to electric shock treatment. Men; honestly.

Doyle then descended the lift to Research, where the poor souls did not even have cubicles but were seated at tables piled high with files and treatises, working away like so many Bob Cratchits. She looked about and saw Owens, who was so absorbed in whatever he was researching that she had to speak to get his attention. "Hallo, Owens—I'm Detective Constable Doyle."

He started and looked up in surprise. He was not happy to see her.

She was a bit taken aback. "I thought I'd come by and wish you luck. I met you at the Somers Town crime scene with DCI Acton."

"Yes." He cleared his throat. "I remember. You were upset."

She ducked her head in rueful acknowledgment. "That I was." *You are never going to live that one down, my girl.* "But I was not so upset that I didn't notice your sharp work—you have a good eye, I think."

"Thank you." He did not offer any further conversation.

Prickly, she thought; *I'd best soften him up—he'll not get far thinking he doesn't need friends and supporters around here.* "Chief Inspector Acton was very impressed; he asked if I would have noticed what you did and I had to confess I would not have."

This seemed to be the correct tack, as Owens visibly unbent and turned around on his stool to face her. "That's very kind of you. I was happy to help."

Remembering that Acton wanted her to draw him out, she offered, "I came by because I imagine you'd rather be doin' field work. If I can get permission, I'll see if you can come along with me or one of the others when we're out and about."

The pale blue eyes brightened. "Thanks—I'd appreciate it. Are you still working that Somers Town case?" He sounded slightly incredulous, which wasn't very complimentary—*not a reservoir of tact, was our Owens.*

She replied in a mild tone. "No, I was ignominiously thrown

off. But if you'd like, I can find out who is workin' it, and perhaps you can lend a hand, havin' opened it up, so to speak."
Doyle well understood the proprietary feeling one got about a
case—she was sorry to let it go herself.

"That would be great," he agreed with equal parts enthusiasm and gratitude. "I would very much like to know how it
goes."

"Do you have security clearance to review the log notes? If
you do, you can see who's on it and how the investigation is
goin'."

"Yes, I do."

Doyle paused, as this was not true; perhaps he did not want
to acknowledge to her that he was not cleared as yet, or it may
have been a male-female thing, although she was getting the
strong feeling that with him, male-female was not something
he was very interested in.

She didn't argue it. "Well, let me know if you need any help,
or I'll give you a ring, if I may—I need all the help I can get,
I'm afraid."

Chuckling, he shook his head and eyed her. "That's hard to
believe—you're working with the chief inspector."

Among other things, she thought, but joked, "That's why I
need all the help."

He unbent enough to lean forward and offer a conspiratorial smile in acknowledgment. "He's a little scary."

"Indeed he is." You have no idea, my friend.

"You were so lucky; I mean, that he was willing to work with
a first-year, given his history." It was evident that although
Owens had not been here long, he had nevertheless managed
to plug in to the gossip. "Was there any particular reason he
chose you?"

The reason, of course, could not withstand the light of day—
or more properly, was best explored at night. "I had a good
record with interrogation," she said instead, which was indeed
the truth.

"Oh." He knit his brow. "I don't think that's my strong suit."

No, thought Doyle, the brusque and bloodstain-obsessed Constable Owens would not be good at handling people. He was much more suited for research—or perhaps forensics. She smiled, "It's the blarney in me, I suppose; I was fortunate to be given the chance, and I have learned a lot." Especially last night; I learned a whole lot—stop it, she cautioned herself—you are going to make a mistake and say something aloud that you oughtn't. Instead she offered, "I should be goin', I have to work on redeemin' my sorry self."

He nodded. "Good luck to you. I really appreciate your coming to see me."

It was true. Well then, thought Doyle; I've charmed him—I'm a charmer, I am.

After exchanging contact information, they parted, and Doyle was so lost in thought on her way back to her building that she almost knocked into Acton, who was coming from the other direction.

"Hallo," she greeted him, the effervescing happiness within her breast powerful in its intensity. "Fancy meeting you here." It was no coincidence, of course; she recalled that he could track her through the GPS unit in her mobile.

"Have a moment?" His lovely dark eyes were fastened upon hers.

"Here?" she teased him.

He gave her a disapproving look, then ushered her into an empty conference room. No sexual innuendos at work, she thought; mental note.

He closed the door and they looked at each other for a long moment, the chemistry crackling between them. "How are you?"

"Well," she answered gravely. "And you?"

He broke eye contact first and ducked his head because he could not contain a smile. "I am well."

This is fun, thought Doyle; I could do this all day.

He raised his head again and reached into his coat pocket. "I bought you a private mobile." He handed it to her, coming around so that he could lean against the conference table beside her. She did not own her own mobile phone, as she considered it an unnecessary expense; instead, she used the CID-issued unit. She turned the small, expensive unit over in her hands, noting that it was already charged and programmed. "Thank you." She knew why he had bought it.

He indicated the contact information, brushing with a forefinger so that it scrolled. "I've programmed my work line and my private line."

Gently, she asked, "How often would you like me to check in?"

He met her eyes and hesitated. "I don't want to suffocate you."

"I know," she replied. "How about every hour? We'll try to work on trimmin' it down over time."

"Thank you," he said quietly. "I appreciate it."

She was thoughtful. "I will be the percentage sign—my very own secret symbol."

"All right—although in an emergency, text an exclamation point on the private line." He was dead serious.

Interesting, she thought. I wonder what's afoot; he's definitely spooked, although at dinner last night he said it was nothing he could identify. She put the unit in her pocket, hoping that his anxiety would decrease once they became more accustomed to each other. It could be that his—condition—had intensified simply because their relationship had intensified. No question that he was anxious and striving mightily to hide it.

"Any leads on Capper?" She threw him a look. "Real ones, I mean."

He didn't miss a beat. "As a matter of fact, we have information that he is rooming with Willard Smythe's relatives. He'll be brought in any time."

She mused, "Smythe was the barkeeper—it's a small cast of characters."

"I'll give you a ring when he's in so that you may observe the interrogation."

"Done." He needed a truth detector, then. "D'you mind if I ask Owens along? I was just speakin' to him."

He crossed his arms. "Were you? What do you think of him?"

Doyle didn't want to queer the pitch if Acton thought Owens would make a good detective; on the other hand, she wanted to be honest. "He'll never make chief inspector. He's a bit rude—says things he oughtn't."

"Not like me," Acton teased her.

"Not at all like you," she protested. "You are unfailingly polite and I'll not hear a word against you."

"Bring Owens," Acton said, standing up to leave. "But don't devote too much time or energy on him; the jury's still out."

"Don't worry, he's not my type." She added the unspoken thought, I believe it's a situation where you are his type—those *beaux yeux.*

CHAPTER 14

He was hesitant to tell her for fear of her reaction; for fear she would weep again, which was the next thing to unbearable. But she should know, if for no other reason than to be made wary.

Doyle spent the greater part of the day doing background work and phoning potential witnesses who were by and large unhelpful. She texted her symbol to Acton on the hour and wondered if he would want to see her again tonight or if he was too busy catching up with his caseload, what with the recent spate of murders—perhaps there was to be no fieldwork today. Unless he had gone out without her. This thought gave her pause and she decided to ring him; she phoned him on his business line and he answered immediately.

"Constable."

There must be others about. If she was truly wicked, she would say something provocative. She was not, however, and so didn't. "I've been lookin' into Smythe and Capper. While Smythe is a known associate of the trainer, Capper is not, and his phone records show no contact."

"I see."

I am telling him nothing he doesn't already know, she thought. Exasperating man.

She persisted. "Which brings us back to your question—why would Capper risk so much to talk to the trainer in person?"

After a moment's hesitation, she suggested, "Perhaps Capper was the killer, after all." This would contradict all working theories, but it would certainly tie up the cases nicely.

"Any indication that the trainer had a falling-out with anyone recently?"

"Not as yet; or no one wants to speak of it leastways. As it turns out, there is a connection with Giselle, however. The trainer was goin' to visit her folks' house in Yorkshire, according to one of the owners."

"Was he indeed?"

Ah; here was something the omniscient DCI did not already know. Pleased she had been of some use and had also managed a vocabulary word, Doyle continued, "It's a wrinkle—by all accounts he was gay and there is no indication the acquaintance was long-standin'."

Acton's tone was thoughtful on the other end. "It is interesting. Perhaps he felt he had to go to ground where he couldn't be easily found; I imagine Giselle had a connection to the track."

"A beautician, she was," Doyle pointed out doubtfully. "Unless she was braidin' the horses' tails or somethin'."

"We'll see; it's a significant fact, that he may have been trying to go to ground—it means he knew he was a target. Good work."

Doyle made a wry mouth into the mobile. "Then he should have gone to ground sooner, and recall that you are not to humor me."

"I am not humoring you," he protested, and it was the truth.

She could hear voices in the background that sounded a lot like a field team, and debated for a moment whether to ask, then decided there was nothin' for it. "Where are you, then?"

"We've pinned down Capper and are waiting for a warrant."

"Are you? Well, that is excellent."

He must have heard her carefully concealed disappointment. "I'll need you in the gallery for his questioning."

"Of course. Give me a ring; I'll be here. "

She rang off and contemplated her mobile's blank screen. She wished he had asked her to go with him, mainly because she would have overseen Capper's arrest with relish after the trick he had pulled on her. Acton knew this, of course, but didn't ask her to come. On the other hand, it was undeniable that Acton would have her close to hand at all times if he had his druthers. So—she thought with an attempt at stoicism—there is a reason I was not asked, and I have to try not to be such a baby about it. I have to be careful not to start thinking I have the ordering of him; it is that personal versus professional thing again.

"Who was that?" Munoz asked through the partition.

All it needed was Munoz, needling her. "You shouldn't eavesdrop, Munoz. It is impolite."

"You sounded as though you were trying to make it up to Acton."

"I'll not dignify that remark with a response."

Munoz appeared over the partition. She is the only person I know, thought Doyle, who still looks good under fluorescent lights.

"What did Drake want?"

Doyle made a face. "To look down my top, mainly."

Munoz laughed, swinging her long hair back. "I told you. Did you let him?"

"No."

"I don't know why he bothered, there isn't much to see." Munoz had a very fine figure.

Doyle remembered that a certain chief inspector had found nothing to complain about and felt generous. "I can't hold a candle to you."

Habib appeared in Doyle's entryway, his dark eyes bright. "What is this? Do I hear that Munoz bests you, Doyle?" He was trying to be funny in his own awkward way—he had a giant crackin' crush on Munoz, as did everyone else with an XY chromosome. Except Williams, apparently. And Acton, of course.

Munoz gave Doyle a sidelong look. "We were speaking of my spreadsheets, which are far superior."

"Sad but true," Doyle conceded. "Many admire them."

Pleased to be participating in the banter, Habib spoke to Doyle but allowed his eyes to stray to Munoz. "You can better yourself."

Gravely, Doyle demurred, "I think not, sir; it's a gift, is what it is."

Munoz could not contain herself and sank down, away from sight.

With regret, Habib dragged his gaze back to Doyle. "I am hearing the chief inspector will bring in the prime witness on the Kempton Park racecourse murder."

"Yes, sir. I am hearin' the same—he has requested that I attend." This so that Munoz would not have the satisfaction of thinking she was in the doghouse.

"Has a link been established between the cases?" He fixed his dark eyes on her.

He is like Acton, she thought; it is hard to tell what he is thinking. "Other than the second victim was shot shortly after speakin' to us, no."

"He was on the scene for both, though. The witness."

Doyle knit her brow. "I don't know if we have him on the scene in Giselle's flat as yet, sir. Not enough to pin him down for a time frame."

Habib tilted his head in a gentle admonition. "Nevertheless, sometimes the best suspect is the most obvious."

This was inarguable and a basic tenet they taught you on day one at the Crime Academy—that, along with the dire consequences of becoming sexually involved with a superior officer. "Do you want me to ring you when the interrogation goes forward, sir?"

"Oh, no, no," he said immediately, shaking his head. I am only interested from afar." He withdrew.

A very odd duck, thought Doyle; I'm having my share of them today.

Munoz's voice was heard. "I'd like to attend the interrogation. Let me know."

Doyle had the immediate conviction that Munoz was casting a proprietary eye on her case and bristled. "Why?"

"I'd like to watch Acton's technique." Munoz's tone was as mild as milk. It was true; Acton was famous for his interrogations.

Doyle was reminded, "I should call Owens, too. He'd like to work on his interrogation technique."

"Who is Owens?"

"A new TDC." Doyle hid a smile. "I think you'll like him."

CHAPTER 15

He didn't understand the killer's motivation—although perhaps there wasn't one. Nevertheless, he didn't like to think that she may be at risk, and considered assigning someone to her—he had to be careful, she was still feeling her way.

As it turned out, there was no shortage of observers in the gallery when Danny Capper was escorted into the adjacent interrogation room. Owens had come to join Doyle, grateful for the invitation and asking her questions about the status of the case. He is warming up to me, she thought—it's a saint in the making, I am. She hoped he wouldn't want her to make a commentary while the interrogation was going forward; she needed to concentrate on what Capper would be saying, which tended to be more difficult when there were others crowded around her. Drake and one of his detective sergeants entered, and Munoz immediately gravitated into their orbit.

It's like a cocktail party in here, thought Doyle with disapproval as she observed Munoz and Drake making eyes at each other. Unprofessional, it is. With a guilty start, she recalled that it was a case of the pot and the kettle and decided to mind her own business.

"Acton is making him wait," said Owens into her ear. This was true; Acton used an arsenal of interrogation tactics—he'd make the witness wait or sometimes he'd pause in the questioning and say nothing for a long space of time. The witness would then start talking to fill the silence and would oftentimes divulge too much. That would be me, thought Doyle; I'd be gabbling.

Acton entered and took his seat across from Capper and his solicitor; the attending sergeant then began the recording machine and recited the particulars for the interview. Doyle sized up the participants and decided Acton would probably start strong—Capper was looking tough and defiant, and sometimes that type needed to be shocked a bit so as to bring home the seriousness of the situation.

"Where have you been? We've been looking for you." With a quick movement, Acton spread the grisly photos of Giselle—or what was left of her—before the witness.

Sullen, Capper bent his head and averted his eyes from the photos. "I dinna know it. I was stayin' wi' me mates, is all."

Stupid culchie, thought Doyle with a flare of temper at hearing his voice again. Now it's your turn to repent fasting.

"Your mates have questionable politics."

Capper glanced up, scowling. "I wouldn't know." Interestingly enough, this was true.

There was a pause while Acton regarded him steadily. "You left the scene before you were released."

But Capper had a reasonable answer and shrugged. "I wanted to get out before you saw that I was banned."

"Then why didn't you leave as soon as you saw the man had been killed? Why identify yourself?"

"I was in shock. Then when the colleen started askin' me questions, I realized I should have cleared out."

Shifting uncomfortably in her seat, Doyle very much hoped the next sequence of events would not be reviewed in detail. However, Acton said only, "It made a very bad impression, your leaving—as though you were guilty."

"I didn't kill him," Capper insisted.

"Did you kill her?" Acton gestured to the photos, but the man would not look.

"No."

The question was for her benefit and Doyle duly noted that he told the truth.

"Who did?"

"I dunno." This was also true and Doyle experienced a pang of disappointment; this strange case was to reveal not a shred of a lead, apparently.

"Anyone you know unhappy with her? From what the neighbors say, she had a lot of different men, in and out."

Doyle watched with interest; Acton was trying to goad the witness into saying something he oughtn't, but she was not hopeful—Danny Capper was a tough customer; she had come across many of his ilk on the streets of Dublin.

"I told you, I dunno who would do this." The question had made him uncomfortable, though, and he glowered at Acton. "You got nothin' on me—you're not going to mock me up with a false charge; I have rights, I do."

With some shame, Doyle realized they could have held him on a charge of obstruction of justice for locking her in the tack room, but Acton had spared her the humiliation and it had cost him some leverage on this case. You are a baby, she chastised herself; and now look what you've done.

But Acton was unmoved, having his own leverage over the witness. "How often have you violated the ban, Danny?"

Reminded, Capper subsided and replied sullenly, "Only the once."

It was true.

Acton waited a few beats, but this witness was not prone to fill in the silences, and so he continued, "What were you doing there?"

The witness hesitated and met the solicitor's eyes. The man nodded and Capper hunched his shoulders. "Giselle sent me. She wanted to talk to him and his mobile had stopped workin'."

"Why did she want to speak with him?"

"They were goin' to Yorkshire, to see her folks."

Acton leaned back and made a show of satisfaction for the

solicitor's sake. "So—your girlfriend was going away with another man and they both turn up dead with you placed at each scene."

Capper was aware this didn't sound good and dropped his head, staring at his hands. "It wasn't like that. They were mates, is all."

"She was friendly with a trainer at the racecourse? I wonder how that came about?" It was clear from Acton's tone that he already knew.

Capper crossed his arms, on the defensive. "She liked the course—liked the horses. She was over there a lot."

Ah, thought Doyle, leaning forward. Here is something.

But Acton didn't need her help. "You had your girlfriend running your numbers for you because you were banned."

"Don't answer," instructed the solicitor.

Acton didn't pursue it and leaned forward again. Doyle could tell from his posture that he had come to the same conclusion she had—they would get little of interest from this witness. "I don't understand, Danny. Why would you do her a favor? Giselle told me you had quarreled."

Capper lifted his head, genuinely surprised. "No. We hadn't quarreled."

Acton thought about this. "What were you to tell the trainer?"

Capper clenched his fists in frustration. "I don't know what was goin' on. She said he was spooked about somethin' and wanted to get away until it blew over, so she was goin' to help him out. Then his mobile stopped workin' and she got all a'fret. If she was seen talkin' with him, someone might guess where he went to, so she sent me instead."

"Spooked about what?"

Capper shrugged. "Dunno."

This was not exactly true.

"Did you overhear any conversations?"

"Nothin' of interest. I told her to stay out of his problems— it weren't her concern."

"Were any names mentioned? Foreign names?"

The man shook his head. "No. No names."

Thinking about those Russians, again, thought Doyle. He's got Russians on the mind, he does.

Acton sat unmoving and continued to watch Capper. "So the trainer thought he was in danger."

Capper met his eye, exasperated. "D'ye think?"

The solicitor gave the witness an admonitory look and the man subsided.

"Did you know he was associating with suspected terrorists?"

"No."

This was not true.

Acton contemplated him for a space, but Capper met his eyes and held steady.

"When did you last speak with Giselle?'

"I went to the pub and told her"—he caught himself—"that I was goin' to stay with me mates."

"And that the trainer had been murdered."

Capper dropped his gaze. "That too."

"And what did she say to this news?"

The witness took a breath. "She was spooked."

Yes, thought Doyle; she was indeed.

There was a small silence, and Capper suddenly allowed a trace of emotion to show through his façade of toughness. "I told her the cops was after me, and that I would go to ground till it blew over—I should have stayed with her." He lifted his head and contemplated the far upper corner of the room. "I should have stayed with her."

Doyle had to close her eyes briefly; the raw remorse simmered just below the surface, and inwardly she flinched.

Apparently, Acton was willing to offer cold comfort. "If you'd stayed with her, Danny, I guarantee you'd be in those photos, too."

Pulling himself together, the witness asked with a show of bravado, "Are we done?"

But Acton was the one asking the questions. "Did you speak with her again that evening?"

"No—I tried to ring her up a couple of times, but she'd turned her mobile off."

Acton then asked him some rapidfire questions about what he'd said and done upon finding the trainer's body. Sometimes the question would be a seeming *non sequitur*. Capper gave consistent answers.

"He's had too much time to rehearse," said Owens in Doyle's ear.

"Or he's telling the truth," Doyle reminded him, which was in turn the truth.

Acton spread out the forensics report and the solicitor leaned forward, suddenly intent. "There was a healthy bit of Danny DNA within the decedent. How do you account for it?"

The solicitor intervened, no longer passive. "This means nothing. He told you he was her boyfriend."

"She was going to implicate him in the trainer's murder," counter-claimed Acton, "but she didn't get the chance."

"You've got nothing to hold him. Call me when you have something more than a fairy tale." The solicitor stood, sure of his ground, and the interview concluded.

"Nasty piece of work," Owens commented, referring to the solicitor.

Doyle explained, "I know it looks like they're ready to have a go at each other, but he's just doin' his job. He and Acton are actually quite friendly."

Owens had found the interview intensely interesting, Doyle could see. "Do you think he did it?"

Doyle tried to be diplomatic, although once again she was made aware that perhaps Owens wasn't really suited for detective work. "It seems unlikely that a knowin' boyo like Capper would kill his girlfriend in her own apartment. Might as well be wearin' a target for the police."

He nodded in concession. "What does Acton think?"

Doyle remembered that Owens didn't have security clearance. "I'm not privy at the moment."

He made a sound of sympathy. "Are you off this case, too?"

"Hangin' by my fingernails." This was more or less true; she had a very pleasant memory of raking her fingernails across Acton's back.

They watched Acton confer with the solicitor, then the two men shook hands and parted. Acton then made his way into the gallery and began a low-voiced conversation with Drake, discussing their take on the interview. Munoz promptly stationed herself within Acton's line of sight and tossed her hair back. Brasser, thought Doyle, and wished she had thought of it first.

After the conversation, Acton approached Doyle and Owens. "Do you have any theories, Constable?" He wanted a preliminary take.

"No," she said bluntly, which was her way of letting him know that the witness had told the truth, more or less.

"I have a theory," Munoz interjected.

"Let's hear it." Drake smiled at her in an indulgent fashion.

"He was set up to take the fall for both murders."

Drake humored her, having recognized a fellow traveler. "So one killer, but it's not Capper—I suppose it's possible."

Munoz preened. "Just a theory."

The detective sergeant, however, was not going to allow beauty to trump common sense. "But there was no point in setting up Capper as the stalking horse; there is no evidence against him, either—although the victim made no defensive struggle, which points back to Capper."

All good points, thought Doyle. This is indeed a strange case.

"I'm afraid I must go. Thank you for your input." Acton nodded to the group and left with Drake, the two men checking their mobile devices for messages.

The remaining group in the gallery began to break up. Munoz lingered to argue her point with the handsome detective sergeant, and Doyle's mobile buzzed as she headed toward the door. It was Acton. He texted, "Cereal?"

She smiled at the screen. Last night—or more accurately early this morning—she had carefully vacated her bed and crept into the kitchen, her bare feet silent on the linoleum. Suffering some discomfort from this first sexual experience, her original intent was to apply ice to the afflicted area. Before she opened the freezer, however, Acton had followed her into the kitchen. She was not about to tell him what she was doing—the man might be remorseful and swear off. So instead she had improvised, telling him that she was hungry and inviting him to join her in a bowl of cereal. She began pouring out her favorite frosty flakes, but Acton had been distracted, standing behind her to lift her hair off her neck so that he could kiss it. They soon adjourned to the bedroom with no cereal consumed, and she had to wait until he left in the morning to have recourse to the ice tray.

"Done," she texted. Apparently he wasn't too busy, after all.

Much heartened, she went back to her task of cross-indexing track personnel, known associates, and Watch List but kept coming up empty until Habib wandered in to watch over her shoulder. This was a habit of his that greatly annoyed the other detectives, but Doyle figured it never hurt to spot-check, so to speak, and so she was not resentful. After a moment he asked about the interrogation. "What did you think of him?" He would never admit to it, but he respected her intuition.

Doyle paused and considered. "I don't think he murdered either of them, but he knows somethin'—I think he knew more than he was sayin' about the trainer's troubles."

"Perhaps who killed him?"

No—but she couldn't very well announce this to Habib. "Perhaps. I think he is afraid, and he is not one who scares easily."

Habib nodded, saying nothing, and Doyle had no idea what he was thinking. I am losing my touch, she thought; that or Habib is a space alien, which is always a possibility.

"I understand you are not to handle the Somers Town case."

"Yes, sir." She did not refute the implied rebuke mainly because it was irrefutable.

"You are wise to submit to the chief inspector's orders without question." There was a note of approval in his solemn voice.

You have no idea, Doyle thought—he'll definitely have the ordering of me tonight, my friend. Immediately, she felt much better.

He took his leave. "Very good. I believe this case will be resolved shortly—this does not seem the type of case that will go cold."

"No, sir," agreed Doyle. And neither will I, tonight.

CHAPTER 16

*H*E CHECKED THE GPS AND SAW SHE HAD GONE HOME. HE NEEDED *to be more patient—after all, she was new to this. He thought about the soft sounds she made in her throat and looked at his watch. It was three minutes later than the last time he had looked.*

Doyle left work late because she knew she would not be doing any follow-up tonight at home and she needed to finish off some loose ends. When she emerged from her tube station, she stopped by the dreary little Sav-Mart on the corner and pondered what to pick up—she had no idea what Acton liked to eat, except for Chinese food. He didn't seem to eat much; he was so tall and lean. She could feel herself blushing right there in the produce aisle between the tomatoes and the peppers. Brasser, she thought; take hold of your lustful self.

She bought some essentials and then stood in line at the cashier under the flickering fluorescent lights with the other poor souls who were also in need of sustenance. The middle-aged woman in front of her was on her mobile, emanating an anxious sadness. Speaking in a low voice, she left a message; she was having trouble reaching him, she said, and she wished he'd let her know where he'd gone—would he be home for dinner? An alternate universe, Doyle thought, and dutifully texted her symbol to Acton. She then froze, suddenly struck;

that's odd. The person in line behind her began to mutter, and thus recalled, Doyle moved forward.

She returned home and put her groceries away, turning over possibilities in her mind. She'd ask Acton about it—that is, if there was a chance to get a word in tonight. On the one hand it was flattering, his being so avid, and all; but on the other hand, she had the very strong impression that even when they were havin' at it, he did not let his guard down, he would not let her in.

As she sorted out the fruit, replacing the old with the new, she thought about it; it may be he was afraid that he would frighten her with the intensity of his—his fixation. She didn't scare easy, though, and she already had a fair estimation of the nature of it. Despite this, she had stepped into this whirlpool without a tremor—if nothing else, she was true to form; he had called her impetuous, but in reality it was part and parcel of her abilities. When you could sense the things she could, it was almost impossible to do nothing and this was why it was all so difficult for her. I wanted to help Acton, she realized, although she knew he would be surprised to hear that she thought he needed help. And he is so very attractive—the attraction itself is attractive in its own way. And there is that other thing—we are freakish, the both of us; trying to pretend we're normal when we're not. And it is so tedious to try to find someone compatible, especially when no one—*no one*—could remotely hold a candle to Acton. She closed the cupboard with a soft click. That was the reason, and that alone. No one else came close, and no one else ever would.

Her instinct was to humor him; wear the ankle holster, text him every hour, happily accede to his sexual overtures with the hope that over time, his symptoms would ease. She was no psychiatrist, however, and didn't know if this was the best course. Perhaps she would begin researching it to see what she could find out—but the thought was rejected almost immediately; he wouldn't care for a confrontation and it would feel like a betrayal. She knew down to the soles of her shoes that she was good for him and that was enough—she would do the best she was able.

Her mobile buzzed, and he texted her that he was on his way. She watched him park his car from the window and then withdrew, feeling self-conscious. No need to be spying on him—there was enough of that going around. When she opened the door to his knock, he leaned down and kissed her gently as he came through. She worried for an unguarded moment that her neighbors could see, and then took hold of herself and smiled. "I didn't know what you'd like to eat."

"I will eat whatever you put in front of me," he said, pulling at his tie, "but not just yet." He hoisted her up and she obligingly wrapped her legs around him as he propelled them into the bedroom. He broke his mouth away from hers to ask, "Have you practiced shooting?"

Looking down at him with her forearms resting on his shoulders, she teased, "You need to work on your sweet nothin's, Acton,"

"Practice."

She bit his earlobe. "I'll practice you one, I will," and laughed as they fell into the bed.

Later, she sat with him at her kitchen table eating ham and butter sandwiches, wearing his shirt with one leg tucked beneath her. "I thought of somethin' that doesn't make sense. D'you recall when we were at the Laughin' Cat and we went over to sit with Giselle?"

"Yes." Acton watched her mouth as she ate. He had a lovely, lovely torso.

"She was textin' on her mobile and smokin', but she was unhappy; d' you remember?"

"Yes."

Sensing that she would have a limited amount of time to get this out before her presence would be requested in the bedroom yet again, she cut to the nub. "Her mobile records show no text messages that night, and Capper said her mobile was turned off."

This caught his attention, and he drew his brows together. "Let's double-check the mobile and the provider—she may have had other accounts." He thought about it. "Or it was not her mobile."

"Capper's records also show no calls or texts after six—which contradicts his story of tryin' to contact her."

He tilted his head. "Perhaps he used a different mobile. He was in hiding, remember."

"I know, but we did see her textin', and I got the impression she was annoyed at the time—perhaps because she couldn't get through."

Acton was silent for a few moments, thinking. "What did you think of Capper?"

"He didn't kill her, as we'd already guessed. He was afraid—and he was truly sickened by the photos. He was not involved in the Sinn Féin splinter group."

"Do you think he was afraid because we caught him running numbers after he'd been banned or do you think he was afraid of the killer?"

She shook her head. "I can't break it down like that, I'm afraid. But if he's afraid of the same thing the trainer was afraid of, it means he's more frightened of the killer than of us and our paltry numbers-runnin' misdemeanor. Perhaps you could apply some more pressure? Rattle your sword and search his place for evidence?"

Acton regarded her patiently. "What pressure I can bring to bear is no match for the photos of Giselle's face."

"Oh," she said. "I see."

"But a search is a good idea," he added, as though speaking to a bright eight-year-old.

She made a wry mouth. "Remember, you are not to humor me—I am content to learn at your feet." She licked a dab of butter from her finger and could see from his arrested expression that her action had started an altogether different train of thought. "We can speak on it tomorrow," she concluded, and allowed him to pull her onto his lap.

Some time later she lay in her bed with her head on his chest, looking at the sliver of moonlight coming in through the lace curtains that did not quite meet in the middle. He was awake, his hands moving on her arms, gently stroking. If someone had told her a week ago she would be thus situated, she would have told them they were out of their minds and should be shriven besides. Acton had said nothing for over an hour and she was thinking wistfully of the ice tray.

"I would like to give you something."

"Somethin' else, you mean?" She giggled.

She could feel him chuckle in his chest. "Yes."

She giggled again. It had been a long time since she'd giggled.

"I would like to pay Dr. Lennox."

Dr. Lennox was the cancer specialist who had treated her mother. The National Health Service had not covered him, but she had hired him anyway; he had been worth every penny. So Acton had been into her finances, small surprise. Another felony. "Thank you. I would appreciate it."

He was surprised she acquiesced so easily and his arms tightened around her. "Any other debts I didn't discover?"

"No. Only my rental."

"Move in with me, then." There was an underlying intensity to the words.

She tried to be light. "And leave all this, Acton?"

But he was not to be dissuaded. "I cannot come every night— and my flat has better security."

He was worried again, but she experienced her own jolt of anxiety at the thought that their relationship would be exposed to the world. A bit defensively, she replied, "You said that no one need know until I had become accustomed."

"And you have not." It was a statement.

"No," she confessed, "I have not."

The stroking paused. "What can I do to change that?"

"Is this a discussion?" she teased.

"Yes." He was not to be diverted. "Have you thought about what is next for us?"

Mother of God, she thought; there is an "us" now that has to be thought about. She didn't know what to say and so said nothing.

He began lightly stroking her arms again. "Are you not sure?"

She was quick to reassure him and tightened her fingers on his chest with affection. "I am very sure. But it will cause quite the ruckus—a nine days' wonder—and it will be just the kind of thing I'll hate, I'm afraid. I'll be wantin' to gird my loins, so to speak."

He was quiet for a moment. "Does it matter what anyone else thinks?"

Propping herself on her elbows, she turned over to look at him in the dim light, and he watched her actions with his dark eyes. She replied honestly, "I know it shouldn't, but it does."

He lifted his hands and held her face between them. "Nothing matters to me but you."

It was the pure truth and it frightened her—I cannot be solely responsible for this man's happiness, she thought, panicked.

He must have sensed her emotional skittishness because he pulled her head to his chest. "Forgive me; I am impatient and I shouldn't press you."

"Truly, I am adjustin'—I promise, Acton." She felt a bit ashamed that she was not as committed as he—even though committed was perhaps not the best term to use. Gently pulling at the hair on his chest, she chose her words with care. "It may be for the best—to find our way at a slower pace, I mean. This—interest—of yours may dissipate; you never know." She managed a light tone. "You wouldn't want to wake up one fine mornin' and realize you and I are quite the mésalliance." A fancy word, and French besides. But there it was.

He lifted his hand to stroke her temple and slowly pulled a tendril of her hair through his fingers. "I would appreciate it," he said as he watched the strand fall to her shoulder, "—if you never say such a thing again."

He meant it, too. She rushed to cover her gaffe and dropped a kiss on his chest. "Nay," she said in her broadest accent, "it's a lucky man, you are. And to think I never got the chance to attend me find-a-mate seminar for which I parted wi' twenty hard-earned quid."

"Two weeks." His tone was a bit grim as he pulled her atop him to kiss her, her hair falling around his head. "Two weeks to gird your loins."

My loins, she thought, have been thoroughly girded already, thank you very much.

CHAPTER 17

*H*E LEFT THE BED WHEN HIS MOBILE VIBRATED AT 5:00 A.M. HE *closed the bedroom door and listened to the message. He was not surprised. She was asleep and hadn't moved; she was tired, her hand curled into a small fist on the pillow. She was off this case.*

Doyle was sleepy and wondered as she dropped into her chair how Acton was faring—they hadn't slept much. She groped for the latte that had been left on her desk by the messenger and that was thankfully not yet cold. Having overslept, she woke to find Acton gone. He must have left before the birds were up, but he never seemed tired—one of the benefits of being certifiable, she supposed. Smiling, she stretched forth her arms. You're certifiable yourself, my girl—God help us both, but this schedule is brutal.

Habib popped up at her entryway, making her spill her coffee in surprise. "You see," he said, his dark eyes glittering with suppressed excitement. "I said it would resolve."

"I haven't checked my messages, sir." She dabbed at the stain and was grateful she was wearing black. "What's afoot?"

Habib's clipped words spilled over onto themselves. "DCI Acton is at the crime scene with DCs Munoz and Williams. The suspect for the racecourse murders—the one who was here for the interview—"

"Capper?" prompted Doyle, suddenly wide awake and wishing he would get to the flippin' point.

"Yes. He and another were in a shoot-out in an alley near Leadenhall Market. Both dead."

"Holy Mother," breathed Doyle.

"Indeed," agreed Habib. "Remember that I said as much."

"You are indeed prescient, sir." It was an excellent word and one she had feared she'd never have opportunity to utter. It didn't seem as satisfying, however, in light of the cataclysmic news that Munoz was at the crime scene and not her. "Could I go, sir? I have been workin' the case, after all."

Habib hesitated. "Remember that you were taken off the Somers Town case—do you think the chief inspector is unhappy with your performance?"

No, she thought; in fact, if I detailed to you how happy he was—last I checked—you would blush to hear it. "I think he couldn't reach me, sir," she prevaricated instead. "I was a little under the weather this mornin' and came in late."

He hesitated, not sure what would best please his superior, and she pressed her advantage. "I'm certain he'd like me to help them process the scene, sir—I have a lot of information on the case."

"All right," he agreed with some reluctance. "But if you are not needed, please return. There has been a rash of thefts in Pimlico."

Doyle didn't trust herself to answer. Grabbing her rucksack, she pelted down to the crime scene, checking her messages to verify that Acton had not attempted to contact her—he had not. With an effort, she tried to control her temper as she rode the tube; perhaps he had gone without her so that the others would not conclude they came from the same place. With a grimace, she discarded the theory immediately; no one would assume such a ludicrous thing, which was one of the reasons she dreaded breaking the news to the unsuspecting public. Perhaps he hadn't heard the report until he was on his way in, but this did not explain why he hadn't called her. Instead, he called Munoz and Williams, and they were working her case while she was at home, sleeping like a dosser.

Take hold of your foolish self, she scolded, and just do your job. Emerging from the station, she strode out quickly for two blocks and then came upon what was usually a welcome and familiar sight—the early morning discovery of a fatal confrontation the night before. The bodies were in an alleyway, between two dumpsters and bordered on three sides by commercial buildings. Even at this hour, PCs were busy keeping the bystanders back and the scene was cordoned off with forensics tape. As it was a business district, the gawkers tended to be more discreet and better dressed, but evidenced the same fascination with sudden death that was a hallmark of the human race. Acton's tall figure was easy to spot; he was speaking with the SOCOs and indicating what he wanted done. Munoz and Williams appeared to be taking measurements and marking evidence with yellow numbered markers.

Munoz was a brasser and a nasty piece of work, but Doyle— giving the devil her due—knew she did excellent work and would not allow an opportunity to impress Acton pass her by. Williams's work was always first-rate. Doyle bit her nail, tired and annoyed and consumed with a burning sense of injustice; apparently she had been relegated to performing an altogether different line of work for the illustrious chief inspector.

It didn't help matters that, now that she had arrived at the scene, Doyle felt a little foolish. She was debating what to do when she saw that Acton had spotted her. He showed no surprise, but indicated she should approach. He looked fresh as a daisy, wretched man.

She stepped under the tape and moved next to him where he stood, reviewing the scene. "Our suspect has been conveniently dispatched."

If she hadn't been so annoyed, she would have considered the nuance in his remark. Instead, she said stiffly, "So I heard from Habib."

At her tone he glanced sideways at her, considering, as other personnel moved between the bodies, carefully bagging evidence and taking photographs. She refused to meet his eyes.

"I did not want to disturb you," he explained quietly.

"I would appreciate it," she ground through her teeth, "if you never say such a thing again."

There was a surprised pause. "Fair enough."

A silence fell between them and continued while the team began the process of loading the body bags. In a small voice she asked, "May I help in some way?"

"Witness statements." He glanced up at the many windows that loomed overhead. "Although this is a commercial area, perhaps someone was here late and heard something."

"I'm on it." She turned and walked away, pulling her fancy mobile from her rucksack. When she had cleared the corner of the nearest building, she stopped and texted: "I M wretchedly sorry." She waited for a moment, feeling miserable until the return message came: "Don't be."

You are such a crackin' knocker, she thought, running her thumb over the words on the screen. Lucky for you he's fatally stricken. Pulling herself together, she went to knock on doors and take down information from the businesses surrounding the scene, the members of which were stationed at the windows and watching the proceedings in the alley. As usual, there was a feeling of excitement among the bystanders; of being involved in the big story. Sometimes this sense of excitement resulted in a fish tale, where a witness would claim to have heard or seen something to inflate his own importance. Fortunately, she was well-suited for sorting the wheat from the chaff and gave those attention-seekers short shrift.

As she was taking notes, her hands paused; the killer had watched the Teddington crime scene—perhaps he was here, too. Paying careful attention, she began asking the potential witnesses if they worked in the building and she found no one prevaricating. She thought about texting Acton to canvass the bystanders outside, but she decided it wasn't necessary—Acton would know to do it, and if there was anything to observe, it would be duly observed. He had an amazing capacity for detail, whereas she, by contrast, had an amazing capacity for losing her temper.

Despite the fact there seemed to be little of interest, she kept at it; someone may have been working late in an office or on a cleaning crew and heard something. It was tedious work, going floor to floor, but she felt the need to atone and worked conscientiously and without inward complaint. It was nearly noon when she finished canvassing the last of the buildings surrounding the site and concluded there were no leads to speak of, but she did get the contact information for the cleaning crews and asked the office managers to check and let her know if any other personnel had been working late last night.

Doyle leaned back in the lift as it descended and took a deep breath. She was exhausted but knew it was important to get as many leads as possible early on. Mentally reviewing what she had gleaned, she decided to return to the Met and begin contacting the cleaning companies immediately.

Acton had not texted her since that morning, but this was to be expected, what with the double murder to process. As she exited the building, she beheld the welcome sight of his Range Rover, waiting at the curb. Think o' the devil, she thought, and smiled at him in relief; apparently she was not in the dog house, thanks be to God.

He reached across to open the car door for her and she slid in. "Are you hungry?"

"Contrite."

"No," he said as he pulled away. "You had every right to be angry."

She blew out her breath in exasperation. "No, Acton; I should not have spoken to you as I did. I took gross advantage of our personal relationship and it was wrong, wrong, wrong." She emphasized the words with a finger.

"But we do have a personal relationship," he pointed out. "I owed you an explanation because of it."

Wary of saying something insulting again about which was more important, she chose her words with care. "When we are at work, you are my superior. I should not treat you with less respect than you deserve."

He glanced at her. "And I cannot treat you as I would any other DC—any other person. It would be impossible."

Now it was her turn to be thoughtful. "While we puzzle this out, d'you think we could find some crackin' strong coffee somewhere?"

Turning onto Gracechurch, he remarked, "You need more sleep—my turn to be wretchedly sorry."

She glanced at him sidelong. "I don't think either one of us is sorry at all."

This pronouncement was rewarded with that rare genuine smile. "No."

"That's just it," she confessed, leaning back and closing her eyes. "I was that tired, and I heard the news from Habib instead of you, and Munoz was takin' my place—"

"Is she a problem?"

Feeling like a petulant child, she complained, "I just don't want her takin' my place, Acton; she fancies you."

He gave her a look that made her chuckle. "You are remarkably foolish."

"Yes," she sighed. "I know this, I assure you."

"Do you want her to be transferred?"

"Faith, no." Her exasperation returned with full force. "This is exactly what I am talkin' about; you should not even offer to do such a thing for me."

"There is little I wouldn't do for you." It was the pure truth.

"You are doin' it again, my friend." She subsided, having the growing conviction that she was starting to argue against herself. "Do you think we can come to terms over somethin' to eat?"

He turned the car. "Candide's?"

She hid her surprise. She went to Candide's after church sometimes with Nellie when they were in the chips; Candide's had wonderful, strong coffee. She regarded him narrowly. "What time do I attend Mass on Sundays?"

"Nine o' clock," he answered easily.

She considered this. "I don't know your middle name."

In a mild tone he soothed, "I am not surprised—there are quite a few."

CHAPTER 18

SHE HAD BEEN ANGRY WITH HIM. SHE WAS VERY ATTRACTIVE WHEN she was angry.

Acton's mobile vibrated as soon as they were seated at the restaurant. He glanced at the ID but did not pick up, and Doyle was recalled to the fact that he was in the midst of a brand-new double homicide on an already difficult case. "Please do not humor me—if you need to go, I completely understand." She added, "Leave your credit card."

He didn't smile in response. "It can wait. I need to talk to you."

Oh-oh, she thought. Trouble.

His expression became serious as his eyes met hers. "There is no easy way to broach this; I'd like you off these cases."

She stared at him in surprise and felt the prickling one feels about the eyes when one is about to cry. Knocker, she scolded herself. Buck up—after your fine speech about how he is your superior, don't you dare. Instead she said as calmly as she was able, "All right. Do you tell Habib or should I?"

Watching her reaction, his words were gentle. "I'm sorry, Kathleen. It is no reflection on your work."

At this crucial point their coffee was served, which gave Doyle the opportunity to regain her equilibrium. The waitress then took their order, and although she had lost her appetite, she ordered anyway because she didn't want him to think she was upset. Such a wretched, miserable day it was; truly. And it wasn't noon yet.

To avoid giving off the impression she was sulking, she made her report. "There was nothing startlin' to discover in the surrounding buildings; there were only commercial tenants, and no one was reported as workin' late. I have the names for the cleaning crew who worked up and down the floors on the east side durin' the night. Do we have an estimated time of death?"

"Just after one."

She brightened a bit. "Then they may have heard somethin'—they were about."

Their food came, and Acton watched her and made no attempt to eat his omelet. Despite her steely resolve not to act like a baby, she could only push hers around her plate. With all the sincerity she could muster, she met his eyes. "Please do not let your feelin's for me supplant your better judgment. Of course I'm disappointed, but I'll recover." She could see that he was debating whether to tell her something and added, "It's all right, Acton—truly. I'll go home early and take a nap."

"I believe you may be in danger."

Faith, this was a surprise. She blinked, then suggested, "I think we're back to our original discussion, about the personal gettin' mixed up with the professional—"

He interrupted, "Do you remember the Somers Town couple?"

Puzzled, she tried to keep up. "Yes—yes, of course—"

"The dead man was your father."

The silence stretched out for a few moments while she stared at him in amazement. "Truly?"

He nodded, watching her.

Completely taken aback, she thought about this, plumbing herself for an emotion. There was none, and she shook her head. "It's not as though I would recognize him on the street, Acton—he meant nothin' to me." In fact, her only reaction seemed to be relief; now she knew why Acton had pulled her off the case.

He released his breath—he had been worried about how she would react—and touched one of her fingers with his own. "It's an extraordinary coincidence."

Struggling to come to grips with it—truly, this was the wrinkle to top all wrinkles—she replied, "Meanin' you don't think it's a coincidence at all."

"No."

Knitting her brow, she met his concerned gaze and tried to follow his train of thought. "You think it was the same killer as the racecourse killer? And that now he's comin' after me?"

He frowned. "Perhaps—I don't know what I think. But I will not take any chances."

But Doyle was finding that this killer who made no sense continued true to form and slowly shook her head. "Perhaps it *is* only an extraordinary coincidence, Acton—there seems little point in killin' me da when I don't even know it's me da."

Acton reminded her, "The killer may not have known you were estranged. And someone has been into your personal file."

Aside from your fine self, that is, thought Doyle. "Who has access?"

"Only those with security clearance. But a first-class IT would be able to hack in—it's always a contest to keep ahead of the latest crop of them."

They sat in silence for a moment while she tried to assimilate this rather cataclysmic revelation—no question that Acton was certain, he knew to put her father's name on the wedding register, after all, and he wouldn't be mistaken about something like this.

His mobile vibrated again and he checked the identification. "I need to take this one." He answered and said, "Acton," then began taking notes, occasionally asking a question—it sounded like forensics to Doyle. "I'm coming in soon, don't go anywhere." He rang off. "I am wondering if you should stay at my flat."

She considered the idea seriously because she knew he

would worry less if she did. Shaking her head, she demurred. "I know you are worried, and I respect your judgment. But all in all, it would have been an easy thing to kill me off already if he wanted to—which makes me think that is not his intent."

This pragmatic remark did not seem to soothe his fears. "Your flat is not very secure," he reminded her. "You live alone."

"Not lately I don't," she corrected him with a small smile. "And I have a very fine weapon to boot. I will be on high alert, I promise—I'm glad you told me." She paused. "Does anyone else know?"

"No."

"Good." She did not hide her relief; she'd rather not have the brethren at the CID in on the sordid fact her father was a petty hoodlum who had come to a bad end—she'd never get that concealed carry permit, else.

Acton was silent, and she was aware he was frustrated that she wouldn't follow his desires on this—perhaps she was being unreasonable, and foolhardy besides. It was indeed an incredible coincidence, with the emphasis on incredible. She met his eyes with all sincerity. "If you want me to go to your place, I will—I don't want to distract you."

She could see he was trying not to suffocate her. "Just be ready."

"All right—I'll pack me bag, I will."

He made an apologetic gesture with his hands. "I'm afraid I must go back. May I drive you?"

"You may." She tried not to think how it would look to the others when she was taken off the racecourse murders as well as the Somers Town murders. It was ironic; they would think she was in Acton's black book when in fact it was just the opposite. She wondered what he would tell Habib that would convince her supervisor that she was not a dead weight dragging down his team's reputation. No point to broaching the subject; on the ride back in the car, Acton was constantly on his mobile and it was not the time to ponder her own paltry career, such as it was. He seemed intensely interested in the forensics; he spoke to Williams about the ballistics and someone else about trace and fiber. Upon arrival at the premium garage, he came around to open her door and looked into her face, assessing. "Are we all right?"

She smiled into his worried eyes. "Of course, Acton—I mean it."

"Be very careful."

"Yes, sir," she responded, teasing him.

"You will pay for that," he said, "later."

It was almost a relief to collapse in front of the laptop at her desk. Tumultuous, she thought, pronouncing the word slowly in her mind. That's a good word. With a ragged sigh, she tried to marshal her thoughts and decide which task was needed next. If she kept busy at her deskwork, maybe she wouldn't think about how miserable she was to be taken out of the field—and apparently there were misdemeanor thefts cryin' out for justice in Pimlico. She was interrupted by Habib, who was suffering from some strong emotion difficult to interpret.

"Hallo, sir." With some trepidation, Doyle wondered what could possibly befall her next.

"Chief Inspector Acton has called and asked that you be assigned to his current homicide docket as well as the Class A cold cases." Habib looked a little harassed.

Acton, Acton, she thought, the constriction in her breast easing. You just can't help yourself. "Yes, sir." She tried to behave as though she were already aware of this, although she had no clue that her Section Seven was going to make it up to her in such a spectacular fashion. The assignment was not at all appropriate for a first-year, particularly one who was not particularly apt at forensics.

Habib pursed his lips and clearly wanted to make a comment but was having difficulty choosing the words. Doyle took pity on him. "The chief inspector can be very high-handed—I hope he is not upsettin' our team's assignment schedule."

"Not at all," Habib conceded with good grace. "He seems to value your services inordinately."

Why is it, thought Doyle, that everything Habib says to me is a *double entendre?* Keeping her countenance, she replied in a grave tone, "I am fortunate to have the opportunity."

"He mentioned an afternoon assignment that will take you away from the office."

"Yes," she countered, "but I told him I would have to check with you."

Apparently she had gone too far in trying to sweeten Habib, as he reacted with alarm. "No, no—the chief inspector takes precedence—there is no question."

"Thank you." She wasted no time in heading home.

Remembering what she had promised Acton, she was extra vigilant as she let herself into her building but noticed nothing unusual; she was certain no one observed her. She locked the door behind her, fell into bed, and was immediately asleep. She was awakened hours later by Acton, who folded her into his arms as he slipped in beside her.

"You have a key?" she asked, sleepily surprised.

"Yes." He spoke as if to a simpleton and kissed the mole near the base of her throat to which he seemed much attached. "Are you rested?"

She smiled. "Does it matter?"

"No."

She suspected that he was there out of caution as much as to put a mattress to her back, but she was content either way. "Habib is annoyed."

"Good." He said no more.

CHAPTER 19

*H*E REALIZED HE COULD NOT FORCE HER TO QUIT AND LIVE SE-
questered with him. The solution, therefore, was to eliminate the threat.

Acton must have been tired from his long day because they
spent most of the night sleeping. In the morning Doyle woke
at dawn to hear that he was in her shower, which was a first. She
pulled the pillow in a bunch under her head and considered
the light that emitted from the crack at the bottom of the bathroom door. From the onset, she had decided there was no
point in making excuses; her flat was a grim little economical
place and there was little she could do, aside from new linens
and towels, to obscure this sad fact. When she had first moved
to London, she had very little in savings and few options; when
her mother became ill, she moved in with Doyle and money
became even scarcer. Now that she was making a respectable
salary, she continued to endure the place so as to pay off her
debts and save up a down payment as quickly as possible.
These good intentions didn't change the fact that when Acton
was there, she felt as though a thoroughbred were slummin' it
in a hack pen. He was too well bred to intimate that the ac-
commodations were less than satisfactory—and it was evident
he found her bed to his liking—but nonetheless she cringed a
bit to think of him fitting his frame into that miserable,
cramped shower.

When he turned off the water, she knocked on the door. "I'm awake; you don't have to be quiet."

He opened the door and leaned through it to kiss her. He was wet and had a towel wrapped around his hips. Seated on the edge of the bed, she watched him, trying to resist the urge to goggle. "What am I to do with my new assignments? In case Habib asks me, I should pretend to know." He began preparations to shave; she had never seen a man shave before and was fascinated.

"All other homicides in my docket," he said shortly, applying his razor. "Whatever you will."

"Thank you." She was grateful to the soles of her shoes—rescued from misdemeanor purgatory; put that in your pipe, Munoz.

He said nothing more and continued shaving. He must not like to talk in the morning, she decided—not during sex and not in the morning; mental note.

Watching him, she realized he brought overnight things with him in a small valise, along with a change of clothes in a garment bag. This is real, she thought, the bottom dropping out of her stomach—this is real; we are a couple. Before me is a man who was the next thing to a stranger a week ago and now he's got shaving things in my medicine cupboard. She dropped her gaze, trying to tamp down a burgeoning feeling of panic. Even when her mother was alive, she had always been fiercely independent; it was the by-product that came along with knowing the things that she knew. This is all happening far too fast, she thought. Mother a' mercy, lass—what were you thinking?

"Kathleen." She looked up to see that he had finished shaving and was now watching her from the bathroom door, a face towel in his hand. "What is it?"

Struggling miserably, she tried to find the right words to explain to him that she was having an anxiety attack because she was not yet ready for this reality. "I love you, Michael," was what came out instead. They stared at each other. She didn't know who was more surprised.

He walked over to her and, taking her head in his hands, crouched down to press his forehead against hers, his eyes closed. They didn't move for a moment. "You know that love does not even begin to describe it."

His voice resonated against the bones of her face and she nodded, the emotion in her chest suffocating her.

Still in his towel, he took her hands in his. "I cannot stay."

"I know." She gave him a wobbly smile. He was elated; she could feel it. "I will see you later," she whispered. He dressed and left, his mobile already vibrating.

In the resulting silence, she sat on the edge of the bed and stared at the door. I suppose I truly must love him, she thought in surprise. Fancy that.

Rising, she walked over to the bathroom, opened the medicine cupboard, and looked at his shaving razor sitting on the shelf within. She closed the door and regarded herself in the mirror. Silly knocker, she thought. Take hold of your foolish self.

After her own shower, she had a bowl of frosty flakes and strapped on her ankle holster. Despite Acton's urgings, she hadn't tried to shoot it, although she had practiced aiming and loading. No question but that it gave one an additional sense of security. She would be extra vigilant; it wasn't just about her anymore—if anything happened to her, she didn't like to think about how Acton would react. Still, in all honesty, he appeared to be worried about precious little. If this killer wanted to kill her, there was no doubt she would already be dead.

Mentally reviewing the cases, she dressed for work. I should make a point of wearing nicer clothes, she thought, looking over her wardrobe. I never seemed to have an incentive before, but I shouldn't continue in my slapdash ways. He always seems so effortlessly elegant and I . . . well, I am the antithesis. Good one; a vocabulary word.

Back to the murders. There were four now that seemed to be connected—or six, if the Somers Town murders were connected in some way, although she still wasn't certain about that, despite what Acton seemed to think. The way the woman was killed was apparently the link that made Acton uneasy. And as an added bonus, there were plenty of Irish people floppin' about the landscape; her father was Irish, the trainer was Irish, and Capper was Irish. But it may be merely a coincidence, after all—the Irish were thick on the ground around here. Someone had been into her personal file, where presumably her father's identity could be traced if one was willing to do some sleuthing, as Acton had done. So the Somers Town murders may have had everything to do with her and nothing to do with the other murders, or they had nothing to do with her and the fact that her father was a victim was a total coincidence. Bullets and casings had been found at the Somers Town scene because the killer had staged it to look like a murder-suicide, and therefore removal of evidence would have queered the pitch, but the evidence was carefully cleaned from the racecourse and Giselle's flat. All in all, the murders were more different than they were similar.

As she pulled her hair into a low ponytail at the back of her head, she decided that the most likely path was to concentrate on whoever had hacked into her file—presumably this was a smaller universe of suspects. All CID personnel ranked chief inspector or higher had top security clearance. If the hacker was a high-ranking officer, it would not be difficult to determine who had been doing the digging, since passwords were required. She also had a vague idea that the user could be traced to a particular device, although she wasn't very tech savvy. But Acton—who obviously could cover his own tracks—had suggested it was a first-rate hacker, so he must not have been able to trace the user. Therefore, the list of suspects opened up to include any anonymous techie in greater London, so some other angle would have to be pursued in order to narrow the universe and find a lead, let alone a working theory.

She rode the tube to St. James's Park, jostling against her fellow commuters and trying to shut out any incoming perceptions. The Met's security system was presumably first rate; it would probably be easier for someone who already had access to the system to cover his tracks rather than for someone to hack in from the outside, undetected. As she was no expert, it was just a theory but the thought was chilling. If the killer was someone at CID with access to forensics and the files, God help them.

Her latte was already waiting when she arrived at her cubicle, where she texted Acton with her symbol. And another thing, she thought as she began sorting through Acton's docket on her laptop—why would someone want to kill her father so that she would discover his mangled body? A very cruel and despicable act, for the love o' Mike. She didn't think she had any enemies. Why, she didn't even think that anyone she knew had enemies—except Acton, of course.

Going still for a moment, she pursued the thought. Acton probably had a basketful of enemies; it came with the territory. She examined this angle but it still made no sense. No one at CID knew about their relationship; she was certain. If a rumor even existed, Munoz would have never let her hear the end of it. Doyle was suddenly reminded of Acton's persistent questions on the way to the China Flower about whether she had told anyone about them. So, he had been to this point already and must have come up empty, as she was coming up empty. Truly, it made no sense. Perhaps someone thought she was pretty or something and wanted to take an innocuous look into her file as Acton had done. And her father's murder was a strange coincidence, which would have gone unremarked and unrecognized except for Acton's own transgressions into her personal records.

In all fairness, she understood why Acton was uneasy—that theory seemed far-fetched. Taken together, the murders did not make sense, but the fact remained that her da was dead, Irish people were dropping like flies, and someone had looked into her personal file and presumably decided to murder her father as a result. Small wonder he was worried about her safety—and he was certainly one to worry. Idly, she wondered for a moment what *had* happened with Acton so as to start him in on her—perhaps someday she would get the story, if he was willing to relate it. Best to tread carefully; she knew he did not like to speak about his condition. What he had said this morning after her own profession of love was as close as he would come—he said that love did not even begin to describe it.

Her thoughts were interrupted by Munoz, who was banging about her cubicle in an annoying and triumphant manner. Nothin' for it, thought Doyle with resignation. You'll have to listen to her crow. Try to keep your thoughts on a higher level—how Acton looked in his towel, for example.

"Doyle," said Munoz, inserting her head into the cubicle and tossing her hair over her shoulder. "I'm really busy. Can you help me out?"

"Yes, ma'am," replied Doyle, as though Munoz were her superior officer. "What is it you're needin'?"

"Holmes wants me to access the technology used by the dead men." She cast a wicked glance at Doyle under her lashes. "I'd like to access *him*."

Access denied, thought Doyle, and felt considerably better. "You are all talk and no action, Munoz."

The other girl conceded, "I have to be subtle. He's all business."

"Do you even *know* how to be subtle, Munoz?"

"Watch and learn, Doyle."

Doyle reflected that she was fast becoming aware of what pleased Acton sexually, and it did not appear to feature subtlety. This, however, was a piece of information Munoz need never know. "I am all admiration, my friend." As much fun as it was to egg on poor deluded Munoz, Doyle realized that eventually Munoz was going to find out that she and Acton were an item—the days were counting down. Therefore, she decided with no little regret that she should drop the topic. "What do you need me to do?" She hoped it was not something high profile, which would require her to confess to Munoz that she had been taken off the case.

"Go through the emails and files. There's a laptop and a tablet on my desk. Williams has their mobile phones. I'm needed back in the field." Her beautiful dark eyes slid to review her companion, a hint of malice contained therein. "What's your assignment?"

"I am sortin' through Acton's homicide docket," Doyle replied airily.

The other girl straightened, her expression incredulous. "*You* are doing analysis?"

"That I am."

Munoz made a silent whistling sound. "What did you do? Run him over by accident?"

If you only knew, thought Doyle, but aloud replied, "He's very busy just now and trusts me to see what needs to be done with his caseload."

Munoz started to laugh, and Doyle had to restrain an urge to fly out at her. "No, Doyle, really."

"You may believe me or not as you choose. It makes no difference to me." Doyle resumed typing.

With what could only be described as a smirk, the other contemplated her while Doyle wished she would just go away. "You aren't any good at research. Your only talent is interrogation."

"Oh, I am good at many things, Munoz." Doyle hid a smile.

The other girl cocked her head. "I will find out what you did to disgrace yourself, you know. I am relentless."

"Fine. Take your relentless self back to the scene."

Munoz tossed her hair in triumph. "See what you can do with the tech stuff."

Doyle saw an opportunity to do a little probing of potential suspects and took it. "Done."

CHAPTER 20

*H*E PHONED TO CONFER WITH FIONA, OFF THE RECORD. SHE HAD INDEED *found third-party DNA evidence on Smythe's body, not that he needed proof. He knew.*

Doyle picked up the dead man's laptop from Munoz's desk and went to search out Habib, who was in his office doing scheduling. He looked up as she stood at the doorway, his dark eyes opaque and unreadable.

"How are you at hackin' into computers, sir?"

Habib looked a little affronted. "I hope you are not making a stereotypical assumption based upon my heritage, DC Doyle."

"Not at all," Doyle soothed, reflecting that personally, she'd much rather be typecast as a computer wizard than a terrorist, which was the lot of the Irish. "I'm just not very strong on it and I need to know who is."

"Forensics has IT people," he replied shortly, turning back to his task. "Ask them."

"Yes, sir." She wondered why he was annoyed with her—perhaps it was because she was now the apple of the chief inspector's eye. "All right, if Munoz phones in to check on my progress, tell her I'm working on it."

Habib looked up. "You are helping Munoz? I understand she is in the field with Williams."

Ah, thought Doyle, seeing an explanation for his foul mood.

Munoz, Munoz; another one down. "I think she was walkin'
out to return to the scene, sir. She asked if I would look into
this."

His manner became more conciliatory. "I'm sorry, DC
Doyle; actually I'm not very good at IT." He attempted a joke.
"It is my only lack, I believe."

Feeling a bit sorry for him, she rallied. "Never say so, sir—
you are without a weakness." Except one very unprincipled DC
who shall remain nameless but with whom you stand absolutely
no crackin' chance. Doyle wasn't sure why she thought Habib
might be a suspect—other than he was unreadable and a little
odd—but when he had claimed no expertise in tech, he was
telling the truth, so he wasn't the infiltrator and therefore presumably not the killer. As she walked away, she thought about
Habib's unhappy distraction and decided it served her right
for thinking everything was always about her. This inspired another train of thought and made her wonder if perhaps Acton
was looking at this puzzle from the wrong angle.

Making a long and meandering progress down to Forensics
IT, she stopped occasionally to ask various personnel the same
questions about hacking into the laptop. Although some admitted to an expertise, she did not get the feeling anyone was a
potential suspect. I should stop, she thought reluctantly; if
Acton knew I was doing this, he would be most unhappy with
my sidelined self.

She thought about her idea and debated whether she should
bother Acton before tonight—assuming he would see her
tonight—no plans had been made as yet. He would see her,
though, and all there was to see besides, because he wouldn't
be able to stay away, the poor, crazed man. Her mobile vibrated
and she smiled.

"Cereal?"

"Very hungry," she texted back rather daringly. That should
give him something to think about in her absence, what wi'
Munoz at the scene and swingin' her hips about.

There was one more person Doyle wanted to test out before

she took the laptop to Forensics IT. Entering the research room she saw Owens, sitting on his stool and absorbed in his task.

"Hallo, Owens," she said cheerfully as she approached him.

"DC Doyle." Not as unhappy to see her this time—the fruit of good works.

"Are you interruptible?"

"Always," he replied with relative good grace. "What's up?"

"Do you know how to hack through a password?" She indicated the laptop under her arm.

"Let me see." He cleared a space on the table, moving various dry-looking treatises aside, and glanced up at her. "Is this sequestered evidence? Do I have to worry about proper protocol?"

"Well—not exactly." She gave him a conspiratorial look. "I'm supposed to take it to Forensics IT, but it's already been dusted for prints and I would so like to have a look at it first—it belonged to one of the victims from Leadenhall."

He began to fiddle with the keys and glanced at her again. "Trying to impress Holmes?"

She smiled that he knew the nickname already. "Yes," she admitted. "It's dog-eat-dog in the lair of the DCs. Any advantage is a boon."

"I am sorry you fell from grace."

This wasn't true, which meant that Owens now counted himself among the dogs in the lair. Everyone must think she was in Acton's black book and, like Munoz, hoped to gain an advantage from the situation. "I hope it's only temporary—I miss fieldwork."

"I think he's put Williams on this case in your place. Do you know Williams?" Owens looked up to her, curious.

Doyle said only, "Williams does fine work."

Owens gave her a half-smile and returned to his task. "You are too nice, I think."

"Whist, Owens—as if there is such a thing. We're all workin' to the same end."

The man's fingers flew on the keyboard as he tried different approaches—he definitely knew his way around the binary system. "Have you heard anything from the scene?"

"No. The field personnel aren't back, so there's no news circulatin' as yet. I doubt there's been a big break, though—we'd have heard. It does appear as though our prime suspect has saved us a lot of trouble by bein' kind enough to get himself killed."

Owens shrugged as he continued his work. "I don't know how much trouble it would have been anyway—he seemed the obvious choice. The trainer was probably muscling in on his numbers gig, and then after he killed him, the girlfriend was going to grass to the police—or blackmail him or something. Motive and opportunity; the door seems slammed shut."

"I suppose," she conceded, thinking this did make sense for those who were not privy to information about the eerily clean scenes or the carcass of her dear departed da. "It just seemed a little too obvious to me."

Smiling indulgently, he glanced up at her. "You read too many mysteries, maybe."

"Maybe," she agreed. Although not a lot of reading going on lately.

"What does Holmes think? Does he think the case is put to bed?"

Making a rueful face, she reminded him, "I am not privy, I'm afraid."

"Chin up," he rallied her. "Will you meet him for lunch? Perhaps you will hear something then."

It seemed an odd assumption, considering she was in supposed disgrace and Acton was at the scene. "I imagine he's too busy. If I do hear anythin', though, I will let you know."

He eyed her, tilting his head. "If you get the chance, put in a good word."

"Oh, he is well-aware you are talented, my friend. Perhaps I shouldn't be too nice."

Smiling in appreciation, he worked for a few more moments until he gave up and shrugged his shoulders. "I'm sorry. It has a sophisticated encrypter. They'll have the program in IT."

"Ah well—thanks for tryin'. I'll let you get back to it—sorry to interrupt."

"Always a pleasure."

At long last Doyle arrived at Forensics. Owens was an odd one—and keen on Acton besides—but she had canvassed him as carefully as she was able and hadn't noticed anything amiss.

She would have liked to linger in Forensics IT, as this would presumably be an excellent place to find an IT hacker who was well versed in forensics and had access to her file. However, she wasn't on friendly terms with any of the personnel, and her attempts to cast a few lures at the personable young men met with little success. In the time-honored manner of tech people, they were abrupt to the point of being rude and had little interest in discussing the murders with her fair self. Although she said her name to the evidence custodian a little too loudly, no one showed a special interest in her or even looked up as she relinquished the laptop and explained what was needed. Filling out the forms with a sigh, she asked if someone could be sent to fetch the tablet and returned to her cubicle; it had been an unproductive hour and she needed to get some work done.

It was almost eerily quiet in her area—Munoz was in the field, which brought the noise level down considerably. Apparently all available hands were working on the murders; Acton wanted this case solved, no doubt so they could establish some sort of normal routine consisting of early evenings and a lot of carnal goings-on. Also, he was well aware she hated deskwork and it wasn't where her talents lay; the city would suffer if she weren't out in the field, asking questions of its citizenry.

After calling the commercial cleaning companies, she caught a break; there was a crew who would have been finishing up on the lower floors around one o'clock because they worked from the top floor down. She contacted the individual workers and struggled a bit as each side tried to understand the other's unintelligible accent. Interesting, she thought as she rang off—another item to report to Acton. Hopefully she could draw out her report long enough to avoid having to cook something; she wasn't much of a cook.

Doyle decided there was no time like the present to delve into Acton's homicide docket—and it may also be interesting to have a look at Acton's Class A cold cases while she was at it. Class A cases were old cases that had turned up some promising evidence but not enough to prosecute. The Class B cold cases were literally hopeless, with little evidence and no real suspects. Both classes remained on inactive status in the event someone had an attack of conscience or a newer case revealed a connection. Although she checked in with Acton on the hour, he did not respond; he would be frenetically busy, as was always the case in the first twenty-four hours of a homicide. She fidgeted and chafed at her assignment—it was hard to bear, not knowing what was happening in the field. Solve the problem, Acton, she pleaded mentally; I'm wasting away here.

When it was late afternoon, she was surprised to see the messenger who brought her the lattes in the mornings come by, holding a plain envelope. "For you, miss."

Within was a hotel room key card and a note in Acton's writing that said *Grenoble Hotel, room 1200.* She turned it over, but that was the extent of it. For a wary moment she hesitated, but she recognized Acton's distinctive handwriting and the usual messenger, and decided she would like nothing better than to escape her cubicle, exile, and find out what the cryptic note meant. Packing up swiftly, she headed out, deciding against checking the hotel's location on her laptop. Acton had warned her that she should assume everything she did on the device was being monitored, just to be on the safe side. She had the strong impression it was something he knew about firsthand, in his career as a Section Seven.

CHAPTER 21

*H*E FELT VITAL, AND SO VERY LUCKY TO BE ALIVE. EXTRAORDINARY *how things could change, how fate could take a hand. All danger would be discreetly eliminated by tomorrow and then he could more properly concentrate on setting up their life together.*

The Grenoble Hotel was an exclusive establishment, small, elegant, and understated, located in the Kensington district. Doyle could feel her color rise as she passed through the revolving door entrance into the marbled lobby—she felt out of place and half-expected the fancy doorman to seize her and push her out again. As this did not occur, she found the lift and inserted her key card so as to have access to the twelfth floor. Room 1200 turned out to be a palatial suite the likes of which she had never seen before but probably would become accustomed to if she indeed clung to Acton like a barnacle. Standing on the threshold, she tentatively spoke his name aloud, but she already knew he wasn't there. With an air of bemusement, she then wandered through the sumptuous rooms and duly noted that the bedroom alone was larger than her entire flat. A huge fish tank complete with exotic tropical fish was prominently featured in the main room, and the furnishings were beautiful; every detail reflected an understated luxury. She was a stranger in a strange land.

A bouquet of roses resided on the parquetry table in the bedroom. Propped beside it was a note that read, *I'll be there as soon as I can. Order something.*

Doyle held the note against her mouth to hide a smile and considered her reflection in the huge gilt mirror on the opposite wall. Apparently the reward for telling a man you loved him was a night in the lap o' luxury. Mental note.

After showering at leisure, she wrapped herself in one of the hotel's luxurious robes to lie propped up against the many pillows on the bed, fiddling with the remote controls and reading the room service menu. Although she was hungry, she decided she would wait for Acton, as she didn't know if she had the wherewithal to deal with the hotel personnel just yet. Instead, she passed the time watching television until she heard a card in the door. Clicking off the telly, she arranged herself on the bed, pulling her hair in front of her shoulders and running her fingers through it. Acton appeared at the bedroom door and was brought up short.

"You are a sight." He approached to put his hands on either side of her so as to lean in and kiss her. He then collapsed and lay back into the pillows beside her, exhaling slowly and loosening his tie as he kicked off his shoes. They regarded each other for a moment, both sunk into the pillows. "I'm sorry I kept you waiting. It's been a long day."

With an effort, she refrained from replying that she had spent the most tedious day imaginable and instead said, "Not to worry. I've been entertainin' myself feedin' gold nuggets to the tropical fish."

He was on alert and gave her a searching look.

"It's so wonderfully grand, Michael. Watch this." Sitting up, she pressed the remote button that made the bedroom's elaborate fireplace burst into gas-furnished flames. Another button caused the lights to dim. She did not look at him but sat with her arms around her bent knees, watching the flames. His hand reached to stroke her back and she knew he was watching her, unsure of her mood. Don't spoil this, knocker, she thought with a mental shake. Face facts. Turning to him, she drew up a corner of her mouth. "Am I bein' transitioned, then?"

He paused, gauging what to say. "Yes. I would like to give you the choice, but I can't."

Placing a palm against his cheek, she assured him, "You didn't have to do this, Michael—I understand. Better to just tell me what you need from me—I will come around, I promise. Remember you are not to be careful with me."

The dark eyes watched hers, the intensity of the emotion behind them very powerful. "I wanted to give us a chance to be away from it for a night. I wanted to give you something."

It was the second time he had said such a thing to her, and she considered this, her brow knit as she traced a finger on her knee. "I think I am afraid to accept anythin'. I am afraid about what I spoke of the other night but I am not supposed to say again."

"You are afraid to relinquish yourself to me because you may be hurt."

That was exactly it. "Yes. Apparently I have my own demons."

With a gentle hand, he pulled on her so that she lay back and settled into his arms. He didn't try to convince or cajole her, but instead kissed her temple. "All right."

He knows me very, very well, she thought, breathing in his scent like an addict. If we go on like this, I am going to get overly emotional again as I did this morning—I hardly recognize myself. To get past the moment, she dug her chin into his chest and addressed him in a tart tone. "If you think I am goin' to be content to bill and coo all night in this remarkable bed, Michael, you have another think comin'. I am dyin' to talk to you about the case and hear what has happened."

He lifted his hand and ran his fingertips down the base of her throat and between the overlapping edges of the robe, where it fell away from her breasts. "Could the billing and cooing come first?"

"Done." She shrugged off the robe.

Later, they lay together, she in the crook of his arm, watching the fire. It did seem a million miles away from her poor flat in Chelsea and two million from the kill site at the alley.

"Michael." She pulled gently on the hair on his chest. "Have *you* told anyone about us?"

He was suddenly alert and wary; she could feel it. "Why?"

"I was thinkin' that you may be lookin' at it from the wrong end—perhaps it was someone from your set who dropped the information, albeit innocently." She hoped he appreciated the deft use of "albeit." "That is, if we assume my father's murder was connected in some way to my relationship with you."

He was silent for a long moment. "I did tell someone, but I did not disclose your identity."

Her ears perked up; here was an item of interest. "Drake?" she guessed.

"Good God, no. Why would I tell Drake?"

At his reaction, Doyle smiled into the side of his chest. "I am told on reliable authority that men boast to each other of their conquests."

"You are not a conquest." His tone brooked no argument.

"I don't know," she teased him, "I feel as though I may as well be drawin' up terms of surrender."

He ignored the remark. "I had a casual relationship with a woman at work—we are old friends, and occasionally we would meet for sex. It stopped about six months ago."

Doyle was surprised but not, on reflection, too surprised. It was clear he knew what he was about in the bedroom, and as he had not been linked publicly to any particular woman, that left clandestine affairs or prostitutes. She much preferred the thought of clandestine affairs.

His arm tightened around her. "It was nothing like this."

She had to smile again. "God have mercy if it was. I'm not jealous, Michael, nor even surprised."

The arm relaxed. "I'd rather not tell you her identity."

Ah. Always the gentleman, he was. She countered, "As long as it's not Munoz, I don't care."

"Good God," he said again, and she chuckled. She didn't want to know. Whoever she was, however, Acton's summarization of their casual relationship was way off the mark—there was not a woman alive who would willingly relinquish him to another, however friendly the context. Doyle hoped he wasn't overlooking a potential motive, but decided he wasn't that dense.

"Do you have any leads?" She wanted to hear his thoughts and hoped that she had put him in a compliant mood. It had certainly seemed that way a few minutes ago.

"They are developing."

She made a wry mouth, remembering that she should not take advantage of the personal relationship to obtain an advantage in the professional. One could hope to be thrown a bone, however, and surely there must be *something* he could tell her. "Do you think the danger to me may be still lurkin' about?"

He chose his words carefully. "I believe not; the investigation is going in a different direction."

This obscure response prompted some prompting, and she raised herself up on an elbow to look at him. "But you don't believe the deaths of Capper and Smythe were a kill-on-kill; you think it was the handiwork of the original killer, who tried to make it appear as though it were a kill-on-kill." This only made sense; Capper and Smythe were mates and unlikely to engage in a gunfight in such an unlikely place, even if they had had a falling-out. She remembered Acton's remark at the scene to that effect, back when she was sulking and not paying attention—no question that this was his working theory.

But his response was cautious. "We will see where the evidence leads."

This, of course, was not how she plied her trade as she was more a leaper to conclusions; but she had to concede that a chief inspector did not have that luxury. Impatient with such niceties, she cut to the nub of the matter. "Can I go back into the field, please?"

"Not as yet—soon." He began to trace her fingers, which were spread out on his chest.

This seemed encouraging, so she decided to leave well enough alone and change the subject. "Do you think Capper's interrogation spooked the killer—made him decide to take him out?"

"Possibly."

Twining her fingers with his, she offered, "I wondered about it—I wondered if it could be someone on the inside."

She felt him become wary again. "It could be someone who has infiltrated, yes."

With a small frown, she suddenly realized that he was answering in equivocations so that she could not spot what was true and what was not, which seemed a bit counterproductive;—oftentimes they reached a very satisfactory result when they brainstormed together, and this was not the case for him to decide to play it close to the vest. Soldiering on, she offered another item of interest. "There was a cleanin' crew in the lower floors at the estimated time of death. They would have heard the shots, one would think, but they heard nothin'.." No question but that the shots should have been noticeable in such a quiet neighborhood and at such a quiet time. The obvious conclusion was that a silencer was used, which again would support the theory that it had all been staged by the true killer.

He began to gently stroke the arm that lay across his chest, back and forth—she noted this was a habit he had developed; he hardly seemed aware he did it. As the stroking continued, she reasoned aloud, "The real killer is hopin' we'll close the case, the same as Somers Town."

"Perhaps."

Trying to control her annoyance, she remembered what Drake had said and took a cast. "Do you think Solonik is behind it?"

There was a moment of surprise, quickly suppressed. "There are times," he mused, "—when you are almost frightening."

She lay back down and retorted crossly, "Remember that, if you please, the next time you make me play twenty questions to winkle a decent answer from you. Honestly, Michael."

Thus admonished, he gave her an honest answer but with palpable reluctance. "It is not Solonik's style, but I believe it is possible that he may be involved. Or the interests he works for may be involved."

She considered this revelation in surprised silence because it pointed back to the original theory of an assassin, a professional killer. That in itself wasn't so strange, certainly; a racecourse was historically attractive to the organized underworld, and although she had never worked those kinds of cases, Acton certainly had and knew of what he spoke. Sensing there was something he was not telling her, she wondered for a moment why he was so reticent, but then the penny dropped and she remembered why this one was different—she was such a knocker sometimes. "So, how does my departed da fit in?"

He hesitated and again chose his words with care. "I believe it may have been a bit of egotism. A chance to show off his abilities."

But she remembered that Drake had said Solonik—whoever he was—was not a show-off. She frowned into the darkness. Better research Solonik and who he worked for—mental note—and in the meantime try to puzzle out Acton's unwillingness to throw her a flippin' bone. If she didn't know better, she'd be tempted to leap to the conclusion that Acton knew the killer's identity but did not want to disclose it, which made little sense. If the killer was hired by an underworld figure, why not just say so? Although perhaps it had something to do with Acton's own dark doings, which would explain why he didn't want to tell her. The wretched man didn't realize she'd already guessed about the gun-running and was doing her best not to think about it—one crisis at a time.

While she was puzzling this out, a silver lining presented itself. "If that is the case, Acton, then it was nothin' personal—I'm not in danger." And can I please, please go back into the field with you, she pleaded mentally—and make sexual innuendos just so you will disapprove. Faith, it would be heaven.

"Perhaps."

She made a sound of extreme impatience.

CHAPTER 22

HER BODY WAS BECOMING USED TO HIM, WHICH WAS EXHILARATING. He took some photographs of her while she slept.

Doyle woke the next morning to find that Acton was seated at the parquetry table, already dressed and watching her. "Good morning."

He was very content, she could tell. I believe I am rather good at this, for a novice, she thought as she stretched. "A fine mornin'." She pronounced it "foine" to tease him, then sat up and drew the covers around her, as she had nothing on. By his arrested expression, she realized she'd better distract him or they'd be abed again and that may not be such a good idea. "I'll need to go home to get a change of clothes before I'm back to my wretched desk detail."

"I brought some clothes from your flat," he explained in a mild tone, nodding toward the closet.

"Did you? Then I suppose I needn't." They regarded each other. "Am I never goin' home again, Michael?"

"Tomorrow evening, but not before. I want to stir up your routine, just to be safe."

She nodded. "We're here again tonight, then?"

"Yes, if that is acceptable."

Smiling, she ducked her head. "Oh, it's very acceptable." There was no question that it was nice to have a bigger bed.

Tracing a design on the bedspread with her fingertip, she thought, there is nothin' for it; time for another discussion. Here goes.

"We probably shouldn't have sex for a few days." She could feel herself color up.

"You are ovulating." It was a statement, not a question. Trust him not to spare her blushes; he probably knew more about it than she did.

"Yes, I think so." She had slipped the literature from the church vestibule into her bag and had read it carefully at home, thermometer in hand.

He said nothing for a moment and she had no idea what he was thinking. "All right."

Mother a' mercy, could it be possible he would not have minded a pregnancy at this juncture? It was the last thing they should be thinking of, for heaven's sake. Dropping her gaze, she fought the panic that threatened to rear up again.

His matter-of-fact voice cut into her thoughts. "I have some estate business I've been neglecting and I must drop by Layton's; I may go this evening, if I can get away."

Righting herself with an effort, she nodded. Layton was his man of affairs who had offices in the center of the business district. Acton had stopped by a few weeks ago when they were out in the field and asked if she wanted to come and wait inside while he conducted some business. She had declined, privately thinking that it looked like the sort of place where alarms would go off if the likes of her darkened its doorway. "That's all right, it's the monthly reconciliation service at church tonight and I'll go with Nellie. I'll wait to have dinner here with you, if you'd like."

He watched her for a moment, his expression unreadable. "Is that like confession?"

She made a wry mouth. "They call it reconciliation now, hopin' we won't realize it's the same grim thing. They're very wily that way."

"May I accompany you?"

Curled in the cocoon of expensive sheets, she hid her surprise. "If you'd like." Listening to her own equivocal tone, she amended, "Of course you may. It's at seven."

"I will meet you there." Kissing her, he then left for work and she watched him go, wishing she knew what was afoot and subject to a vague uneasiness—the kind that never seemed to bode well. It was clear to her that he was no longer anxious about these cases, even though ostensibly the true killer was still at large and trying to get away with it. Interesting, she thought. And doubly interesting that it's such a shrouded subject.

Doyle decided she should order breakfast, as she had not had any dinner the night before—instead they had raided the honor bar when they had come up to breathe—and took a look in the closet whilst she awaited its delivery. Acton was a wonder; several outfits she had worn to work on previous occasions were contained therein, complete to the details. She dressed with no real enthusiasm, wishing she were looking forward to fieldwork and bitterly resenting the DCs who were taking her place on this case just when things were getting interesting—stupid Munoz and stupid Williams. She took a last look in the gilt mirror and sighed. Get on with it, Doyle—you'll survive. And no question everything is ten million times better than it was at this time last week—quit being such a crackin' baby and trust the man.

This resolution, however, did not last long because once at work Doyle watched for Munoz to arrive and then shamelessly flattered her for half an hour to glean information about the Leadenhall murders. Munoz, preening with importance, revealed that Forensics had determined that the murders had indeed occurred in the alley and the bodies had not been merely dumped there. The weapons this time were a 9 mm and a .22, respectively—both illegal.

So, the large-caliber gun from the earlier murders was not used, thought Doyle. The killer is indeed spooked and is covering his tracks.

"Holmes's working theory is the two men drew and fired several times upon each other almost simultaneously," Munoz continued with a superior air. "The bullets and casings found at the scene are all from the same weapons and indicate erratic targeting."

"And?" prompted Doyle.

"Then Smythe was hit, but not fatally; when Capper came closer to assess the injury Smythe raised his weapon and fired close-range."

That may be the killer's fatal error, thought Doyle; too hard to contain the DNA evidence when the shot was at close range—unless the killer was wearing a bunny suit like the SOCOs did; anything was possible in this strange case. "And Smythe died of his wound?"

"Yes, bled out."

"Were there silencers on the weapons?"

Munoz's expression was pitying and she spoke as if to an imbecile. "No, Doyle; there were no silencers on the weapons."

Doyle bit back a retort because Munoz did not know of the cleaning crew—apparently no one did, except her and Acton. By all accounts, the true working theory should be easy to piece together; the killer lured them there, one at a time, and killed them—he knew that time of death can never be precise within an hour or so. The staging was not perfect, however, because he did not know of the cleaning crew nearby who had heard nothing—no arguments, none of the multiple shots—which put a huge dent in the theory Acton was putting forward. And another thing; the ballistics report should confirm there were silencers used—which in turn wouldn't make sense given the wild shoot-out theory. Surely the ballistics report was available by now—perhaps the information was being withheld for some reason; she remembered Williams was working ballistics for Acton. And another angle came to mind; she asked Munoz, "Any prints or DNA?"

Munoz tossed her hair. "They're going over it with a fine-toothed comb, although it seems pretty straightforward. I think they are looking to match one or both of the victims with the earlier murders at the racecourse."

One murder at the course, corrected Doyle silently. The other was at Giselle's flat. And I imagine they will find something—fibers maybe, which links one of the dead men to at least one of the earlier scenes. The killer wants to put this to bed and will have planted the evidence. But for reasons that were unclear, Acton was promoting the false theory and—here she paused, much struck—and had taken the fair Doyle and her conclusions-leaping abilities off this case.

She listened to Munoz with only half an ear while she thought over this rather startling conviction. Acton was up to something, then—something under the radar. Perhaps it was some sort of sting operation, hoping to catch the now-complacent killer by pretending the case was closed. Perhaps it was being kept so quiet that he couldn't even tell her for fear she'd queer the pitch by blurting out the wrong thing to the wrong person—not an unfounded fear, after all, given her track record.

But she doubted it. She knew that man—on one hand she hardly knew him but on a more elemental level she knew him very well indeed—and there was something he was keeping from her, which in itself was alarming, given his condition. She thought of the crime scene in Teddington, when Acton had offered to loan her money even though it was against protocol. He had not been able to resist the urge to come to her rescue, even though she might be embarrassed by the offer, which indeed she had been. When it came to her, he could not help himself. Frowning, she was struck by a tantalizing thought that hovered just out of reach; this was important for some reason.

"Snap out of it, Doyle. What is the word on the tech?"

Doyle blinked. "Oh. I'll check."

Munoz jerked her head in frustration. "Sooner rather than later; Holmes wants a report and I'm all over him. I mean it." She slid Doyle a smug, sloe-eyed look.

Instead of making a suitable retort, Doyle tried to regain her thread of thought—the one that seemed important. She drew a blank and so instead wondered if Acton had consciously chosen her as an object of obsession or if he had been powerless. Imagine, for example, if he had become fixated on Munoz (who was going on and on about something self-important; Doyle had lost interest) and Munoz had turned him down flat or had threatened to go to HR. What would he have done? But such a thing wouldn't have happened—someone like him would never allow himself to be at the mercy of a girl like Munoz. He'd never allow it, she thought slowly. Now, what is it I'm trying to understand, here?

Her phone pinged, and she texted her symbol—she'd forgotten and was a few minutes late. She considered the mobile's screen, debating whether to ring Nellie to warn her that his lordship was going to join them at church tonight, but decided she'd spare her the foreknowledge. Nellie was a Filipino immigrant and fascinated by the peerage.

Realizing that Munoz had asked her something, she lifted her gaze. "Sorry, Munoz, I was woolgatherin'. What was it?"

"Who is that you were texting?"

Doyle smiled. "My secret lover."

Munoz laughed aloud and Doyle held on to her temper. It is possible that I will very much enjoy it when Munoz discovers that Acton is mine, she thought, and was surprised by her own spite.

But Munoz apparently was willing to render some aid to the enemy, and arched a graceful brow. "Speaking of such, Williams was asking me things about you."

"What sort of things?" Doyle wondered if Williams could hack his way around a personal file. He didn't seem the murdering type.

"Just general asking. We're going to lunch at the deli. Maybe you should come."

The deli was just that—a deli located down the street from their building. In the warmer months it was a popular place for lunch. "Done," said Doyle, thinking to scope out Williams the questions-asker. "Come get me when you go."

Two hours later, Owens came by to visit, hanging on her cubicle partition as though he owned the place and looking over her shoulder at her screen. Saints, thought Doyle, looking up at him. How I miss being in the field.

"Anything new?"

Doyle reflected that Owens was in the same boat as she was, dyin' to be out in the thick of it but left to glean information from others more fortunate. Taking pity, she told him what she knew, editing out anything she had heard from Acton and repeating more or less what Munoz had told her. She didn't mention the cleaning crew or her suspicions about the silencer; she still wasn't sure about Owens—or any of them, for that matter. With this in mind, she thought she'd do a little listening. "I'm meeting Munoz and Williams for lunch at the deli. Why don't you come by and you can quiz them to your heart's content."

"Thanks, I owe you." He winked as he left.

Creepy, she thought, turning back to her screen. But it may be he's creepy because he is an ambitious weasel with a crush on my man and not because he's a killer. She paused and regarded her hands thoughtfully; as part of her campaign to improve her general grooming habits, she was trying to grow her nails. I am remarkably unkind today, she realized. And I hope it is not because I look forward to being in church with Acton instead of abed with him, because that, my girl, is unacceptable.

CHAPTER 23

*H*E WAS LOOKING FORWARD TO THE END OF IT. THERE WAS ALWAYS *a sense of elemental satisfaction.*

Just after noon, Munoz, with a replenishment of perfume that Doyle could smell from the next cubicle, announced it was time to go downstairs. "Did you find out about the tech report?" Munoz used her best impersonation of an impatient DCI dealing with a dosser.

"Nothing of interest," Doyle reported. "Forensics IT got past the passwords, but there was very little to glean—they weren't the types to record their doin's on their electronics, unfortunately. And the calls to each other were only sporadic."

"I'll need to submit the report—forward it to me, please."

"I'll get it by this afternoon." It's a very fine lesson in humility I'm to be having, she thought, resisting the urge to grind her teeth. In all things, give thanks.

"Samuels is joining us," Munoz revealed as they emerged from the lift and headed out the main entrance. At Doyle's blank look, she explained, "He's from Drake's unit." Munoz then gave Doyle a critical glance. "It wouldn't kill you to try to flirt with the men a little, you know—or if you wore a little makeup once in a while. If you made the least attempt to be more alluring, you'd have more of a social life and you wouldn't have to go to those horrible singles mixers."

"It wasn't a singles mixer and I didn't wind up goin' anyway," Doyle replied hotly. Ironic that she had skipped the seminar and the compatibility rubric and had proceeded directly to the pleasures of the flesh—saved a lot of time and trouble, it did.

They walked out of the building and down the broad sidewalk of Victoria Street to the deli, which was crowded with police officers, as it was a very fine day. Williams was already holding a table with Samuels, whom he introduced to Doyle. She and Munoz then went to order sandwiches and returned to join the men. They ate and talked and no one minded when Owens walked by and asked if he could join them.

There was a great deal of good-natured discussion about their caseloads, and Munoz was in her element, flirting with everyone—even Owens. Save your powder, Munoz, thought Doyle. He doesn't play for your team.

Williams seemed a bit more subdued than usual; he certainly didn't appear to be as interested as Munoz had intimated. She must have been exaggerating, which, all in all, was just as well; it was more likely Munoz just wanted a handmaiden to accompany her while she held court. Not for the first time, Doyle considered the general reaction from the DC corps when her relationship with Acton was revealed, and she almost shuddered at the thought. To take her mind off it, she turned to Samuels, who seemed rather shy but could be drawn out on the all-engrossing subject of homicides.

He hunched his shoulders in chagrin. "I haven't had a chance to work a murder yet. I'm jealous of the rest of you—you're all so lucky."

"It's Doyle who broke the ice." Williams saluted her with his glass of iced tea. "Holmes found her useful and now he's willing to assign the occasional DC to a homicide."

Doyle bowed her head in mock humility at the homage, all the while thinking that she may not have broken the ice so much as been plunged headlong in a fast-moving torrent and the devil take the hindmost.

"Nothing short of miraculous," agreed Samuels, who joined in the toast.

Munoz, unhappy with the shift in focus of attention, raised her own glass. "And here's hoping she'll be out of Holmes's doghouse sooner rather than later."

Doyle blushed and the others looked a little embarrassed. "Happens to the best of us," Williams assured her. "We can't forget our humanity, after all."

I would very much like to forget both humanity and humility and strangle DC Munoz, thought Doyle, grinding her teeth. And Williams, bless him, always seems to step in to my rescue—very unlikely he's murdering people left and right.

"What's happened with Holmes?" asked Samuels, looking between them. "Or is it a sore subject?"

Doyle refused to answer because she couldn't tell the truth or they'd all fall out of their respective chairs. Munoz, realizing that she had not shown to advantage, added hastily, "Nothing that won't blow over—Holmes is a little tough on her, is all."

Doyle intercepted a quick look from Williams that she couldn't interpret but that seemed to indicate a difference of opinion. She demurred in mock humility, "Whist, he's been very fair—think on it, I'd never taste the joys of Class A cold cases, else."

"He is a hard taskmaster," added Owens, who was apparently yet another champion in Doyle's defense. "He's keeping me very busy with the bloodstains materials."

Doyle and the others looked at him in surprise. "Did Acton give you a project, then, Owens?" Faith, what had gotten into the man? Owens must be over the moon.

Pleased to have something to tell them, the trainee explained, "Holmes is giving a lecture at the Academy on bloodstains in two weeks. He remembered I had an interest and has me editing his materials and assembling photographs and diagrams from his cases. I'm working in the adjunct next to his office."

Why is it, thought Doyle with profound irritation, everyone seems to be working with Acton except me? She then recalled that he did his best work at night and comforted herself with this thought.

Her mobile vibrated, and she pulled it out to read the text. "Where RU?"

She texted, "Deli."

Immediately, another one came. "Who?"

Feeling a little foolish, she typed abbreviated names as quickly as she was able, holding the mobile under the table.

Munoz teased her, "Who is it this time?"

"My parole officer," Doyle replied absently. "Wants a word with me, he does."

There was general laughter and then Munoz added archly for the benefit of the unattached males at the table, "Do you have a secret boyfriend, Doyle?"

Doyle replied mildly, "Not at present, no."

As she could see that Munoz was winding up to make another smart remark, Doyle forestalled her. "Anythin' interestin' come up with respect to the Leadenhall murders?"

Munoz was happy to be the center of attention again. "I heard a rumor that there were fibers on one of the men from the murdered girl's sweater, which pretty well slams the door. There's no official report yet. It's just a rumor."

Ah, thought Doyle—just as expected. "Are you helping with the ballistics report, Williams? Anything unusual?"

Instead of answering directly, Williams deftly turned the subject. "Where do all the illegal guns come from, anyway? Everyone has one—it's like the bloody Wild West out there."

Doyle carefully pulled her left leg further under the table.

"Too much money to be made," agreed Samuels. "The runners always find a way."

Time to change the subject, thought Doyle. "Aren't you working on contraband, Samuels?"

"I am. It's like herding cats; you have no way of measuring your progress. Very frustrating."

Interestingly enough, this last was untrue. I wonder what that is about? Doyle thought, brought up short; perhaps I am losing my touch.

"Put in for a transfer," suggested Williams.

"Yes, come join me in the archives," teased Doyle.

"I'll stick it out for the time being; I don't want them to think I'm a complainer." He glanced up the street and announced, "Look, its Holmes."

They all turned to see Acton's tall figure striding along the sidewalk, heading back to the Met. Munoz called out to him and he paused, spotted her, and then approached their table.

Saints, thought Doyle, hiding her surprise. Does he want me away from here? She waited to see if he would give her a cue as they all stood up and greeted him, Munoz looking like the cat at the cream pot.

"We were discussing the proliferation of illegal weapons," said Williams, his tone deferential.

Polishing the apple, thought Doyle. Good one.

"A major problem," Acton agreed. "The more restraints that are attempted, the more the black market flourishes." Doyle was grateful he made no attempt to meet her eye.

"Is the Leadenhall case near a resolution?" asked Munoz, who decided she had ceded the floor long enough.

"I believe so."

"I have the final ballistics report for you," offered Williams, which earned him a sharp look from Doyle.

"Come, then." To the rest, he looked at his watch and said, "Who is saving the city?"

They immediately disassembled.

Doyle was forced to listen to Munoz chortle as they retreated back to their basement. "Did you see him come over when I called? He is so tall—and you know what they say about men who are tall."

"Munoz," warned Doyle, and then was not sure what it was she wanted to say.

"I know, I know—I'm not his type. I'm just having fun."

Munoz lowered her voice. "There's a rumor that he's very friendly with that woman from the morgue."

Doyle blinked. "Fiona?"

"Yes, but it's not clear whether it's anything other than friendship—they went to school together or something."

Fiona, thought Doyle. She remembered the inter-team conference when Fiona was eating her doughnut and expertly fielding Acton's questions at the same time—they did have an easy camaraderie. She tried to picture Fiona and Acton together and decided she'd rather not. One thing was clear; he didn't have a preference when it came to women—Doyle was very slender; her mother had always referred to her fondly as a bundle o' bones. Well then, mystery solved. Fiona seemed like a nice, kind person. She glanced sideways at Munoz. It could have been much worse.

CHAPTER 24

HE WOULD EXTRACT ANY INFORMATION HE COULD BY ANY MEANS HE could, but he didn't want to come back to her too late; she needed her sleep.

Doyle left work with plenty of time to arrive early at the reconciliation service at St. Michael's—she didn't want Acton to arrive before she did and have to fend for himself. Waiting in the church vestibule, she tried not to be anxious about this anticipated clash of civilizations even as her eyes flew to every congregant who came through the door. It was a good sign that he was willing to come; she should be welcoming and not a bundle of nerves. It was just that people who hadn't been steeped in it from birth may find the whole thing a bit off-putting. She tried not to think about what she would do if he found the whole thing off-putting.

Next to her was the fund-raising chart, which showed the anemic progress the parish was making toward a new roof, and she decided she should move away from it so as not to make a bad impression from the start. It was a small parish and not in an affluent area, so there was always an ongoing appeal for funds. Nellie was a wizard at fund-raising ideas; she had instituted a raffle for the pastor's parking spot at Midnight Mass and had raised nearly five hundred pounds. Her latest plan was to institute a weekly bingo night, but Father John, who abhorred gambling, was standing firm. Doyle put her money on Nellie.

Acton appeared in the doorway and came toward her. Taking her hand, he bent to kiss her cheek as though it was the most natural thing in the world, which, of course, it wasn't—not in public. Struggling to catch her breath, she blurted out, "You know you may not have sex with—with anyone else anymore."

He regarded her for a moment, his expression unreadable. "Yes, I am aware."

Horrified, but unable to control her tongue, she continued in a rush. "Because I know the aristocracy has a different view a' these kinds of things." Pausing, and well-aware she sounded slightly hysterical, she then added in a small voice, "I would be very unhappy, Michael."

He said nothing for a moment and she could see the glint of humor in his eyes. "Is this part of the service?"

"No," she confessed. "I am havin' a fit o' the absurds."

He squeezed her hand gently. "Let's go in. I promise I won't embarrass you or ask anyone to have sex."

"Thank you," she replied, gathering up her dignity. "I would appreciate it."

They entered the nave and slid into a pew near the back—she wanted him to know that the place did not show to advantage in the evening. "There are lovely stained-glass windows, but you can't appreciate them at night. One is of St. Michael and is quite fine."

He took her hand in his and she calmed down; she always talked too much when she was nervous. As the service was not heavily attended, Doyle's presence with a male companion attracted a few covert stares from the regulars. She and Acton sat in silence for a few moments, until Doyle realized—once she stopped worrying about what everyone else was thinking—that Acton was full of news.

"What has happened?" she whispered.

"To what?" he whispered in return.

"Have you solved the case?"

She had caught him off guard, she saw, but he recovered and said in a neutral tone, "I have some information that is helpful."

"Can you tell me?"

Running his thumb over the back of her hand, he bent his head, thinking. "I'd rather not, I'm afraid."

Maddening, is what it was, but she refused to be annoyed at church. "Don't forget," she reminded him, "I'd rather not be humored."

"I won't," he assured her.

She shot him a look, not clear on whether he wouldn't humor her or wouldn't forget, but he had moved on to the next topic. "I'm afraid I'll need to do some work later tonight, and in the meantime I may have to take a call from—Forensics."

She knew he was going to say "Fiona" but caught himself, which showed that he'd guessed that she knew. Honestly; the way she was behaving it was a small wonder he didn't want to tell her anything about the case. Grow up, she castigated herself; he told you it was over and now he is all Doyle, all the time. Change the subject. "What exactly happened at lunch?"

This, however, was apparently another shrouded subject. "Aren't you supposed to be praying?"

With ill-concealed exasperation she replied, "I am prayin' for patience, my friend, but it does not seem to be workin'."

Relenting, he chose his words with care. "I continue to be concerned about your safety—if I overreacted today, I apologize. It would be best, perhaps, if you stayed away from crowds for the time being."

She eyed him, aware that he had probably never overreacted to anything in this life—with the possible exception of that memorable occasion when she kissed him at the Somers Town crime scene—but that was understandable, considering how she threw herself at him like a Montgomery Street brasser. And another thing—she didn't think it was the nameless crowd he was worried about; he had wanted to know who was with her at lunch. Pointless to try to pursue it; he wouldn't tell her.

A touch on her shoulder heralded the arrival of Nellie. Acton stood for their introduction and Doyle did the honors as they shook hands. Nellie was the mother of nine children, a grandmother to three, and was the kind of capable, efficient woman upon whom churches tend to rely. They had met when she helped Doyle with her mother's funeral arrangements, and the two had become friends—Doyle suspected her motherless self served as a project for Nellie's capable nurturing skills. At present, Nellie was shooting Doyle a glance that promised severe repercussions for failing to fill her in on this very interesting development.

They sat through the half-hour service, Acton observing while Doyle and Nellie stood, knelt, and responded where appropriate. At the conclusion, the penitents lined up at the confessionals, awaiting their turns. Doyle preferred to be shriven by Father John, who tended to remind her that she was only human, after all, and not to be so hard on herself. When it was her turn, she entered the confessional booth, thinking carefully about what she would confess and wondering if she could get away with speaking in broad generalities—she didn't want to give Father John an apoplexy. "Bless me, Father, for I have sinned," said Doyle through the screen.

"Is that Lord Acton out there?"

"Yes," Doyle admitted. "It is."

"Well, I don't want to be pesterin' him, Kathleen, but do you think he would mind if I introduced myself?"

Father John was an avid follower of sensational crimes, which he would explain was strictly a professional interest. He would often listen, rapt, as Doyle described some of the wages of sin she witnessed on a regular basis.

"I will introduce you, Father—that is, if you absolve me from my sins." Perhaps this would be easier than originally anticipated.

"Is he an Anglican?"

Doyle paused. "He hasn't said."

"Ah."

"I've had some impure thoughts," she ventured, hoping she needn't be too graphic.

"D'you think he's sweet on you, if I may be askin'?"

She couldn't lie to a priest. "Yes."

"Ah."

"There's been a bit of wrath and envy," she offered cautiously. It did seem as though broad generalities were acceptable tonight.

"You're a fine girl. I'm not surprised."

She realized they were speaking at cross-purposes and decided she would have to wait to catalog her transgressions at a later date, given the circumstances. Accepting absolution, she promised herself she would do a more thorough job next time, when the officiate wasn't starstruck.

When she rejoined Acton, he was in conversation with Nellie—trust Nellie to make short shrift to beat Doyle back to the pew; she was bent on buttonholing Acton without Doyle there to monitor the conversation. Doyle wasn't sure who would prevail; Nellie was the irresistible force, but Acton was the immovable object.

"Father John would like to meet you, if you don't mind." She knew Acton avoided all admirers and well-wishers and generally disliked having to carry on a conversation that wasn't work-related, but he waited patiently while the final blessing was said, shook the priest's hand when introduced, and was very gracious. Father John expressed his admiration for Acton's work and asked several intelligent questions, the substance of which he had gleaned from his conversations with Doyle. Give over, Father, thought Doyle—you'll not be sweetening him into taking Holy Orders.

In this, however, she proved to be somewhat mistaken. After a pause in the conversation, Acton asked, "To whom do I speak if I am interested in taking instruction?"

To his credit, it took only the barest moment for the priest to recover from his astonishment. "Why, myself. If you will call for an appointment, I can explain the process." Doyle stood by, blushing and silent, and noted that both Nellie and Father John carefully refrained from staring at her in stunned amazement, although it couldn't have been more obvious that she was the cause of this unlooked-for conversion. Good one, Acton, she thought with grudging admiration. The cat is well out of the bag.

CHAPTER 25

*H*E SHOULD HAVE HEARD CONFIRMATION BY NOW. HE DARED NOT *call in the event his location could be triangulated.*

Doyle noted that Acton paused as they stepped out of the church door to survey the immediate area, his eyes hooded, before proceeding down the sidewalk. He is still cautious, Doyle thought, despite whatever breakthrough that he won't tell me about, wretched man. Wretched Roman Catholic man, apparently.

They turned to walk up the block, their footsteps echoing on the damp pavement; there must have been a rain shower while they were inside. "You are a basketful o' holy surprises," she observed in a mild tone.

"It is important to you." He said it as though this was a sufficient explanation and she supposed that, for him, it was. To compound the effect, he had also presented the priest with a check toward the building fund. Doyle did not need to ask how much it was for; it would be a ridiculous amount—Father John had the look of a man who had personally witnessed the Transfiguration.

Doyle took Acton's arm as they walked past the corner grocery, its door and windows gated up. She felt a little shy; she had never physically claimed him in such a way before but for once, he did not react to her touch. She noted he surveyed the area by looking in the window's reflection—an old trick they were taught at the Academy.

She found that her mouth was dry, for no reason she could discern. "Back to the hotel?" she asked, trying to gauge the situation.

"Yes." He was distracted and checked his mobile for messages. He then stopped at a distance to remotely unlock an unmarked police vehicle that was parked on the street, taking another quick glance around. He didn't want to drive his own car, then, Doyle thought. Interesting.

When they got into the car, she leaned over to him and pulled on his lapel. Taking the hint, he kissed her. "Sorry."

"You are distracted," she said gently. "Can I help?"

His expression impassive, he considered her in the dimness, and she was reminded of that night on Grantham Street when he had made his unexpected proposal. "I'm afraid not."

As they drove in silence to the hotel, she thought about what had happened at the church. Acton was subtly and efficiently arranging things so that she had no option for retreat. It was masterful, truly, and a shame that he felt such a campaign was necessary. She knew now that retreat was unthinkable—she had been on pins and needles worrying more about Acton and what the priest would think than worrying about her own immortal soul. I'm done for, she thought. I'm aiding and abetting a Section Seven and ever shall be. Amen.

Unexpectedly, he pulled over and parked next to a busy pub. "Will you come in with me for a minute? I have to make a phone call."

"Lead on." She was careful not to let her gaze rest on the mobile phone at his belt.

He watched the street for a moment and then left the car to open her door. With his hand on her arm, they entered through the swinging door. The place was quite a bit more crowded than the reconciliation service due to a rugby game on the telly, which probably was a reflection on the trying times in which they lived or some such thing—Doyle was too preoccupied with Acton's behavior to finish the thought. It was clear that he did not want her to be more than arm's length from him.

Moving toward the public phone in the back, he took a long, sharp look around the pub before he bent to dial a number. He waited, glancing up again to survey the place, waited, then hung up when there was no answer. Taking her arm again, he escorted her out the door and they returned to the car. He made no comment and she asked no questions. This is very serious, she thought in acute dismay; I wish I knew what I should do. It was as though a black, ominous mood had descended on her companion and she was powerless to penetrate it.

As they drove toward the hotel, she noted he was paying very close attention to the other cars around them. She could feel the weight of the weapon in her ankle holster and thought about the Leadenhall murders, which everyone had been led to believe was a kill-on-kill, and the ballistics report that Williams didn't want to discuss—the one that should have revealed that a silencer was used but apparently did not. It all pointed to one conclusion: Acton was content to create the appearance that the racecourse murders case was now closed. Except that it wasn't and the killer was still out there, the one who had killed her father, the hoodlum. The one who was connected, in some way, to those pesky Russians who haunted Acton's every thought. No, she corrected, actually it is I who haunt Acton's every thought. Her scalp tingled and she was reminded that Acton had said there was little he wouldn't do for her.

She swallowed and said into the silence, "You know, Michael, you can't just go about killin' people."

There was a pause, and he said with an attempt at lightness, "First you prohibit sexual liaisons and now this. Are you always this unreasonable?"

"Positively puritanical." She found the heaviness in her chest would not allow her to match his light tone, and bit her lip. "You must leave retribution to God—God and the CID, I suppose."

The silence stretched out as they wound through the Kensington traffic, Acton alert and watchful. "I cannot allow a threat to you." He admitted it as though they were discussing the weather.

She drew breath, almost relieved that her half-formed fears were out in the open. "I understand the feeling; none better." As had any other enforcement officer, Doyle had experienced the exquisite frustration of *knowing* a suspect was guilty but not having sufficient evidence. Vigilantism, however, was not an option. The safeguards of the justice system were there for a reason, and besides, she believed in an ultimate justice. "But—"

"I cannot discuss it," he interrupted. "I am sorry, Kathleen."

Trying a different tack, she said as lightly as she was able, "Michael, if you are put in prison, I will have to bring you a cake with a file in it and I have never baked a cake in my life."

But he would not be cajoled. "It will not come to that."

She closed her eyes briefly. "You canno' know that."

He turned to look at her. "It will not come to that." She knew the discussion was at an end.

They circled the block once before parking the unmarked in the hotel's parking garage, Acton intent on their surroundings. Once they came to their suite, he motioned for her to stay by the door as he walked in before her, his weapon drawn. Turning on the lights in each room, he took a quick look around, even in the closets and the shower, before he holstered his weapon and indicated she should enter. In the bedroom there were fresh roses and a fruit tray on the table, and unsure of her strategy, Doyle sat and nibbled on a strawberry whilst he took off his shoes and his tie, then sat on the edge of the bed, his head bowed and his hands clasped between his knees. The black mood hovered.

"Can I order you somethin' to eat?" she ventured.

"No—thank you. I ate earlier."

This was not true and she contemplated what was best to be done as she ate some more of the fruit—she was hungry and a body had to eat, even in the midst of an unexplained crisis. "If you need to go somewhere, Michael, I swear on all the holy martyrs I will stay here locked away as though I were in the Tower itself. Safe as houses."

"No." Then with an effort he focused on her. "Forgive me, Kathleen. It's nothing; I am tired, is all."

This was also untrue. Contemplating him, she decided the situation called for drastic measures, and so she stood up and stretched her arms over her head for a moment, arching her back and sighing before she began unbuttoning her shirt. "Well, then, I'm for bed."

It turned the trick; suddenly he was amused, his gaze sliding over toward her. "I know exactly what you are about."

"Is it workin'?" Pulling off the shirt, she unbound her hair, shaking it about.

"Too well." His tone held a note of warning.

She was brought up short, remembering they were supposed to abstain. Surely one little lapse wouldn't result in a pregnancy, would it? Perhaps she shouldn't take the chance. On the other hand, she was aware there were other avenues to pursue, even if she was untrained. Moving toward him with what she hoped looked like confidence, she began unbuttoning his shirt and kissing the skin beneath.

He did not want the distraction, however, and stilled her hands with his own. "I think I would like to lie next to you, if you don't mind."

She paused, dubious. "Truly?"

He was amused again and stood to take off his shirt. "You will have to try to control yourself."

She ducked her head to hide a smile. "I don't know if I can, Michael—you are a fine specimen."

"Do you want me to sleep in the other room?" He was serious.

"Good God, no," she replied, imitating him.

"Well, then. Get in." As he lifted the comforter, she complied, and it was rather nice. In the past they had only lain together thus after a torrid session of sex—not that there was anything wrong with that, either. She lay in the crook of his arm as they watched the fire in the dimness; he was emanating a dark emotion and she wasn't certain how to proceed. Holding up her hands, she explained to him with some pride, "I am tryin' to stop bitin' my nails. "D'you see?"

He folded her hands in his and pulled them to his chest. "Don't change anything on my account. It would be a wasted effort."

She kept talking. "Samuels says he hates contraband but he doesn't, not truly."

"Who is Samuels?"

"A DC from Drake's team. He was at lunch." Best not to mention Munoz was trying to set her up. "And Williams was in a strange mood, for Williams."

"I am sorry I spoiled your outing."

"How did you know I had left for lunch?"

"The GPS in your mobile phone."

"Oh." Not at all a surprise that he kept such close track of her. "Can I do it, too? Does yours have one?"

"Mine has been disengaged."

"D'you want me to stop talkin'?"

"No."

So she kept talking of whatever topic entered her mind while he listened and said nothing. Something is very wrong, she thought in dismay, and eventually the pauses between the topics she expounded upon became longer and finally she could no longer stay awake. She remembered as she drifted off to sleep, feeling his long fingers tracing hers.

CHAPTER 26

*H*E HAD UNDERESTIMATED HIS MAN.

The next morning Doyle awoke to find Acton dressed and leaning over her, looking grim.

"What has happened?" She was instantly alert.

"I have to go secure the lab and the morgue." His words were clipped. "Stay at your desk until you hear from me. Don't go off."

"Yes, sir," she said out of habit.

"I've left a passkey and the security code for my flat. You will stay there tonight, even if I am unavailable." He paused. "I'm afraid that's an order."

"I will," she said simply.

"Don't forget to check in with me."

"I won't." And he was gone.

Saints and angels, she thought, rubbing her eyes with the heels of her hands—I wonder what's happened. She scrambled into her clothes and wondered for a moment whether she was supposed to pack her things and check out of the hotel. No, she thought, I'm to follow instructions.

Acton's mood had transferred to her. As she left the hotel, she was very vigilant in making her way to work amidst the other commuters, uncomfortable as she always was in crowded quarters. Doggedly blocking out the cross-currents of emotion, she tried to concentrate on this latest crisis; something had gone wrong in Acton's plan to put this case to bed and he didn't want to tell her what it was. He must not think she was in danger, though, or he'd lock her in a basement somewhere and never let her out. Considering the possibilities, she carefully moved away from the unhappy gentleman who stood to her right and emanated a bleak misery.

Last night Acton had been full of suppressed excitement, waiting for the call from Forensics—a call that was coming after hours from a woman at the morgue who was loyal to him, a call that would confirm something so that he could go forth and dispose of the killer. It was pure speculation on her part, but it was based upon her trusty instincts, which rarely let her down, and Acton's implied confession. Doyle chewed her thumbnail and wondered for a brief moment what she would do if she knew without a doubt that Acton was manipulating evidence to suit his own ends. Nothing, she decided, feeling nearly as bleak as the unhappy gentleman—she was yet another loyal woman. Heaven help her, it was that personal versus professional thing and it did appear that the personal was reigning triumphant. Instead, perhaps she should worry about saving him from himself; although how to do it was another kettle o' fish—she couldn't very well buttonhole Fiona or Williams and demand to know what was going on. Wait and see, she decided. And hope for the best, although hoping for the best never seemed to serve her very well.

Once she arrived at headquarters, it did not take long to discover what had happened. Munoz couldn't even wait for Doyle to put her rucksack down before she descended upon her. "Fiona's been murdered." She sounded a little too excited. "Remember? We were just talking about her."

"Mother of God," whispered Doyle. "Michael."

"What?" said Munoz.

"What's happened, Munoz? Quickly."

"They found her by her car early this morning in the parking garage—they think it happened last night as she left. Her purse and briefcase were taken."

"Shot?"

"I think so. They are reviewing the surveillance tape."

But it won't show anything, thought Doyle as she leaned against the cubicle partition, utterly dismayed. This one was more difficult for the killer because security personnel monitored the cameras round the clock as an antiterrorism measure; he must have hacked in a false image—he was good at that type of thing. It was the same killer, of course; Munoz didn't know it, but then she hadn't spent the evening with Acton, who had been expecting a confirmation from Forensics—from Fiona—that never came. Pulling out her mobile, she debated what to text, feeling ashamed of her silly jealousy and aching for him. She decided to text her symbol, only repeated multiple times across the screen.

Habib came to join them, his manner brisk. "Anyone using the parking facilities will be escorted by security until further notice." He made it clear that if Munoz required any heroics to protect her, he was at her disposal. Munoz thanked him in her best imitation of a helpless maiden, but Doyle was not taken in; Munoz had the best hand-to-hand combat scores in their class after Williams.

Doyle noted that Habib exhibited the same concealed excitement as Munoz—they couldn't be blamed; it was only human nature. They didn't have a personal stake in Fiona's death, and it was big news. Acton texted her with his symbol.

"Is there any information?" Habib asked as he watched her take the message.

"Not that I am aware, sir." Best be careful; she did not know what she was supposed to know. It was interesting that Habib assumed the message was from Acton, that he was aware Acton would text her even in the midst of the crisis.

"Please continue with your assignments, then. I will inform you as news comes in."

"Perhaps I can help process the scene, sir," suggested Munoz at her most beguiling.

He was reluctant to disappoint her. "I believe Williams has been recruited."

Doyle could swear she heard Munoz grinding her teeth as she retreated into her own cubicle to think about what was best to do. Williams was on the scene, and Williams—with his mysterious ballistics report—apparently served as another loyal stalwart to the chief inspector. It was a surprise, truly; he seemed so straight-arrow and by-the-book.

"Doyle," whispered Munoz, "come with me."

"We can't," Doyle replied at the same decibel level.

Munoz's head appeared over the partition, glancing down the hallway to ensure she was not observed. "I want to find out what's going on, and if I go alone, Habib will write me up."

Habib would no more write Munoz up than he would fly to the moon, and Doyle imagined the girl was well-aware of this little fact. "That won't wash; what's the real reason?"

Munoz's beautiful mouth assumed a mulish pout. "Williams will tell you more than he will tell me."

Doyle couldn't resist. "That's because I am so much more attractive than you, Munoz—you should try wearin' less makeup."

She waited for the explosion, but the idea was so preposterous that Munoz did not take offense. "Good one," she said, imitating Doyle's accent. "Now come with me."

Doyle shook her head. "Sorry—I truly can't go; I am under strict orders from Acton."

Munoz tossed her head in frustration then disappeared, only to reappear in Doyle's entryway, keeping a weather eye out for Habib. "Text Williams, then; find out what's going on."

This seemed a harmless request, although Doyle knew a moment's qualm that Williams would divulge to Acton that she was asking. Not that it was a sin, but she imagined Acton wouldn't want her talking with Williams and hence checking facts before

Acton had a chance to manipulate the flippin' evidence. "Anything?" she typed.

Williams's reply came promptly. "Not good. Talk later."

Showing Munoz the screen, the two stood silently for a moment. "I hate Williams."

"Whist, Munoz; he does fine work." Best not to mention the whole falsifying evidence theory.

Her dark eyes flashing, the other girl insisted, "I don't get any homicides and my work is just as fine."

"You worked the Leadenhall murders," Doyle reminded her.

"Only because you were hung over," Munoz shot back, refusing to be placated.

The other's temper was such that for once Doyle didn't escalate the argument, instead saying mildly, "I don't drink, Izzy; have done."

"Williams is like a brick wall."

Ah—here was the nub, apparently. Doyle tried to tease her out of the sulks. "Never say your fatal charm hasn't enslaved him."

"It's early days—he'll come around," Munoz retorted with some fire.

"That's the spirit; take no prisoners."

"They'd better not promote him before me." Apparently Munoz was equal parts enthralled and threatened.

Doyle did not voice her own opinion, which was if Williams was hip-deep in Acton's doings, he would be promoted forthwith. But before she had a chance to fashion a reply, Munoz ducked out because Habib was approaching with rapid steps. Their supervisor explained there was to be a general meeting and he would announce the details shortly. Because he lingered next door to discuss Munoz's caseload, it allowed Doyle to get back to her laptop, which she regarded with a knit brow and a heart full of disquiet. The best thing I can do, she decided, is to follow instructions and not cause Acton any more worry. With this in mind she began to sort the cold cases by priority, which was busy work and did not require concentration.

She culled the ones with the best-preserved evidence to consider first; the science was literally improving every month—a case that had stalled two years ago because the only evidence was a partial smeared palm print was now solvable. It was only a matter of queuing up for the proper enhancements and then processing a comparison to the database, which was also expanding exponentially. The scientific strides made it a lot harder for the criminals to escape justice, which only made the present murders all the more frustrating; this killer knew his forensics and was behaving accordingly.

Doyle texted Acton every hour exactly on the hour. Maybe I can develop my own OCD, she thought; we could relate better if I developed a neurosis. This seemed unlikely; she was very easily distracted, which came with the territory.

When it came time for lunch, Doyle asked Munoz if she would bring back a sandwich from the canteen when she went up. "Chained to my desk," she explained when Munoz looked very put-upon.

After Munoz returned with the sandwich, she lingered to complain. "All the fieldwork is on hold—the brass are all working on Fiona's case."

"Did you hear anythin'?" Doyle wished she could ask after Acton.

"I heard it was a clean scene and looks like robbery." She paused. "It could have been any of us."

No, thought Doyle; it was Fiona for a reason, and Acton knows what that reason is. She assured her colleague, "If it was you, Munoz, I wouldn't rest until I'd collared 'im and put 'im in the nick."

Munoz was unmoved. "I appreciate that, Doyle. You still owe me for the sandwich."

Habib swung by to tell them there was to be a meeting with all hands in the main conference room at two o'clock to discuss the latest developments.

Good, thought Doyle, a chance to see Acton—to see how he was faring; she longed to comfort him. Her fit of the dreads when she had watched him shaving now seemed like the reaction of a silly girl who was in no way related to her present self. Acton was right; it didn't matter what anyone else thought. They were well-matched, and what the world may think didn't matter a pin, even his fearsome mother.

At the appointed time, Doyle filed into the main conference room with her team. It was crowded with personnel and the mood was somber as befitted the occasion, which would make for a very uncomfortable hour for her. Acton, Drake, one of the superintendents, and the detective chief superintendent were seated at the front table, and Acton's eyes met hers across the room; even from that distance it made the adrenaline jump in her veins.

The DCS stood when they were all assembled and made a very heartfelt speech about the terrible loss to the CID family. He told them that all available leads were being pursued and that changes in security measures would be instituted immediately. Funeral arrangements were to be arranged by the decedent's family and they would all be informed of the details.

Doyle couldn't keep her eyes from Acton, who listened with a grave expression. He looked weary, poor man. Samuels was there but she didn't see Williams. She remembered her theory that her personal file hacker was an inside person and wondered if the killer was present in the room—this killer who made no sense.

Maddening that Acton wouldn't tell her what he was about. Whatever it was, it wasn't according to protocol and had a great deal to do with the fact that the unclaimed man in the morgue was actually her long-lost criminal father—that, along with the danger that a good barrister might convince twelve fine people that the presumption of innocence was somehow involved as opposed to Acton's own notion of justice. Religious instruction was coming not a moment too soon.

As she listened to the DCS make his closing remarks, she

considered her plans for the rest of the day. Acton had said he may not be home this evening; she hoped he could snatch some rest. She longed to stay here with him and help, but she would follow instructions and not cause him worry—therefore, she would retreat to his flat to abide in all patience. The only problem being she didn't know where he lived.

CHAPTER 27

*F*IONA WAS DEAD BECAUSE SHE KNEW THE KILLER'S IDENTITY, AND AS *he was the only other person who knew, he had to be careful; there was so much to live for, now. He would keep her well away from it.*

At the conclusion of the meeting, some left to return to work and some gravitated into small groups to deplore the murder in low voices. Trying to appear unobtrusive, Doyle worked her way over to the gathering that surrounded the DCS, Acton, and Drake. They were in conversation with another man whom Doyle recognized as the head of Forensics, although she could not recall his name. Lingering on the fringes, she waited along with several others for an opportunity to make a comment or ask a question. In grave tones, the four men were discussing something having to do with the lab, and Doyle listened in to the conversation already in progress and tried not to feel self-conscious. Hopefully Acton would realize she needed to speak to him privately and would break away for a moment.

"No," the head of Forensics said with emphasis. "I tested it immediately; there was no breach."

Doyle was so startled that she was frozen for a moment. Then she brushed her hair off her forehead. After waiting a few seconds she glanced at Acton, who was watching her. Meeting his eyes, she then looked at the floor.

"And nothing was out of place?" asked Acton.

"Nothing," said the nameless man firmly. "No sign of tampering."

Doyle brushed her hair back.

"There is nothing to indicate that Fiona's work was a factor in her death," Drake noted, observing Acton's intense interest with a doubtful expression. "It appears to have been a simple robbery."

But Acton would not concede and continued to scrutinize the other man, who was not enjoying the experience. Nervous, thought Doyle, despite his bravado.

Watching Acton's reaction, the DCS commented, "It does seem a strange place for a random crime—there was no easy exit for the shooter where she was shot."

"There was no record in her log of anything unusual," Drake noted. "I had DC Williams check it out immediately."

Wretched Williams, Doyle thought. On the fast track to detective sergeant, he was; Munoz will have an apoplexy.

There was a pause while the men considered the issue, and Doyle awaited her next cue. In due course, it came; Acton asked the head of Forensics, "Did you check the lab for unknown prints?"

"Of course." The other man sounded as though he was annoyed by the persistent questioning but was aware that he shouldn't cross a DCI. Doyle brushed her hair off her forehead and tried not to think about how simple it would be for the head of Forensics to murder people and then manipulate the evidence; she kept her gaze fixed on the floor for fear she would gape.

Acton turned to the DCS. "I would like to convene in my office, if you can spare a few moments."

"Certainly." The DCS gave Acton a sharp glance.

He is no fool, thought Doyle, and knows it is no casual request.

Acton included Drake and the Forensics head. "Come join us, if you would."

The men began to leave and the others who were hovering in the vicinity gave way, recognizing that no questions would be answered at this time. Acton turned to Doyle. "Did you need something, Constable?"

Still shell-shocked by the implications arising from the previous conversation, it took a moment for Doyle to remember why she was there. "Only that address, sir—it can wait." He nodded and left with the others.

Trying with little success to control her acute horror, Doyle retreated back to her basement cubicle. Was this it? Was it this simple? Needful of more information, she went, for once, to seek out her neighbor. "Munoz, who is the head of Forensics?"

Munoz was typing up the final report of her activities on the Leadenhall murders and said without stopping, "Prickett. He's a creep."

"Meanin' what?"

"Put me to the touch. No thanks."

This seemed unhelpful. "Know anythin' else about him?"

"No. You interested?"

"Everythin's not always about sex, Munoz," Doyle said, affronted.

"Usually, it is."

Doyle returned to her desk and settled into her chair, willing her mobile to ping. It did not. What was happening in Acton's office? It was truly a wretched shame she was consigned to her desk and had promised Acton she would stay. Perhaps this was the break they needed; Prickett was their man and it was all over. No more hotel, no more trips to a public phone with a spooked chief inspector. She could go back into the field and wrest her laurels away from Williams. She could make flippant remarks and earn disapproving looks. She could spend her lunchtime with Acton instead of Munoz. Please, please, please. The reflection in her laptop screen stared back at her. Not to mention, she amended, that there would be no more corpses piling up, which was, after all, the greater good. But oh, it would be nice to be back to normal—although she wasn't certain what normal was, as yet—it certainly seemed to involve a lot of sex. With an effort, she halted this line of thought—she shouldn't be thinking about sex, not at such a moment with the cases in crisis and poor Fiona lying in her own morgue. Reminded, she offered up a sincere prayer for the repose of Fiona's soul. *I hope it happened quickly and she didn't know it was coming—there must be nothing worse than facing the man who has killed so many, knowing that you were next.*

Habib wandered by to look over Munoz's shoulder whilst she ignored him and continued with her report. Unable to contain herself, Doyle accosted him as he stepped into the hallway. "I have never met Prickett, the head of Forensics. Do you know much about him, sir?"

Habib's dark eyes betrayed a hint of incredulity. "You are interested in Forensics, Constable Doyle?" Doyle's deficiency in the sciences was not a secret.

"She's sweet on him," threw in Munoz through the partition.

Doyle ignored her. "I was wonderin' about him, with Fiona's loss and all—he'll be understaffed."

Habib regarded her with a hint of disapproval. "I would not advise you to consider him as a potential husband."

Munoz snorted inelegantly.

Controlling herself only with an effort, Doyle assured him, "No—no; I am not interested in him as a husband, I am just curious." *Why is it,* she thought crossly, *that everyone thinks I'm in need of advice?*

"I believe he does excellent work." The praise was tepid; Habib was not going to gossip.

"But not a good man, perhaps?" Doyle had no such qualms.

Habib thought about it and managed to come up with a positive accolade. "I believe he follows Man U." Habib was a huge fan of the football team, which was surprising in and of itself.

Munoz's head appeared over the partition. "Does he? I'm a Chelsea girl, myself." The two then entered into a spirited comparison of the two teams while Doyle retreated back to her desk with the certain knowledge that she would learn no more while the merits of various midfielders and the shortcomings of various coaches were being dissected.

Two hours passed. Doyle was unable to concentrate and checked her mobile every few minutes even though there had been no ping. Acton hadn't texted her since the meeting, even though he must know she was in a fever, and on reflection, this seemed an ominous sign. Laying her mobile on the desk beside her, she regarded it, wondering whether she should try to give him a ring even as she knew she should not; he was well-aware she was dyin' here. She continued to text her symbol on the hour.

On top of everything else, she was not unaware that Acton was himself in danger; he was in possession of whatever information it was that had made him triumphant at church last night and that had gotten poor Fiona murdered. And this strange silence did not bode well. Her fingers stilled on the keyboard. Keep your head, my girl, she thought—you'll do no good by panicking; Acton is well-able to take care of himself. She debated sending him a text other than her symbol but decided against it. If he was not contacting her, he must have good reason, given his need for it.

Munoz was done with her report and could be heard packing up next door. "I'll go home early, this murder has me nervous." She carefully reapplied her lipstick. "I wonder who is doing the escorts?"

"Not Williams—he's helpin' on the case." This was unkind, and a measure of Doyle's own agitation.

"Naturally." Munoz eyed her. "What did you think of Samuels?"

Doyle knit her brow. "I don't know what I think of Samuels." It was the truth; he was very hard to read.

Munoz shut her lipstick case with a snap. "You are hopeless, Doyle. I wash my hands of you."

Doyle shot her a sidelong glance. "Perhaps I'm not needin' a man just now."

"You are forgetting that everything is always about sex. Write it down." Munoz hoisted her rucksack. "Are you coming?"

"I've a bit more to do."

"Suit yourself. Try not to get murdered."

"You're chokin' me up, Munoz."

Her mobile having remained silent, Doyle was not very surprised when the usual messenger appeared with a latte even though it was nearly five o'clock. "Thanks," she said, wondering what was afoot. The man handed her another plain envelope and left.

The note was in Acton's distinctive handwriting and said: Meet at the place we met this morning. Do not text or phone. Leave your mobile at your desk. Do not turn it off.

Re-reading it several times over, she could hardly believe what it portended and then closed her eyes, bitterly disappointed. Prickett must not be their man—unless they didn't have enough to hold him and Acton was worried about his reaction. Ah well, she would soon know; it was pointless to speculate. She folded the envelope and put it in her pocket; trouble, then. If he didn't want her to text or phone, he must believe that someone was monitoring their communications—the killer, presumably. The murdered trainer had been worried that his mobile was being monitored, which was why Giselle had sent Capper to him, despite Capper's ban. Thinking of the texted symbol she had sent to Acton all day long, she bit her nail, uneasy. On the other hand, it may simply be Acton being cautious—no question the killer had outmaneuvered him when Fiona was killed, and Acton was not one who was easily outmaneuvered.

After waiting a few minutes, she began packing up as unobtrusively as possible, sliding her mobile into the top drawer. She left without telling anyone she was leaving and walked past the usual St. James's Park station, instead walking briskly to the next one, Victoria. She passed through that busy station, down a platform, and then exited from the other side without taking a train. Walking on to the next station, she paid close attention to those around her—no one was shadowing her; she was certain. With some relief, she took the tube to the Kensington stop and as she emerged on the pavement, she carefully swept her gaze across the area, looking for anyone familiar or showing an unusual interest in her. She knew their hotel room faced this direction, and so she looked up and smiled—it went without saying that he'd be watching her from the window.

CHAPTER 28

*H*E WAS REMINDED OF THE FIRST TIME HE HAD WATCHED HER THUS, *through these binoculars. He hoped she had not made a bad bargain.*

Acton anticipated her approach to the hotel room door and opened it just as Doyle arrived. She walked into his arms and they stood for a moment, embracing, while the door closed behind her.

"I am so sorry," she whispered. "Not a happy birthday."

He said nothing but rested his chin on the top of her head. She could feel him take a long breath. "That was good work, today."

"More like luck, really. What did he say?"

Acton indicated she should sit on the sofa in the suite's main room and then sat beside her, absently caressing the back of her hand with his thumb. The tropical fish meandered around their tank, undisturbed.

"I confronted him in my office, and implied I knew more than I did. He blustered for a while but eventually confessed he had been using the lab for sexual liaisons with at least two employees that he would admit to—I imagine there are more. When he heard word of Fiona's murder, he knew the lab would be scrutinized for clues and so he panicked and scrubbed it down. Any potential evidence was destroyed."

Doyle took this in for a moment and then observed, much struck, "Munoz was right—it was about sex."

Acton tilted his head, trying to make sense of this non sequitur. "I thought you didn't care for Munoz."

"Doesn't mean she's never right. So Prickett was sacked?"

"Yes; the DCS was furious. But it didn't change the fact that the lab has been compromised."

But to Doyle, this seemed the least of their concerns. "This killer wouldn't have left any evidence behind anyway, Michael."

He said nothing and continued brushing the back of her hand, but she had intercepted a brief leap of emotion from him. "What?"

His eyes met hers. "I beg your pardon?"

"What did he leave behind? What is it you know?"

He turned her hand over, as though examining it. She hoped he didn't notice that she had been biting her nails again—not a good day to give up the habit. After waiting a moment while she could see he debated telling her, she prompted, "Fiona was examinin' some evidence, only off the books." Acton, the tiresome knocker, was going to be careful with what he told her again—she could feel it.

"Yes."

She closed her eyes briefly. "Michael," she pleaded. "Just tell me—I promise I won't have the vapors."

He lifted his head. "She was going to report to me when she made the match, but she never made the report."

"Who is it?" Clearly it was someone from whom Acton already had sample DNA, or they wouldn't be attempting a match.

"I'd rather not say."

At least it was the truth and he didn't attempt to fob her off. He didn't want to tell her because he was going to kill the killer, if the killer didn't kill him first. She could have remonstrated with him once again about the evils of vigilantism but refrained; the memory of Fiona's body was too fresh for her words to have much of an impact. The whole thing made her very uneasy, particularly since Fiona was killed despite Acton's best efforts. "Do you think he is after you? Is that why we are here?"

She tried to ask in a neutral tone and thought she had been largely successful except that he gathered her in his arms and embraced her, saying into her ear, "Please don't worry—I am not taking any chances is all."

She nodded, closing her eyes briefly as she rested her chin on his shoulder. "So we are playin' least-in-sight for the time bein'?"

He paused, and she could feel his chest expand as he took a breath. "I believe Fiona's communications with me may have been monitored—it is the only explanation for the surgical strike at exactly the right time."

Yes, Doyle had already guessed as much when he had asked her to leave her mobile behind—although it was fortunate they communicated using symbols; the killer wouldn't know what to make of it.

Disengaging from her, he reached into his coat pocket. "I have acquired new mobiles—yours is programmed with my new number."

She glanced at it—it was exactly like the last one and she bent to slide it into her rucksack. "Do I keep textin' to check in?"

He hesitated. "Yes, if you don't mind."

She nodded without comment and hoped it was the right thing to do—if the killer had figured out the last set, he may well figure out these, too, but Acton needed to know she was safe, her sweet Section Seven. Trying to sound reassured, she said, "All right. Are you hungry?" She was starving; Munoz was not good at the sandwich-choosing.

With real regret, he shook his head. "I can't stay."

Struggling with it, she decided she couldn't not say. "You must promise you will be very careful, Michael."

He bent his head to meet her eyes so as to reassure her. "I don't think he's after me, for the same reason you didn't think he was after you. If he wanted to kill me, he could have already done so—especially early on, when we didn't know what we were dealing with."

She knit her brow, considering this. "But he's monitorin' you—or at least you think he is. That seems rather ominous."

"He's protecting himself. That's the pattern—he was protecting himself when he killed the trainer, and Giselle, and Capper, and Smythe, and Fiona. The only one that does not fit the pattern—"

"Is Somers Town," she concluded for him. "My father."

"And he may yet have been protecting himself, but we are not aware what was at stake, there—or at least not yet. He's been on the defensive, Kathleen, not the offensive; therefore, he's not a lone wolf. I believe he is aligned with outside forces."

Stupid Ruskies, she thought. Muckin' up my love life.

He touched her face briefly, then withdrew his hand—she could sense that he was trying to avoid becoming aroused, probably because when he became aroused, Katy bar the door. "I am afraid I must drive to my estate and speak with my mother."

Doyle was silent for a moment and then decided she hadn't heard him aright. Now? With all hell breaking loose on this case?

He frowned, considering her. "I can't decide if it would be best for you to accompany me."

Doyle was certain that she paled—she could feel it—and all her fine resolutions about facing the music flew out the window as she stared at him in dismay. But surely it couldn't be a social visit—something else must be at play. "What's afoot, my friend?"

He waited for a few beats, then reluctantly revealed, "My mother claims she was shot at today."

Utterly astonished, Doyle breathed, "Mother a' *mercy*."

"Not exactly."

She stared at him, nonplussed. "Michael, do not joke; d'you think she's a target?"

He was going to say something unkind, she could see, but checked himself. "I doubt it. If it actually happened at all."

Now, here was a fine insight into the Acton family tree that was nothing short of alarming. "Do you think she made it up, then?"

"Perhaps. It is my birthday, after all."

At a loss, she sensed she was treading into dangerous waters and proceeded with caution. "Is your mother—mentally unbalanced?"

"Not clinically."

Doyle reflected that she shouldn't have asked him, as perhaps he was not the best judge of such things.

"She is very difficult," he explained, and it was true.

Thinking of her own gentle and self-effacing parent, Doyle could not relate but did not doubt him. "I see."

His brows drew together. "Unfortunately, I cannot ignore the small chance that it is true and that this may be part of a different pattern altogether."

"Yes." She was suddenly sober. "He is targetin' the women in your life." Although Acton's relationship with Fiona was not generally known. Not true, she corrected herself—Munoz certainly knew of the rumor, which meant anyone could have known. She tried not to dwell on the undeniable fact that at present, her own fair self was the center of Acton's universe.

"Or it may just have been a poacher."

This was exactly what was needed to make her laugh out loud—it felt good to laugh. "A poacher? Will you be puttin' him in the stocks?"

"No." With a small smile, he leaned in to kiss her. "I'm afraid there are no stocks."

Thankfully, she managed to dissuade him from the idea that she accompany him to confront his difficult mother. "I promise I will be very careful, Michael—do I come here after work or do I go to your flat?"

The light mood vanished. "Here. I am concerned my flat is no longer secure."

It was quite a thing to admit; Acton was the grand master of security. "You can't be certain?"

"No. He is very good at covering his tracks." Reminded, he pulled a slip of paper from his inside coat pocket and handed it to her, bending his head as he did so to look up into her face. "This is my address—you really did not know it?"

"No," she admitted, thinking that he probably knew every address she'd ever had, as well as the latitude and longitude. "HR would never give it out without your permission."

There was a long moment while his dark eyes held hers. "I love you. I didn't really say it before."

She was touched; he wasn't good at this. "I know it," she said gently. "You don't have to say—not to me."

"Nevertheless."

CHAPTER 29

SHE WOULD BE SAFER WHERE SHE WAS THAN WITH HIM, BUT HE couldn't be easy. He wondered if he ever would be.

It felt strange having the whole extravagant bed to herself. Doyle missed Acton, which was a novel experience for her, having lived alone and well-content for so long. It was nothing short of amazing that they had found one another—that they were so good together. Although it sounded strange, she felt she could be her true self with him; he was a devoted man and it seemed that nothing she could do could shake that devotion—in fact, her many foibles only seemed to endear her to him. And unlike the other relationships she had attempted, she rarely knew what he was thinking, which actually made the whole endeavor much more enjoyable. He, in turn, was beginning to allow glimpses of his true self; he had been much less guarded during their last conversation, which meant he was becoming more confident that she was not going to flee the scene. I suppose we are each relinquishing ourselves, she thought, remembering his apt use of the word, and it seems to be working. With a mental shake, she swung her legs out of bed. Try to maintain some dignity, silly mawker; next you'll be writing sappy poetry.

She pondered dropping by her poor neglected flat to pick up a change of clothes but decided that Acton would not want her to do so—even though he seemed to believe there was no elevated threat level. Best take no chances; she had promised to be careful. In any event, no one was going to notice if she was wearing the same clothes as yesterday, and she was longing to nip into work to find out if there were any new developments on Fiona's murder. Perhaps Williams would know—she thought about texting him on the new mobile but decided she would keep all communications to a minimum; she didn't like the idea that she had been monitored yesterday, if indeed she had been.

The doorman touched his hat as she headed to the hotel's revolving front door, and Doyle suppressed a desire to flash her identification so that he wouldn't think she was a brasser, leaving in the same clothes she had come in. Instead, she gave a guilty glance around the lobby to make certain she was unobserved and found that such was not the case.

There was a man leaning against the concierge desk and dressed in casual business clothes. He was reading the newspaper. Doyle's gaze rested on him for the smallest instant, but as she continued out the door she knew with certainty that he had been in the tube behind her the day before. He had the look of a man here on business, but any businessman staying at this grand hotel would not be riding on the tube. Her mouth dry, she walked down the pavement and forced herself to think, not panic. He was white, about six feet tall, and in his early thirties. He did not seem familiar, although she didn't get a good look at him. Test it out, she thought.

There was a newsstand on the corner, and she stopped and bought a granola bar although she positively ached for her frosty flakes. As she paid, she pushed her sunglasses behind a stack of magazines. She then began to walk to the tube stop, peeling back the wrapper on the granola bar and eating it with as much nonchalance as she could muster. Abruptly stopping, she turned around to head back to the newsstand, as though she had just remembered her glasses.

She caught a glimpse of him, his head bowed down, turning

aside in the crowd to shadow her change of direction. In an odd way, she felt relieved; he was indeed following her and he didn't know she knew. That was to the good; she had an advantage. After recovering her glasses, she retraced her steps toward the tube.

Weighing her options, she decided she should continue toward headquarters since there was presumably no safer place—Fiona notwithstanding. In the meantime, she would make certain that she was never in an isolated area with him. To this end, she was careful to mix in with the crowd of commuters, for once grateful for the humanity pressing in around her. The man boarded the same train as she did but continued reading his newspaper and seemed completely uninterested in her. Eyeing him from behind her sunglasses, she noted that he didn't seem menacing in the least, but then she reminded herself that Giselle was shot at close range by someone she was not afraid of. Best be safe.

Casually pulling out her mobile, she thought about what she should text Acton, but the new unit wasn't fully charged and didn't come on. As she returned it to her rucksack, she was struck with another possibility—that Acton had hired the man to watch over her. This gave her pause; she had initially considered alerting security once inside her building, where he could not follow. Security could set up a trap and seizure, and they could take him in for questioning. If the man was indeed working privately for Acton, however, such a course would result in some very awkward revelations for the renowned chief inspector.

So, she should contact Acton and ask him about it, but that presented another problem; if he *hadn't* hired her shadower, Acton would come pelting back in a rare lather and no mistaking, leaving his mother exposed. As she entered the building with an inward sigh of relief, she decided there was nothin' for it. If her shadow was not Acton's man, Acton needed to be informed immediately—it was too dangerous to wait, and the man might present an opportunity to catch the killer; indeed, he could be the killer himself. She wondered if she should try to engage him in conversation in an attempt to read him but discarded the idea; Acton would slay her for taking such a risk. The best course was to call Acton and advise him of the situation; if she kept the conversation very short, it might go under the radar, so to speak.

Upon arrival at her desk, she unloaded her rucksack; her old mobile phone lay where she had left it in the top drawer. Don't mix them up, she warned herself as she attached the battery recharger to the new one. As she did so, however, the screen remained blank, which didn't seem right—it should indicate that it was charging. Stymied, she held it in her hand and willed it to work—if her mobile was malfunctioning, it would be another trigger that could send Acton pelting back. Hopefully he would assume she wasn't yet awake and all would be well. Wiggling the contacts and then the plug, she made another attempt to engage the power. Nothing. Saints and holy angels, she thought in extreme annoyance; don't be defective, wretched thing. Ten minutes of relentless attempts later, she still had a dead phone.

On pins and needles and hoping Acton wouldn't start to worry, Doyle pounced on Munoz when she arrived. "Do you have an extra mobile phone battery, Munoz? Mine appears to be defective."

Munoz took a quick look at the mobile in Doyle's hand. "Not my brand." She gave Doyle an assessing glance and added, "Too expensive."

"How about lettin' me use your recharger?" Perhaps this was the cause of the problem—she was willing to grasp at straws at this point.

"Suit yourself." Munoz pulled the unit from her rucksack and watched in silence as Doyle hooked it up and then stared in frustration at the uncooperative screen. "You're out of luck," pronounced her companion.

Distracted, Doyle replied shortly, "Shoot—I have to make some calls."

"Use your desk phone, idiot."

Doyle looked up and had the distinct impression Munoz was eyeing her rather speculatively. "Yes, I will—it's only so much less convenient; I have to look up the numbers." It was more than inconvenient, of course—Acton's new mobile number was programmed into the phone and she had no idea what it was. How could she contact him? Even assuming he had given his new number to his assistant—which he may not yet have done—that worthy was not going to hand over his personal number to the likes of Doyle, a lowly DC she'd never met before.

I'm flummoxed, thought Doyle in frustration as she bent her head, thinking. Munoz interrupted her thoughts by observing in a suggestive tone, "Must have had quite a date; you are wearing the same outfit you were wearing yesterday."

Doyle blushed to the roots of her hair and retorted, "None of your business, Munoz."

Munoz chuckled in a patronizing manner. "Did you leave something at his house and you don't remember his number? Is that what this is all about?"

Doyle did not deign to reply and instead stalked back to her cubicle.

Munoz's voice could be heard, full of amusement. "I must say I am impressed—I didn't think you had it in you."

Doyle ignored her and sank into her chair as she considered her options. Impossible to ask HR for Acton's personal number—they would laugh in her face, if they didn't write her up, and there was no saying they even had it as yet. She could leave a message on his work number, but she remained uneasy about his belief that his communications were being monitored; no matter how cryptic she made the message, it would give the game away and any chance to catch the man would be lost. If there was a danger to Acton, she didn't want to add to it.

However much she hated the idea, she would have to try to call him at his estate on a landline. Unfortunately, this was another number that his assistant and HR were unlikely to relinquish to her. If Doyle didn't check in soon, Acton would wonder why—although, if it was his man shadowing her, he could simply check with him. How annoying that she didn't know if the shadow was friend or foe and how annoying that the wretched, *wretched* new phone didn't work. She pondered her best course.

An option presented itself, even though it nearly made her groan aloud. Nothin' for it, she thought with resignation. "Munoz, let me borrow your windbreaker." Munoz kept a windbreaker at her desk for unexpected trips into the field.

"No one is going to notice your outfit, Doyle. No one cares."

With an effort, Doyle held on to her temper. "No—it's not that. I have to go out on an errand and I'm a bit chilly." This was patently untrue, as it was a glorious day outside.

Munoz's head appeared over the partition. "What kind of errand?" She was clearly hoping to hear revelations about the alleged date.

"It's only for a case, Munoz." This was more or less true, and the other girl predictably lost interest and handed the windbreaker over with poor grace. "Don't get it dirty."

"Thanks." Doyle pushed her arms through the sleeves of the zip-up, pulling up the hood and carefully tucking in her hair, which was a giveaway. Donning her sunglasses, she waited near the lift but out of the view of the security camera until a group assembled to wait for it. She then walked forward to board the lift with the group, keeping her face averted. Ascending to the canteen with them, she disembarked with the group, then ducked into the nearest stairwell to descend to the underground parking garage. Opening the door with confidence, she kept her head down and threaded through the cars, trying not to think about poor Fiona or about the security cameras that were undoubtedly watching her every move. Hopefully she hadn't given the shadow enough time to track her, and since he wasn't aware she had twigged him, he would not be expecting such an early escape.

Arriving at a side door to the garage, she took a deep breath and emerged onto the street near the back of the building.

Without looking up, she continued walking briskly to the busy Victoria tube stop and down the steps. While waiting on the platform, she cautiously looked around for the first time and congratulated herself—her shadow was nowhere in sight.

Once on the tube, she thought it all over again and came to the same decision; she needed to contact Acton and as soon as possible to determine if her shadow was a danger. If he wasn't, there was no harm done. If he was, Acton would create a protocol—unlikely he would want the police involved; as far as everyone knew, the case was closed. A seat opened up and she took it, mainly to get away from the woman behind her who was radiating despair.

As she headed into the business district, Doyle took a moment to congratulate herself on learning her lessons; she felt she had handled this latest situation well, considering how it had all started when the culchie had locked her in the tack room. Small wonder Acton had been unhappy with her—she was lucky Capper wasn't the killer. Well, not lucky for him, of course; crackin' bad luck, as a matter of fact, since he had been doing Giselle a favor, going to the racecourse to speak to the trainer even though he was banned. The trainer's mobile had stopped working.

Doyle sat very still, her scalp prickling. The trainer's mobile had stopped working. Giselle's mobile had stopped working. Quickly reaching into her rucksack, she pulled out the new mobile and dropped it on the seat beside her as though it were a venomous object, then stood and pushed others aside to go and wait by the door, in a fever of impatience. When the next stop finally came, she could not exit fast enough. Holy Mother of God; he was after her. Acton didn't think so because that was the plan—Acton has been made complacent and drawn away from her. The man following her this morning was the killer.

All right, she thought, willing herself to calm down as she emerged into the sunlight again, her head down. Think about this; he doesn't know you've twigged him. He doesn't know you've left the building unless he is monitoring your GPS the way Acton does. She was not certain if the GPS functioned when the phone was dead and wondered if perhaps she shouldn't have left it on the tube. Too late for second thoughts; stick with the original plan and speak to Acton.

When she reached her downtown destination, she stood across the street for a moment, canvassing the area and gathering up her courage. Noting the location of the CCTV cameras, she averted her face and walked into the lobby of the building, then took off Munoz's windbreaker, folding it into her rucksack. After deciding it would be prudent to apply lip gloss, she then walked into Acton's banker's offices with all the confidence she could muster.

CHAPTER 30

SHE HADN'T CHECKED IN WITH HIM YET THIS MORNING AND HIS OWN text had not gone through; there may be a problem with the cell tower in the area. He did not want to think about it.

Doyle entered the elegant offices and approached the receptionist, a very attractive woman in a Chanel suit who wore expensive eyeglasses that Doyle suspected were not prescription but were simply for effect. The woman smiled at Doyle with perfect, even teeth. "May I help you?"

"Yes," said Doyle, feeling as though she were a pilgrim visiting a shrine. "I would like to speak to Mr. Layton, please."

"Do you have an appointment?" The woman continued polite even though she must be fully aware that Doyle was a gate-crashing peasant.

"No, I'm afraid I don't. But if he could spare a moment of his time, I would appreciate it. It concerns Lord Acton."

The receptionist was too refined to show any surprise. "And whom may I say is visiting?"

Doyle swallowed. "Lady Acton."

The receptionist didn't miss a beat. "If you would please be seated, I will see if Mr. Layton is available." She walked away, her stiletto heels tapping on the wooden floor, and closed the hallway door behind her with a soft click. Doyle sat on the tasteful leather settee, eyed some very tasteful artwork, and waited, trying to tamp down the anxiety that threatened to rise up.

After only a few minutes, a neat young man in a three-piece suit came through the door and approached her with a smile, the receptionist in tow. Doyle stood to shake his hand. "Mr. Layton?"

"No, I am his assistant; he is tied up at the moment and I thought I would see if I could help you." Doyle noted the receptionist returned to her desk but didn't take her eyes off them. She is probably supposed to call security at his signal, thought Doyle; can't say I blame them.

"You are related to Lord Acton, I understand."

"Yes." She tried to conceal her nervousness with only moderate success; she was working very hard to control her accent. "I am Lady Acton."

The assistant regarded her for a moment with a small smile. He doesn't think I'm dangerous—just nicked, thought Doyle.

"I believe Lady Acton is an elderly woman who is currently residing in . . . elsewhere."

Good one, thought Doyle with approval—shouldn't give out state secrets. "That would be the dowager Lady Acton, Lord Acton's mother. I am Lord Acton's wife." Her voice sounded high to her own ears.

It was clear the young man didn't believe her and the receptionist just stared, fascinated. Doyle continued a bit desperately. "We were married a few days ago, here in London." Best not to mention it was the same day her father was murdered— too much information and it would only confuse him. "You probably haven't heard as yet because it was quite spur o' the moment, although not on his part, apparently . . ." You are talking too much, my girl, she thought, and firmly closed her lips. They were both watching her as though she were a madwoman.

Remembering her wedding ring, she bent to pull it out from the zipper compartment in her rucksack and noted the movement made her companion start in alarm. She slowed her hands and carefully pulled it out—a small and ancient rose-cut diamond, flanked by even smaller emeralds. Holding it up before him, she explained, "This is my weddin' ring—Acton said it belonged to his many-times-great-grandmother." She had a momentary vision of Acton digging through the family vault to find something that suited her so perfectly, and smiled at it. Truly, it was a pretty ring; she had not looked at it since her wedding day because to do so made her feel a little sick.

It may have been the authentic-looking ring—or it may have been the lip gloss—but in any event the assistant agreed to fetch Mr. Layton. Wise of him to pass on this wicket, she thought, sitting herself down again; doesn't want to kick me out on the chance this fantastic story is true.

While she waited, Doyle thought about her wedding—not your normal nuptials by any measure. While in the car after the Somers Town murders, Acton had wanted her answer with no further discussion and she had simply agreed—she wasn't even certain why she did; it was as though she went along the path that offered the least resistance. He had assured her that she could become accustomed to the idea at her leisure and that no immediate announcement need be made. He was so calm and matter-of-fact that, strange as it sounded, she felt it would be impolite to refuse.

Acton had put in a call to a priest at St. Cecilia's Chapel who was apparently already on scramble drill in the event of just such a contingency—Acton didn't want to give her any time for sober reflection. Upon arrival, Acton took her arm and escorted her from the car to the chapel; she was aware that he was hoping for a *fait accompli* before she came to her senses, which was a very good French phrase, and apt. Much better, for example, than the English phrase, *Marry in haste and repent at leisure.*

There, in the dimly lit chapel, she and Acton had met the priest who had enlisted his secretary as a witness, and the both of them had behaved as though having an Anglican peer demand a Roman Catholic wedding ceremony on a moment's notice was something quite routine.

She remembered that as they assembled at the altar, the sunlight shafting through the diamond-paned windows, Acton had leaned down and whispered, "Michael" into her ear. Because, you see, she was marrying a man who was not at all certain she knew his first name.

Keeping her gaze locked upon Acton's, she had remained calm as they recited their vows. He was euphoric; she could feel it, his voice steady and sincere. She had tried to match him in demeanor and was largely successful—the only time she faltered was when he placed the ring on her finger. It was sized perfectly of course—the man probably knew her shoe size, too—but she had to take her eyes off it and draw a deep breath as her knees suddenly went a bit wobbly.

After the ceremony, they had signed the license and thanked the priest and his secretary, Acton handing him an envelope that undoubtedly contained another enormous check; the Catholic Church was making an unholy profit as a result of the chief inspector's romantic inclinations. Acton had escorted Doyle back to the unmarked—the entire wedding had taken less than thirty minutes—and they sat together in the car for a few silent moments. He had asked gently, "Are you all right?"

"Yes," she had replied. "I only have to become accustomed, is all."

"Take as long as you wish; I rushed you."

Understatement of the century. She didn't like to think about how she would break the news to Father John that she had married the famed Lord Acton before another priest in another parish without even posting the banns. The whole thing had been surreal; she couldn't blame Layton's assistant for thinking it a preposterous tale and for a wild moment, she considered fleeing the scene. Unbidden, she had another memory; that of Acton telling her in no uncertain terms that she was never to imply their marriage was a mésalliance. Lifting her chin, she thought, I will insist on speaking to Layton and I will not take no for an answer. And I will wait until he can get Acton himself on the phone, if necessary. It is that important.

Her resolution was rewarded when an elderly and dignified man preceded the assistant through the door and approached her with his wrinkled features fashioned into a dry smile. "Lady Acton." He bowed.

Doyle was not certain what she was supposed to do and so she nodded her head but couldn't contain an irrepressible smile. "You believe me—thank all the saints and holy angels."

Eyes twinkling, he smiled in return. "You are the former Miss Kathleen Doyle?"

"Yes." She was that relieved. "So Acton told you."

"No." His manner expressed dignified regret. "Lord Acton visited a few weeks ago to name you as the beneficiary of his unentailed assets, but he neglected to mention you were to marry."

"That is very like him," she said fondly, but thought to herself, silly, besotted *knocker*.

CHAPTER 31

*H*E WAS NO LONGER AFRAID SHE MIGHT RECONSIDER, *BUT SHE HAD not worn her ring and he did not know where it was. She still had not checked in with him.*

"I am afraid that my mobile is malfunctionin' and I do not know the landline number for—the estate." Doyle didn't remember what it was called, if she ever knew. She should learn it, mental note. "It is somethin' of an emergency, I'm afraid."

"My assistant will be happy to fetch it for you." Layton gave said assistant a meaningful look, and the man, who was doing only a fair job of hiding his astonishment, pulled himself together and left the room. It was obvious he was not as experienced as Layton in the eccentricities of the aristocracy.

"Please come into my office and make your call; it will give you some privacy. May I offer some refreshment?" After having seen to it that she was comfortable, Layton then closed the door with a soft click and left her alone.

Sinking into the leather armchair, she dialed Acton's estate number with no further ado. She heard it ring and then the phone was answered by a man who sounded as though he looked exactly like Layton. "Trestles."

Trestles? The name conjured up visions of Pemberley, and Doyle immediately lost her nerve. "I am sorry to bother you, but this is Detective Constable Doyle from the CID and I am tryin' to get in touch with the chief inspector—I'm afraid it is important or I wouldn't be botherin' him."

The measured voice on the other end was regretful. "He has gone out to the local town; do you have his mobile number?" The question held the merest hint of incredulity that this avenue hadn't yet been pursued.

Another danger presented itself, and she was left to explain lamely. "I'm afraid it is important that his mobile not be used at present—we are concerned there is a security leak, so please do not forward my message."

"I see," said the retainer, even though he probably didn't see at all.

"Do you have a pencil?" Doyle stalled, thinking furiously. How should he contact her? Not the old mobile, not the new mobile, not at work, not the hotel—the killer had been in the lobby. How?

"Please tell him my mobile is malfunctioning but that I will leave messages for him periodically on Fiona's email." This would answer; any Section Seven worth his salt could hack into Fiona's email and he had probably already done so as part of the investigation—hopefully they hadn't closed the address yet. If the killer had been monitoring it before the murder, he would stay well away now for fear of being traced. She would be careful about what she said, regardless.

The retainer on the other end of the line allowed no hint of the confusion he must have been feeling to enter into his tone as he read back her message. She thanked him and hung up, anticipating the day when she would have to meet him in person and his profound shock if he recognized her voice. Which he would, of course—couldn't hide this accent with a bushel barrel.

She sat in Layton's impressive office and considered for a moment, feeling very acutely how much one relied on one's mobile phone functioning properly—it didn't help that she was utterly paranoid that the killer could monitor all her electronics. Pulling out her tablet from her rucksack, she powered up her email to compose a message but paused yet again. She didn't know if there was a GPS in her tablet. Acton hadn't indicated it was a concern and so she didn't think so, but she was not sure. Cautiously opening the office door, she looked around for Layton; he and his assistant appeared immediately.

"I am not very technical," she confessed, "and I need to know if this tablet has a GPS."

Layton professed to be just as ignorant and deferred to his assistant, who sat down with her unit and checked the bios. "Yes—it has a device installed that traces it in the event it is stolen."

Doyle was glad she asked. "Do you mind if I leave this one here and borrow one of yours?"

They assured her this would not be a problem, and at Layton's sharp glance, the assistant volunteered his own.

"Thank you so much." Using the borrowed tablet device, she typed a message to Fiona that said: "I am being shadowed. My mobile is not functioning and I have abandoned it. I am being very cautious and will contact you when you return."

Re-reading the message, she decided it would put the cat among the pigeons with a vengeance but there was nothing for it. She smiled sweetly. "Is there a back exit?"

"Right this way, my lady." Layton ushered her toward the back hallway as though it was the most natural thing in the world; she made no attempt to explain her actions and no explanation was demanded. I hope they don't think I'm playing Acton false, she thought—I'd rather that they thought I was a bit nicked. As she slunk away, she realized there were clear benefits to being Acton's better half; if it were anyone else, they probably would have called the police in a heartbeat, and she would not have been able to avoid the awkward revelations that would have ensued.

Walking down the alleyway at a rapid pace, she pulled Munoz's windbreaker out of her backpack and pushed her arms through the sleeves. With the hood up, she donned her sunglasses and kept her head down. Instead of descending into the closest tube station, she walked a few blocks, keeping an eye out and deciding what should be done next. She dared not return to the Met—the killer could be watching for her and he would not be so easily shaken off next time. Best stay away.

She assessed. If he tried to trace her through the mobiles, old or new, or her tablet, he would find a dead end. Although she couldn't talk directly with Acton, she could reassure him that she was safe until he returned. All in all, the situation seemed secure. The problem was; where should she go until Acton came back? She was afraid to use a credit card and she didn't have much money in her rucksack—a direct result of staying in fancy hotels and ordering room service on the tab like a pharisee. She considered going to Nellie's house but discarded it as too obvious; the killer may know her habits, so she needed to stay somewhere no one would think of looking.

Anticipating Acton's reaction to her message, she suddenly realized that if he was in danger, she may have compounded it—he would return forthwith without first hearing a description of the suspect and so be at a disadvantage. Nor would he wait to be contacted by her; instead he would start looking for her in the usual places and the killer would know it. He could walk into a trap—although she had a very fair idea that Acton was more than a match for even the shrewdest killer. Nonetheless, if she could lay a false trail, it would be helpful and could keep Acton out of trouble—she needed to throw some dust in the suspect's eyes. And above all, Acton needed a description.

The nearest shop was a nail salon, and she ducked inside to sit for a moment in the waiting room so as to send another email: "Suspect is white male early thirties six foot 180 pounds light blue shirt khaki slacks. I am OK. Will stay at safe place tonight. Will check with the HQ security desk on a secure line to see if you have returned." She read the message, wishing that she knew how to hack into Fiona's email herself so as to receive a return message. It didn't matter; once Acton returned, they would work something out. She then added: "I will lay a false trail, so disregard any contradictory messages." Biting her nail, she contemplated the last sentence; if the killer figured out how they were communicating, then he would also not be misled by any contradictory messages. Ah well; it couldn't be helped and it seemed unlikely that he would monitor Fiona's email—it was a clever idea, if she had to say so herself.

As she signed off, the Chinese receptionist indicated there were personnel at the ready to work on her nails, and Doyle was tempted to lay them before the woman so as to indicate the enormity of the task. At the same time, she saw an opportunity—the desk was cluttered and chaotic, with receipts and tips stacked every which way, a testament to the thriving business. With an easy smile, Doyle stood to lean over the counter so as to display her abused nail beds. With a chuckle, the other made an unintelligible comment and a shooing motion, indicating Doyle was to begone from this place. With a rueful expression, Doyle packed up the tablet and left, but not before she palmed a credit card that had been lying in plain view— she had learned a trick or two whilst rotating through petty thefts.

As she hurried away, she reviewed the card and noted that her name was now Jenny Ho, which seemed unlikely—although she could explain she had married Mr. Ho and they were very happy together. With any luck she could use the card for her purposes before anyone reported the theft.

The next block revealed what she needed: an internet café in a coffeehouse. After noting the locations of the cameras in the area, she slid in the door and made her way to the back of the establishment where the public could have access to desktop computers. Inserting the stolen credit card into the slot, she logged on and opened her work email. Fingers flying, she wrote to Acton, "I'll meet you there as soon as I can. I will check the timetable. All my love to your dear mother."

There; the killer was obviously aware that she and Acton were together—he knew of the hotel stay. Let him think she was unaware of her danger and was instead sneaking out of work to take the train to Trestles. She had little doubt that Acton would now set up a trap and seizure at the train station; hopefully there was one somewhere near the place, wherever it was.

After logging off, she decided to leave the credit card at the internet station in the hope that the next user was an honest soul and would turn it in—she dared not use it again. As she was making ready to leave, she noted that the woman next to her was functioning under duress, miserable and angry at the same time. Unable to stop herself, Doyle rendered a sympathetic smile as she turned to rise.

"Does he love you?" The woman stared at her with hollowed eyes. Apparently she had read Doyle's message.

"Yes." The answer came almost without conscious volition; Doyle needed to leave—not engage in idle conversation with bystanders. Out, she told herself, but could not move.

The woman's eyes searched Doyle's. She was middle-aged and unkempt, not on drugs but unable to focus. "Did you make him love you? Did you get pregnant?"

"I'd rather not discuss it," Doyle said gently. And then, because the other seemed so haunted, she added in the same tone, "I don't think you can make anyone love you; love is a choice."

The woman's expression hardened and she jerked her head toward her screen. "Oh no; I will make him love me—I will give him no choice."

Doyle's eyes were drawn to the screen, where a full page of emails had been sent to the same address. Almost immediately she averted her eyes; she knew the messages would be equal parts threatening and cajoling—the woman was a cyberstalker.

"He won't be my doctor anymore—I wanted to have his baby, but he wouldn't give me the hormones."

"Please," Doyle urged in the same gentle tone, inwardly wincing as she placed a hand on the woman's arm and perceived the rolling waves of thwarted rage. "You must speak with someone who can help you. There is an anti-stalkin' law and you wouldn't want to be arrested."

"I hope I am arrested." The woman's eyes met Doyle's in defiance. "Then everyone will know; he will finally have to pay attention to me."

Doyle stared, mesmerized, and her scalp prickled. This is important, she thought; but I don't know why. "If you call the Department of Health, they can help you with this." She added as an incentive, "Perhaps they will call him in for counselin' with you."

The woman sat back, considering this idea.

Go, thought Doyle. Get out of here, lass—you do not want to start drawing any comparisons here. "I have to leave, I'm afraid. You will call the Health Service?"

"You are a good, kind girl," the other replied, her haunted eyes fixed once again on Doyle's. "I hope he doesn't break your heart."

CHAPTER 32

*B*EFORE *HUDSON HAD FINISHED GIVING HIM THE MESSAGE, HE KNEW.*
He called for his car, struggling to breathe as Hudson handed him his
coat and assured him he would make the appropriate excuses.

Doyle exited out the back way and into the alley, having
snatched a hooded sweatshirt that was laid across the back of a
chair. It's a cutpurse, I am, she thought. It must be in the blood;
back to confession I go. Or reconciliation, or whatever it is.

Folding Munoz's windbreaker into her rucksack, she pulled
on the new one so as to provide a different appearance in the
event the killer was reviewing the CCTV feed. I am giving him
way too much credit, she thought as she carefully covered her
hair, but I would rather not find out the hard way that I underestimated him.

She was trying not to think about her encounter with the
cyberstalker or her instinctive reaction to the woman—as
though what she had said was somehow tied to Doyle's current troubles. It was *not* a reminder of Acton's own neurosis;
not the same thing, at all—the woman was a head case, and it
was obvious that Acton was not a head case—case closed. Only
the case wasn't closed, and the experience had affected her
more than she cared to admit; no denying she had felt the
same sensations she always experienced when she was making
an intuitive connection, but what was the connection? With

complete certainty, she knew that Acton was not a potential danger to her—the same instinct told her this. Then why was she uneasy? Walking along, she remembered to take another covert survey of the passersby and decided it had something to do with the woman's fatalism, her defiance. Again, the connection eluded her and she gave herself a mental shake. Best to concentrate on the task at hand, which was to stay alive until Acton came into contact. She would call the security desk at work on various landlines to check for his arrival, which seemed the best option. He wouldn't go to his flat, as he worried it was not secure, and she hoped he wouldn't go back to the hotel, because the killer had been in the lobby. Assuming it was the killer, of course. There was still the possibility it was Acton's man, shadowing her, and the killer was someone else.

Pointless to speculate; she needed to go to ground and find a place to spend the night, if necessary. An idea had already presented itself, but she was trying not to think about that particular option. And although she was hungry and had little money, she was tired of stealing things; therefore, the best option was to drown her troubles in some blessed, blessed coffee.

Spotting a franchise coffeehouse, she entered the door and breathed in the aroma, feeling like a castaway washing up on shore. Counting out her cash, she ordered a latte and found a stool toward the back, away from the windows. Opening up her borrowed tablet, she emailed Fiona: "I am OK." She checked the time on the screen; it was going to be a long day and she probably shouldn't stay in any particular place very long. After hunching a shoulder so that her face was not visible from the door, Doyle decided she may as well put together a theory on these cases so as to help pass the time. To this end, she visited various crime news sites to see if there had been any breaks in Fiona's case since last night. It did not appear so; there was an article about Fiona and her fine work at the CID; she had been a brilliant scholar and devoted to her job, teaching classes on forensic techniques. It appeared she had never married.

Frowning at the screen, Doyle thought it over. So the killer had killed Fiona, had shot at Acton's mother, and was now after her. Perhaps it was the alternate pattern that Acton had mentioned—the one that he had discounted; the killer was after the women in his life. But he was right in that this seemed unlikely; Acton had no connection with the trainer or Giselle, after all. And Fiona was murdered because she was carrying evidence—evidence that would have implicated the killer. And the dowager was shot at so as to draw Acton away from Doyle—if he had wanted to kill the wretched woman, he wouldn't have missed. But this latest development cast some doubt on Acton's working theory—that the profile was a defensive one; that the killer was not acting as much as he was *reacting* to protect himself. Putting a period to the fair Doyle would not protect him, one would think—unless his aim was to take her hostage and obtain leverage over Acton.

She rested her chin on her hand, stymied. The problem with this stupid case was there were no consistent threads—small wonder they couldn't come up with a working theory. Suddenly struck, she raised her head off her hand and contemplated the biggest inconsistency of all—why would this killer decide at this late date to set his sights on her? Why did he delve into her file, then kill her long-lost father instead of her in the first place? The answer presented itself almost immediately; due to events after her father's killing, she had become Acton's weakness—the killer knew of their liaison at the hotel, after all. It must be a trap for Acton, and she was the bait.

It was a sobering theory, but even this theory made no sense as it came back to her father's murder; the killer couldn't have known of her importance to Acton the morning her father was killed in Somers Town—faith, she had only found out herself the night before, at the fake stakeout on Grantham Street. Who would have known? She couldn't imagine that Acton had discussed her with anyone—except Layton, apparently, and he seemed very discreet and an unlikely candidate, not to mention he probably couldn't heft a large-caliber weapon without assistance.

Flummoxed again, she concluded, and abandoned the effort. The whole thing made absolutely no sense, and maybe they were all trying to find a pattern where none, in fact, existed. Wouldn't it be grand if it was all a flight of fancy—Fiona's killer was already in custody and Doyle had a mobile phone with defective circuitry. Acton would be amused at her fears and he would help her go crawling back to Layton's to return the tablet and offer up her apologies. Unfortunately, pigs would fly first. She knew—the way she knew things—that she was next on the list of faceless dead women. I thank You for the warning, she offered up; let's hope I can outfox him.

Since it wasn't her tablet, she was tempted by the opportunity to do some research on stalking behavior with Acton none the wiser. Scrolling, she began to read of schizoaffective and erotomaniac delusions and almost immediately hit the "delete browsing history" function. I can't do this, she thought. On a fundamental level she didn't want to know what made Acton tick; any analysis would be trumped by her formidable instinct, which told her that their pairing was for the better—there was nothing truly evil within him, and she was good for him. Doyle closed down the tablet and began to trace a pattern in the moisture on the countertop with her finger, wishing that the time would pass faster. She was longing to speak to Acton and he must be climbing the walls after her long silence. By now, the retainer at Trestles—the butler? Master of the Chalice?—had given him the message and Acton had read her emails. He would set up the trap and seizure and then return in short order; she hoped he wouldn't crash his fine car in the process.

Keeping her head down and covered, she made her way to the pay phone in the back as Acton had done that night after church—she was grateful that places such as this still had public phones. After dialing headquarters, she asked to be put through to the security desk.

The operator explained that there was no one stationed at the security desk; due to the murder, all personnel had been advanced to the perimeter. This meant that all security personnel were manning the entrances and the metal detectors. Wonderful, Doyle thought. "Are there any messages for me?" She knew as soon as she asked that Acton would not have trusted any third party with a message. No, there were not.

She rang off and girded her loins for the next call. There was nothin' for it.

"Munoz."

"It's Doyle."

"Well, well, well; how nice of you to call. You left your mobile in your desk drawer and it's been ringing constantly, so I finally turned it off. Habib has been looking for you and so have Drake and Williams. I'm sick of covering for you and making excuses, so get your skinny Irish behind back in here—"

Doyle interrupted the diatribe. "Munoz, I need to ask a big favor of you. I can't go home and I need to stay at your flat."

There was a long pause at the other end. "Trouble with the text-man?"

"In a way. It's very important you don't tell anyone."

Munoz was thinking. "What do I tell Habib?"

"Nothin'. You haven't heard from me. Please, Izzy; it's *imperative* that you say nothin' to anyone."

"You'll be sacked," Munoz observed with no small satisfaction.

I doubt it, Doyle thought—I have just had my first lesson in the power of the peerage. "Please, Izzy."

"All right. Do you know my address?"

"I know the buildin'. Can I meet you in front after work?"

"I'll leave early, then. I'll be there around four."

"Thanks, I owe you." Doyle hung up. Hoisting her rucksack, she made her way out the back exit—best not stay after making the calls. After she walked for a few blocks toward the Knightsbridge area, she spotted a sports bar on the corner. Once again, she found a stool at the rear of the establishment and tried not to smell the chips sizzling as they cooked in wonderfully greasy oil. Rummaging around in her rucksack, she managed to come up with a few spare coins and ordered a plain cup of coffee. Ironic, is what this is, she thought. I imagine I am rich, if Acton's wardrobe and his car are any indication. Thinking along these lines, she pulled out the assistant's tablet and looked up "Trestles" on the internet. There was a photograph of the main building, along with a recitation of the family honors and a synopsis of the history of the House of Acton, starting with the Conquest. "Mother of God," she said aloud, dismayed to the core.

One of her neighbors, a man in a knit cap who was watching the football game on the telly, interpreted her comment as an overture. He sidled up to her, giving her the once-over. Thank the holy saints, she thought; I don't have to do this anymore.

"Are you all alone, then?"

"No." She smiled. "I am waitin' for my husband."

CHAPTER 33

He read the next email and was somewhat reassured; he should not forget how clever she was. He would set out surveillance at the train station and then return to track her down.

The afternoon dragged on while Doyle nursed her pathetic little coffee and pretended an acute interest in the outcome of whatever sporting event was being televised. Finally at a quarter to four, Doyle took a careful look about and walked in the direction of Munoz's flat, five or six blocks away in Knightsbridge. She kept her head down and her hands in her pockets, occasionally glancing behind her. When she arrived at the Edwardian building, she didn't see Munoz and so she leaned into an alcove across the street, waiting for the other girl to appear and keeping her face averted.

"Where's my windbreaker?"

Doyle nearly jumped out of her skin. Munoz was standing beside her, smirking.

"Don't be scarin' me like that." Doyle was annoyed that Munoz could approach her unseen, but on the other hand, Munoz was an excellent detective.

"Enough with the cloak-and-dagger stuff, Doyle—you are overreacting to whatever it is and I'm ashamed of you."

"Can we just go in?" Doyle was in no mood.

The two girls crossed the street to the building, and Munoz

gave Doyle a sharp glance as she ran her security card through the building's front door slot. "I thought you said you didn't have a boyfriend."

"I don't and I never will again."

Munoz shook her head in disgust. "Well, that's a good attitude—you finally convinced someone to have sex with you and now you've ruined it."

Doyle recalled with an effort that Munoz was taking her in and she shouldn't commit mayhem; at least not in a public place.

They rode up in the lift and neither girl spoke. Doyle had been concocting a story in the event Munoz demanded an explanation, but no questions were asked. She thinks I am in trouble with a man, thought Doyle, which is just as well—it explains my odd behavior and at the same time boosts me in her estimation.

Munoz unlocked her door and walked in before her as Doyle hid her surprise; it was a very nice flat, spacious and with expensive furnishings. As Munoz made the same money she did, Doyle surmised that she must either have some financial help from another source or she made some money on the side. It would be surprising, taking into account the long hours of her primary job—as for herself, Doyle never seemed to have a spare minute.

"A very nice place, Munoz," she said with good grace.

"Don't think you'll be staying here long," Munoz cautioned with an admonitory glance. "I like to live alone."

So did I, thought Doyle. But not anymore—getting married throws a rare wrench into it; you start to think you wouldn't mind following him around all day. I miss you, Acton—it's a sad case I am.

"Make yourself at home." Munoz went into the kitchen, took an apple from the basket on the counter, and disappeared into the bedroom. Doyle set down her rucksack and realized that she was very tired—comes from having a rare case o' the willies all day, she thought. Wandering over to look out the kitchen window, she noticed that over the sink hung a small charcoal sketch of the Madonna's head. It was lovely; profound and delicate—Doyle thought it might have been an excerpt from a larger drawing by a master. She was scrutinizing it as Munoz returned to the kitchen, munching the apple.

"She's my hero." Munoz indicated the drawing.

When Doyle found her voice again, she said, "Me too," and resolved that in the future she should do a little less judging and a little more judging not. To this end, she tempered her comments. "Thank you so much for doin' this—I'm afraid I don't have a toothbrush or anythin'."

"As long as you have my windbreaker, I don't care."

Pulling the windbreaker from her rucksack, Doyle handed it over. "Thanks," she said again, and wished she could think of something else to say.

"When Habib asked me where you were, I told him you were holed up with Prickett. I think he swallowed his tongue."

Doyle stared at her in horror, her color rising. "Tell me you are jokin'."

Munoz chuckled. "No worries—I just wanted to make sure you were still in there."

"You can be as unpleasant as you like," retorted Doyle with some fire, "as long as you give me somethin' to eat—I'm starvin'."

"Help yourself." Munoz tilted her head toward the refrigerator.

Doyle dove in and pulled out makings for a sandwich, which she carried over to the counter under Munoz's amused eye. "Prickett's been fired, I hear."

"Of course; they can't be too careful, what with sexual harassment claims looming. I wonder what he was thinking, being so reckless."

Doyle recalled a certain chief inspector's behavior at a certain crime scene and prudently held her tongue while she bit into her sandwich. She thought about it between gulps of orange juice. "Forensics will be depleted, with Fiona's death still unsolved—they'll need more personnel."

Munoz shrugged, her long hair sliding over her shoulders. "They're hard to come by; Forensics people are odd. Which reminds me, Owens came by to look for you—if he's the best you can do, it's no wonder you are hiding out."

"For heaven's sake, Munoz; give over. What did he want?"

"I wasn't about to ask him, thank you very much. I told him you were gone and had left your mobile behind. He was followed by Drake and then Williams, who were told the same story. Between the visitors and your buzzing mobile, I felt like your receptionist."

"I'm sorry. I hope I'm not in Habib's black book."

"Just tell him you have female troubles; men never want to hear of it."

This was inarguably true, and sound advice. "Have you heard anything about Fiona's murder?"

"There's precious little evidence. I think the theory is she was a chance victim, or at least that's what Williams is saying." Munoz indicated a blanket and a pillow she had left on a chair. "You can sleep on the sofa. There's an extra toothbrush in the bathroom drawer, and you can sleep in one of my T-shirts." She checked her watch. "I'm going to meet up with some friends for dinner—you are welcome to come along."

This was true and Doyle was touched. "I appreciate it, but I am that tired and cross. I wouldn't be good company."

Munoz regarded her with an unreadable expression. "Should I stay and hand you tissues or something?"

"Please don't—I am goin' to lie on your fine sofa and watch the telly."

"Right, then, I may be late. Eat whatever you can find and don't take any clothes—they wouldn't fit anyway."

Doyle said dryly, "I truly appreciate it."

"Tell me the details someday," said Munoz, and she was gone.

The details, thought Doyle as she locked the door, will definitely be worth the price of admission.

She lay on the sofa and tried to watch the telly as the light faded and evening set in. She emailed Fiona to say she was safe and sound, and wished she was clever enough to figure out how to read a response. I should work on educating myself, she thought—he is miles smarter than me. With an inward smile, she remembered that he had said she was not to change anything on his account, as it would be a waste of time. I miss that man—I hope one or more of us is not going to be murdered before our one-week anniversary.

Made restless by the reminder, she stood and paced, wishing she knew what was happening and hoping Acton had a plan, as she was fresh out. She paused in her pacing and considered whether it would be safe to check in with Habib for news of Acton's return; Habib was likely to still be at work. Acton was surely back by now and would be bent—as only Acton could be bent—on finding her. It would be a shame to make him worry, and surely no one could trace her here to Munoz's if she called Habib's landline on Munoz's landline. She debated, biting her nails and worrying she would make a stupid decision like the heroine always seemed to do in mystery novels. Picking up the phone, she finally decided it would do no harm to ring Habib; he may have left already anyway.

She dialed his extension and Habib answered and identified himself. Doyle realized belatedly that she was probably *persona non grata* (a good phrase, and apt) with her supervisor at present. She swallowed. "Hallo, sir, this is Doyle."

"Constable Doyle, we have been worried about you." It was said in a scolding tone and, thankfully, not in what one would call a sacking tone.

"I am so sorry, sir; I had to leave work and was unable to return." Remembering Munoz's advice, she implied female troubles.

"Many people are wondering what has happened to you. Indeed, I have a note from Chief Inspector Acton."

Doyle's heart skipped a beat. "What does it say, sir?"

"It says that if you call, I am to tell you that everything is clear and he will meet you at his flat." Habib sounded disapproving. "He said you would know the address."

"Yes." Relief washed over her, almost overwhelming in its intensity. Let Habib think whatever he chose—they would all know soon enough; Acton was on a campaign. "Thank you," she responded happily, unable to contain her reaction. "I will be in tomorrow, I promise."

She rang off. Thank the saints, the coast was clear. Acton must have gotten to the killer, or neutralized him in some other manner. She was in a fever to know the details—perhaps her false trail about the train station had borne fruit; Acton would be that proud of her. This long and miserable day was finally, *finally* over.

Opening drawers, Doyle looked about her for materials so as to write a quick note to Munoz and found paper and a pencil. She then paused; the paper was sketching paper, the pencil was an artist's charcoal pencil. Doyle slowly lifted her gaze to the sketch of the Madonna, transfixed. Mother a' mercy—and I mean that literally, she thought. That's how she can afford this place.

Controlling her bemusement, she wrote a short note explaining she needed to leave and once again conveying her thanks. She then paused long enough to brush her hair before she pulled Acton's address from the zipper compartment of her rucksack where she kept her wedding ring. After puzzling out the best way to get there, she left the flat, her spirits high— no need for the sweatshirt and sunglasses; she was no longer incognito. As she rode on the tube to her destination she remembered with regret that it was not the right time for sex. Vixen, she thought; take hold of your lustful self.

CHAPTER 34

*HE HAD NEVER THOUGHT TO MARRY; NEVER THOUGHT HE COULD
form such an allegiance. It was almost alarming how quickly this had
changed.*

Doyle held the passkey and the security code to Acton's flat
in her hand and drew a deep breath; it was one of those turning points one experienced in living one's life, and it seemed
she had experienced more than her share this past week. For
the second time this day, she stood across the street from an in-
timidating building, working up her nerve. This time, at least,
she was fortified by the sure knowledge that Acton was within,
or would soon be. The building was a lofty and prestigious edi-
fice in the High Street Kensington area, the small and understated brass letters on the granite entry proclaiming OAKHAM
MOUNT MANSIONS. Knocker, she thought. This is your home
now, yours and Acton's—try not to feel as though you've gone
through the looking-glass.

A security guard and a concierge were stationed in the elegant lobby. Both looked up at her entrance and smiled in a
friendly fashion. The concierge asked, "May I help you?"

Doyle debated. She could attempt to present her *bona fides*,
but she doubted these people were as yet aware Acton had tied
the knot, and she didn't want to perform another morality
play by presenting her wedding ring. Instead, she took the easy

way and showed her warrant card. "I am here to see the chief inspector. I have a passkey."

If they thought an after-hours visit by a young woman was in any way unusual, they were too well-trained to betray it. After scrutinizing her ID, the security guard nodded and made a note in his log. "It's the penthouse," the concierge volunteered.

Naturally, she thought as she followed his gesture toward the lift. Nothing less would answer; there's probably a golden door, too. She remembered Grantham Street and Acton's assurance that marriage to him would not change her life much and tried not to trip over the irony that was thick on the ground.

Once in the lift, she inserted the passkey and typed in the security code. The doors opened with a hushed sound onto a hallway paneled with expensive wood and lit by sconces, the carpeting luxurious underfoot. Out of habit, she noted the discreetly positioned security cameras recording her progress.

Once at Acton's door, she felt her natural shyness rise to the fore and knocked softly rather than bang her way in. She waited a moment, but there was no answer—he was not yet here, then. Foolish to hesitate; she had every right to enter and make herself comfortable—in fact, it may be better to have a look around before he arrived, to become accustomed.

Inserting the card key, she entered the flat. Her first impression was that the place was very spacious—it was essentially one huge undivided unit that went from kitchen on the left, to living area, to an offset master bedroom to her far right, which was elevated by a few steps. Several closed doors lined the wall away from the windows—they must lead to utility rooms or spare bedrooms. The furnishings were few and had simple, modern lines; nothing was out of place and everything looked expensive. The man's a neat freak, thought Doyle—not exactly Holmesian. The only illumination came from a series of small recessed lights in the kitchen area and a hallway light. The aspect that drew her attention, however, was the view from the windows directly across from her. She walked over and stared out. "Saints," she breathed aloud. Three huge picture windows that stretched from ceiling to floor overlooked the street below. With the traffic lights, the park and the illuminated city in the background, the view was breathtaking.

She then realized she was not alone. To her left, in the kitchen, someone moved. She turned her head and saw Owens.

No, she thought. No, no, no, no.

After a small pause she said, "Hallo, Owens; have you been summoned also?" She was surprised she managed the words.

"No. Step back, please." He leveled a .45-caliber weapon at her.

"Owens." She feigned astonishment and dismay. "What's afoot, my friend?"

"Come away from the windows," he commanded, all business.

She obeyed, willing herself to function and unable, at the moment, to even remember a suitable prayer.

"I'm really sorry, Doyle. I liked you." He meant it, too. Small consolation since he referred to her in the past tense.

She stared at him for a paralyzed moment and thought, merciful God, help me; if Acton finds me with my face blown away, he will go stark, raving mad. Do what you do best, Doyle. Talk. She asked with a hint of awe, "So it is you who killed Fiona?"

Her assailant was remarkably at ease. "Yes. She found a hair and told Acton. I couldn't take the chance he would match it."

"Is your DNA in the database?" She allowed her tone to be skeptical.

"Not anymore." He smiled his thin little smile.

He doesn't know you are armed, she thought. You have an advantage. Do not panic.

"Are you goin' to kill Acton, then?"

His brows lifted in genuine surprise. "Of course not. Why would I want to kill Acton?"

With due deference, Doyle pointed out, "You are here, lyin' in wait."

"Not for him—for you." He drew down his mouth, a little exasperated that she was so dense. "Acton is not going to come here—I was careless; he figured out someone had been in the security system." The man's face suddenly portrayed a rapt expression, different than the calm façade he had originally presented. "He is really, really good."

"Apparently not as good as you." You were supposed to flatter the taker of hostages; this seemed a comparable situation.

But it was the wrong tack and she could see he was thinking she was dense again. "You must be joking—he is a *bona fide* genius."

Swallowing, Doyle noted the trace of an accent, but she was not very good at accents since everyone who was not Irish had a very strange one—but it didn't seem Russian to her, and besides, the situation was beginning to take an unexpected shape. On instinct, she went with it. "He thinks you are very sharp—he speaks of it often."

"What does he say?" The rapt expression returned, the pale eyes gleaming.

This was tricky in that she wasn't certain what would best please. "That you are very, very, smart." She watched the tepid reaction and amended, "Brilliant, even."

He straightened his posture and hardened his features, keeping the barrel of the gun leveled upon her. "Then you have to go."

Her mouth dry, she shook her head in bewilderment. "And why is that? It seems unkind; I stand your friend, Owens."

Making a small movement with the weapon, his face softened. "It's not your fault—but I didn't realize how much of an obstacle you were. It's a shame, but there it is."

He was very calm, speaking of her anticipated death. I need to sit down, she thought, so as to have a chance to draw as well as ensure my knees won't give out. "We are friends; perhaps we can work out our differences—shall we sit down?" He hesitated and she added with a smile, "You see, I am hopin' this is going to be like those mystery stories where you will boast of your exploits so long that I will be rescued."

He smiled, genuinely amused. "I'm afraid it's going to be more like Patricia Highsmith."

"Oh," she replied, not at all clear on the allusion. Nevertheless, with false confidence she moved over to sit on the leather sofa and he stood across from her, the gun tracking her movements. Trying to sound conciliatory, she carefully crossed her right leg over her left. "Now, tell me what I have done to offend you."

"Nothing—you are too nice, just as I told you. I've never had to kill someone I liked before—it is a lot harder." He appeared willing to delay the inevitable in an attempt to explain the situation to her—a respite that she supposed would not have happened had she not gone out of her way to be kind. Hopefully it would give her enough time to show just how unkind she could be.

"I thought when I killed your father you would go on leave. I wish you had; that would have been better than this. I just needed you to stop working with Acton."

She knit her brow, assimilating this. "You killed my father so that I would go on leave."

"That, and to show Acton what I could do—to make him notice me."

Mother of God, she thought in stunned disbelief, *that's* what this is all about; those fatal *beaux yeux*—only in this case, fatal for me. "You are interested in Acton, then?"

"Oh yes." There it was again, the smallest trace of an accent. "No one else comes close."

Amen to that, thought Doyle; and if it's the last thing I do, I'm not going to let you get your filthy mitts on him. With a renewed sense of focus, she rubbed her left leg with her left hand and admitted, "I didn't know it was my father at the time—otherwise it was a good plan."

With a gesture of amused frustration, he tilted his head back. "I know, I know—I couldn't *believe* you didn't recognize him. And after all the trouble of looking him up, too. Although it did shake you—Acton was not happy you were upset."

"As well I remember." The first time Acton had kissed her.

Don't think about that, she ordered herself immediately. Don't lose your concentration; now you know what makes him tick and you are making progress, here. Unbidden, a vision of the cyber-stalker at the internet café came to mind. Don't think of her, either, she warned. Stay cool; concentrate. She laced her fingers around her right knee and turned her right hip toward him, obscuring as much as possible her left lower leg—she would get only one opportunity, but he was watching her steadily. She would have to distract him, even if it was just for a moment; otherwise she had no chance.

"How many people have you killed, then?" She tried to sound genuinely interested, as though they were discussing gardening, or coin collecting.

"You would be surprised." The pale eyes narrowed.

"But none as kind as me." She smiled, trying to convince him to re-think it.

"No." He smiled in return.

So, he didn't want to boast of his exploits. Perhaps a little gentle prodding would answer. "You didn't like Giselle?"

He said a vile epithet, and she flinched. "Is that really necessary?"

"Sorry," he apologized. "No—I didn't like her."

"So I gathered. I processed the crime scene."

He smiled again at her dry tone. Good; she was making inroads, buying time. "Because she was after Acton?"

He rolled his eyes at her abject stupidity. "As though someone like him would pay any attention to someone like her—it was comical. But I had to kill her before she could tell Acton."

"Tell him what?" Doyle was genuinely curious.

He shrugged. "About me and the trainer. But that was strictly business, and I had to kill him because he figured it out." He paused. "And I wanted to see Acton in action again—I watched him from across the street with my binoculars—but you were there, both times."

"Indeed I was. So you wanted me to go on leave." Doyle was fascinated despite the exigency of the situation. Suddenly all the murders that had heretofore made no sense were starting to make sense. "And you killed the trainer when Drake was at conference so that Acton would take the investigation."

Owens tilted his head. "Let us just say Drake was away; everyone only thought he was at a conference."

Doyle pretended admiration. "It was a close call, you know—the trainer was goin' to ground and you almost missed your chance."

"He figured it out—I didn't think he was that smart."

"My hat is off to him," Doyle agreed. "I certainly didn't figure it out." Just the same way she hadn't figured Acton out; apparently her instinct didn't work so well when dealing with a Section Seven.

Owens shook his head slightly, incredulous. "You are so naïve—especially for someone like him; what does he see in you?"

The words hung ominously in the air; this was not good—if he considered her a rival, she was done for. "I think," she offered diffidently, "—that you are sufferin' under a misapprehension." Excellent word. "My relationship with Acton is innocuous." Even better; small solace if it was to be the last word from her vocabulary list she ever used.

As he regarded her, she could see he was deciding whether or not to tell her something, and taking advantage of his abstraction, she moved her hands to rub her legs absently, to rub her calves. "Listen, Owens, I understand now—and I certainly can't blame you. As we are friends, perhaps we can keep this a secret and I will gracefully bow out. Then you can arrange to work for Acton with my blessin' and you won't have to shoot me." Meeting his gaze with her own guileless one, she tried to sound as though this was a perfectly reasonable course to take.

Her assailant shook his head with real regret. "It wouldn't work. He fancies you."

"Holmes?" She pretended shocked surprise. "I don't think so. Why, I've never even been here before."

"No," he agreed. "I could tell when you came in that you had never been here. That's when I realized."

"I don't think so, Owens," she insisted. "He thinks I'm thick as a plank."

"No." Owens suddenly sobered; the light, almost playful mood had disappeared and he straightened his shoulders. "He fancies you."

"You are mistaken," she said firmly. "Now, let's come to terms."

But he was not to be persuaded. "I'm not mistaken. He has seventeen photographs of you in his mobile."

She stared in unfeigned astonishment. *"Truly?"*

He nodded gravely, as would a headsman getting set to do his duty. Disliking the shift in tone, she improvised, "Perhaps he is goin' to paint a portrait or some such thing—he's an artist, y' know."

"In some of them you are sleeping with no clothes on." A hint of bitterness had crept into his tone.

Amazed, she asked, "Are you sure it is me?" Oh Acton, Acton, she thought in horror—you have sealed my flippin' fate.

"Yes, I'm sure—don't be so stupid." He tried to control his anger. "Can't you see the irony? He is just like me. He is just like me only it's you he wants."

No, Doyle thought, recoiling. He is not just like you. He is not.

"I have photos of him. But he has photos of you. " Owens was angry, thinking about the nude photographs, and she knew he was working himself into pulling the trigger. "So first you have to be taken out, and then Williams has to be taken out, and then he will work with me and I will show him—" he took a long, steadying breath; the hint of an accent back in his voice, "—that we should be together. He will replace your photos with mine."

Doyle recognized she was out of time and that she somehow had to get a shot off. If I'm going, she thought grimly, I'm taking him with me. Trying to appear puzzled, she absently rubbed her left leg with her left hand. "I don't understand it,

Owens. Perhaps he means to sell my snaps on the Internet or somethin'—I always assumed he was gay."

Ah, this got his immediate attention and he stilled. "No—he fancies you." But there was the slightest questioning in his tone, the slightest hint of incredulous hope.

Doyle leaned forward as if to share a deep secret. "I'm not *that* thick, Owens—I've seen gay porn on his laptop. Here—I'll bet there's some in that one over there and I'll prove it." She made as if to move toward the desk by the windows while he stood, frozen. As she turned, she drew her weapon from its holster, unlatched the safety with her thumb, aimed, and shot in one smooth movement, guessing at the trajectory. Throwing herself on the floor as the report sounded, she rolled, clutching her gun and tensing for his return shot as she scrambled behind the sofa. No return shot was heard. Instead, Owens fell backward and hit the floor like a board, a bullet hole between his eyes. Silence reigned.

"Good one, Doyle," she said aloud.

CHAPTER 35

*S*HE WASN'T AT NELLIE'S. HE HAD TRIED TO HIDE HIS ALARM BUT DID *not think he had been entirely successful. There had been no recent emails.*

After a brief moment of sheer exhilaration, Doyle clenched her teeth in agony and clutched at her right leg, rocking back in forth in reaction to the searing pain. The bullet had first passed through her right calf before it had hit Owens. Groaning aloud, she pulled up her trouser and examined the wound. Blood was flowing around her ankle and dripping onto the floor. A through-and-through—it was bleeding but not arterial, which was good; otherwise she would have to tourniquet it. Think—first aid. Elevate the leg and apply pressure to stop the bleeding. She struggled to her feet and hopped into the nearby guest bathroom, which was wonderfully elegant and did not go unappreciated. She sat on the floor and elevated her right ankle by bracing it on the sink, snatching several guest towels off the rack to staunch the flow of blood. Grimly noting the gunshot residue all over her inner right calf, she decided she would worry about infection later, after she had managed to stem the carnage.

After taking some deep breaths, she assessed the situation. She didn't seem to be in danger of bleeding to death or passing out. Best not to make an emergency call; she didn't even want to think about the scandal this little scenario would create for the worthy chief inspector. I will contact him, and wait—it is my only option. She rested her forehead against her knee, in intense pain and sickened by the thought—it would all come out: Owens's obsession, their hole-in-corner marriage, her father's murder, her own murder of Owens. Nothin' for it—would rather be alive, all in all. Thank You, she offered up; in all things, give thanks.

After the bleeding had slowed, she struggled to her feet, trying to keep the leg elevated in front of her. She braced herself against the wall and noted with a grimace that she left bloody handprints, so she paused to wash her hands before she hopped across the room to where she had dropped her rucksack. Steadying herself by hanging on to the back of the sofa, she eased herself to the floor, propping her leg up on the sofa as she pulled out the assistant's tablet, half dreading it would be out of battery which would be very much in keeping with her luck. No, she immediately corrected herself; I am the luckiest lass alive. Thankfully, the tablet worked and she wrote to Fiona: Call your flat immediately. Urgent.

She then hopped over to the telephone mounted on the kitchen wall and called work, leaving a message on both his voice mail and her own voice mail. "Acton, it's me. Please call your flat as soon as possible."

No fear of being monitored anymore; it was a mournful shame she didn't know Acton's mobile number. Her wound had started bleeding again, so she returned to sit on the floor, propping her leg up against the sofa again and pressing both her palms as hard as she could against the hand towel she had tied around her calf. She felt a little dizzy for a moment—don't faint, you knocker. Think about something else. Make a report.

The first item on the agenda was to wonder how a candidate like Owens had managed to pass all the screenings that were required to be a constable, for the love o' Mike. But it hadn't been obvious—he was smart, a smart psycho; he had certainly fooled her and she was not easily fooled. Not to mention he apparently enjoyed creating a thorny crime scene so that he could observe Acton at work. I had a feeling it was something like that, she remembered. But I never would have guessed it was all about Acton. Munoz is right once again; we were puzzling over patterns, profiles, and motivation—but it was really all about sex.

Carefully shifting her weight, she lifted the towel to peer at the oozing wound. Not a good idea, she thought, replacing the towel and taking deep breaths. No more peeking; it was amazing how different it felt when the wound was one's own rather than on a corpse.

To take her mind off it, she resumed her narrative. Owens watched Capper's interview and decided to kill Capper and Smythe so as to eliminate anyone else who could identify him, and at the same time to throw dust in the CID's eyes so it would close the case. But Acton had known it was staged and had alerted Fiona to comb the bodies for third-party evidence. A hair was found; unfortunately, Acton did not know that Owens was monitoring his mobile and when Fiona informed him of the find, she had sealed her own fate. She would have kept the evidence with her; it wasn't logged in because Acton was going to kill Owens himself with no one the wiser.

She gazed out over the lights of the city, trying not to think of the body cooling off a few feet away or the stain on Acton's fancy throw rug. Her father's murder served two different desires for Owens—it drew Acton's attention to himself with some clever detective work and it was supposed to force Acton's current favorite to take a leave of absence. In Owens's fantasy, he would then present himself as a substitute for Doyle, and he and Acton would have begun a relationship. Doyle ran her hands gently over the hand towel. But when she hadn't reacted as planned to the death of her father, Owens had not escalated his plan to remove her because Acton had pulled her off of the cases; he had placed enough distance between them so that Owens no longer considered her an obstacle—it had probably saved her life, until the discovery of the nude photographs, that is. Seventeen photographs, some nude—it was hard to believe Acton could be so reckless. Poor Owens, it must have been quite a shock. No, she corrected; Owens no longer deserves my sympathy; he can beg for mercy from God.

A dark thought was hovering around the edges of her mind, but she refused to allow it entry. There was nothing to compare between the two; have done, Doyle.

Remembering the questions Acton had asked her about Owens as they left the Somers Town crime scene (en route to their wedding), she realized that he must have known straight off that it was staged and by whom. Owens was right; Acton is a genius, she thought in admiration. He must have been keeping a sharp eye on Owens all along, giving him an assignment to keep him close and collecting a DNA sample, then waiting for him to make a mistake that would confirm him as the killer. He never mentioned his suspicions to Doyle, probably because Owens was slated to simply disappear along with any chance that her father's identity would be revealed. And now she had killed Owens, just like that. He had been alive and now he was dead, thanks to her. She was almost surprised to realize she felt no remorse—a good riddance, it was.

The bleeding seemed to have stopped, but she nevertheless avoided lifting the towel. Although she was somewhat thirsty, she didn't have the wherewithal to make her way to the kitchen, and so stayed where she was. All she could do, it seemed, was wait. And admire the view. She thought about her mother and she thought about Acton, and how wonderful it was to be alive. Owens wasn't given another glance. Hurry, Acton, she thought—I don't want to spend the night here with him.

Blessedly, the phone rang about ten minutes later. She had taken the receiver to the floor with her and answered it before it completed its first ring. "Hallo?"

"Kathleen."

"Michael," she breathed, a world of relief in her voice. He was silent. Pull yourself together, Doyle, she thought—you're not out of the woods yet. She was suddenly conscious of the fact the call could show up in a later investigation and said only, "Could you please come here as soon as possible?"

"Is he there?" Acton's words were clipped.

No need to identify who, thought Doyle. "Not anymore."

He paused. "Is your hair in your eyes?"

"No, there's no trap; he's really not here." She added, "Anymore."

"I'll be over immediately. Don't unlock the door for anyone but me."

"Not a chance," she replied, eyeing the body on the rug.

CHAPTER 36

*H*E WOULD KILL THE BASTARD SLOWLY, WHICH IS WHAT HE SHOULD *have done to begin with.*

While she waited for Acton, Doyle had a chance to think about his probable reaction to this latest disaster. As a result, she pulled her trouser leg down over the bloody towel and hopped up to array herself on the sofa so that she would not appear quite so *hors de combat.* Listen to me, she thought a bit giddily, livin' in a palace and talkin' like a nob.

In short order, Doyle heard Acton inserting his key into the slot. As he entered the room, his eyes were drawn to her position curled on the sofa and then, to the body lying on the rug. He halted for a moment in surprise. She mustered up a smile. "I'm afraid we have a bit of a problem."

He walked to her, ran his hand over her head, and leaned over to kiss her. After running his hand over her head a second time, he then crouched down beside Owens and took a long look. "Well done."

"I'll have no more o' your aspersions about my shootin' skills."

He smiled without answering and casually pulled the .45 from Owens's hand. He wasn't wearing gloves, and Doyle's well-trained sensibilities were a little shocked by the application of his bare hand to the weapon.

Steeling herself, she said, "I have somethin' to tell you and you must promise me, on your honor, you won't be overreactin' or runnin' amok."

Acton fixed his sharp eyes upon her, still crouching with his forearms on his knees. "It doesn't matter if he raped you, Kathleen."

"Michael," she said in exasperation. "He didn't rape me—he was gay, for heaven's sake."

He bent his head for a moment and Doyle thought he was hiding his relief. Oh, she realized; I am ovulating—small wonder he was worried.

Lifting his gaze to meet hers, he asked, "What is it, then?"

"I had to shoot myself through the leg to shoot him." She didn't think she needed to tell him it was unintentional—that part would be her own little secret.

He stared at her for a moment and then rose. "Show me."

She propped up her knee and rolled up her trouser leg to expose the bloody towel. He came to sit near her feet on the sofa and helped her gently pull the cloth from the wound, as it had begun to stick.

She said suddenly, "I think I am goin' to be sick."

He deftly pulled a wastebasket over and held her hair back while she was sick as a cat. "Sorry." She was embarrassed. "I was goin' grand 'till now."

Running his hands down the sides of her head, he said, "You are going wonderfully. Let me get you a cloth and some water." Seeing that he was headed into the elegant bathroom, she winced and called after him, "Sorry about the mess in there."

When he returned, he said only, "I thought you were going to stop apologizing to me."

She smiled, relieved. He was handling this better than she had expected; good one, Acton.

He helped her to tidy up and she drank the water—she was thirsty from the loss of blood. As she lay back on the sofa, he asked, "Ready?"

She nodded, and he carefully eased the cloth away from the

wound with gentle fingers. She decided that this time she would watch him and not look at the wound; in the future she resolved to be more sympathetic to the witnesses at the crime scenes who were apt to become green around the gills.

Acton examined her, scrutinizing the area carefully. "This will require some attention."

Not a surprise—she already knew this; she hated doctors and the very thought of needles. And there was another prob-lem, too. In a small voice, she noted, "It's a gunshot wound, Michael." Any medical practitioner was bound by law to con-tact the police.

"Yes, it is." Pulling out his mobile, he scrolled through his programmed numbers while she watched him.

After ringing a number, he spoke into the mobile. "Timothy, it's Michael. I wonder if you can come to my flat at your earliest convenience." He paused. "Thank you. Best bring your bag." There was another pause while Acton glanced at Doyle. He added into the phone, "The surgery kit may be necessary—B positive." He disconnected.

Doyle attempted a false heartiness. "Shouldn't I be drinkin' brandy or holding a bullet in my teeth or somethin'?"

He smiled, but only to humor her. "I'm going to move TDC Owens into the spare bedroom before the doctor arrives." With-out ceremony, Owens's body was then rolled up into the rug it lay upon and dragged into the spare bedroom. When Acton re-emerged, she could see that he was deep in thought—planning logistics, no doubt, being as how there was a dead body in the flat and the place was awash with security. It had been apparent from the moment he took Owens's weapon that he had no in-tention of contacting law enforcement.

Doyle could not endure the silence and spoke into it. "The doctor is a friend o' yours?"

Pulled from his abstraction, he answered, "Yes. A good friend. A mackerel snapper like yourself."

"Well then—if all else fails, he can administer last rites."

Acton did not respond to her teasing, did not even lift his

head, but she was suddenly aware of the effort this was costing him. Don't be flippant, she cautioned herself—let him know you're going to be all right.

Coming back over to stand beside her, he resumed stroking her hair—it appeared he could not stop touching her head with his hands. Overcome with emotion, she had to bite her lip to keep it from trembling. I don't know which of us to feel sorrier for, she thought unsteadily. Wrapping an arm around his hips, she pulled him to her, resting her head against him. She tried not to think about what would have happened had Owens killed her and Acton come home to witness the aftermath. Life was so very precious.

He continued the stroking. "The doctor should be here in thirty minutes or so."

"Time enough." With a sudden movement, she lifted her head and began pulling at his belt to unfasten it. "Come here, husband."

Surprised, he grasped her hands with his to still them. "Not such a good idea, Kathleen."

"Michael," she said through her teeth. "Do this or I will shoot you as I did Owens."

Still holding her hands, he crouched down to look up into her eyes, smiling to reassure her. She was not fooled. "Later, perhaps."

It was a lie. "Do as you are told, Michael." She pulled him to her, her mouth seeking his.

He resisted. "Kathleen," he said gently. "I don't know if I can—I'm not a performing bear, you know."

It was funny and so—*aristocratic* that she began to laugh, which was what he had intended. Then she began to cry; huge gulping sobs she couldn't control. He put his arms around her and she clung to him and caught his mouth with hers for a moment, then broke away so she could gasp for air and sob. Murmuring endearments, he carefully climbed atop her, pulled away the clothing that was impeding him, and performed very well indeed.

Afterward, as they lay spent, Doyle thought about what she had learned this evening. Acton was, in fact, all too willing to whisper sweet nothings to her during sex but only if first, she had been shot, and second, she cried about it. Mental note. "Thank you."

"My pleasure." He kissed her mouth and then her eyelids. "Now may I straighten up?"

"Yes. Will you fetch me a brush, please?"

She made herself presentable as best she could, hoping the doctor wouldn't guess what they'd been at—there would be enough explaining to do as it was. To this end, she tried to come up with a plausible explanation for her wound and drew a blank. Ah, well; he was Acton's friend, let Acton explain. Speaking of which, she asked, "Where were you?" She regretted the words as soon as they were out; she didn't want him to feel guilty.

"I was out looking for you. I'm afraid Nellie may be alarmed."

"Not to worry. I'll call her. How ironic that I was here and this is the last place you'd think I would be."

"He lured you here?" Poor man; she could see he didn't want to talk about it, but he wanted to know how this had all come about.

She responded in a level tone—hopefully she would not fall into hysterics again, although the cure for the hysterics was not unwelcome. "Yes—he left a note with Habib pretending it was you. I should have been more wary; I knew I was next on his list."

He pulled up a leather chair so it was next to her and sat down. "How did you know that?"

"My mobile stopped workin'. I remembered the other victims' mobiles stopped workin'—and I just knew."

He nodded, well-aware of how sometimes she just knew. "Did he say anything?"

Here was a crackin' minefield—the persistent dark thought still hovered around the edges of her mind; Owens had compared himself to Acton, saying Acton was just like him. He was not, but she was not even going to allow the comparison to be raised, so instead she answered, "He said he killed a lot of people—I think he was some sort of assassin."

Acton was watching her response, and she had the impression he was aware she was leaving something out. It was hard to put anything past this husband of hers; mental note. "Did he say for whom?"

"No, he didn't." Leaning back against the cushions, she attempted to look wan. "Could we not talk about this just now?"

Immediately he moved to her and held her head in his hands again. "Of course; forgive me."

The buzzer rang. Saved by the bell, she thought.

CHAPTER 37

*H*E SAW HER BLOODY HANDPRINTS ON THE WALL AND TRIED TO *control his rage. On an elemental level, he craved retribution.*

Dr. Timothy McGonigal was a genial man about Acton's age who came through the door carrying two black canvas bags. Doyle smiled at him from her perch on the sofa, nervous. She hated doctors but was forced to make an exception for Acton's friend—the first one she'd met. She would rather have held him off at gunpoint.

"Kathleen, may I present Timothy McGonigal. Timothy, my wife, Kathleen."

She had never heard Acton refer to her as his wife and she found it very agreeable. If the doctor was surprised, he hid it well, shaking her hand in a friendly fashion. "Very pleased to meet you, Lady Acton."

I will never get used to that if I live to be a hundred, she thought.

"Now, let's take a look." Putting on his glasses, the doctor pulled up another chair. He asked Acton to reposition the lamp, and the two decided they should bring the reading light from the desk over also. Once this was arranged, he unwound the bloody towel and examined the wound. Doyle looked out the windows at the lights and Acton sat next to her, running his thumb over the back of her hand repeatedly.

Feeling the toes on her right foot, the doctor asked her to wiggle them. He then took her blood pressure. He asked no questions at all, other than to inquire if she had any allergies and whether she was pregnant, which made her start guiltily and blush to the roots of her hair.

"Not that we are aware," answered Acton smoothly.

The doctor then leaned back and addressed them both. "I'll need to clean it out pretty thoroughly, and with this kind of thing we like to do a debridement. We'll leave it open for four days or so and then give it a stitch or two. A strong dose of antibiotics should keep any infection at bay. I'll give you a shot of medication that will help to take the edge off the pain along with a tetanus shot—you've lost some blood but I don't think it's necessary to have an infusion. Drink lots of water and rest. You're young; you'll do."

When he pulled a pre-filled syringe from his bag, Doyle turned her face into the back of the sofa. Don't be such a baby, she scolded herself; you've been shot, for heaven's sake.

"Where are you from, Lady Acton?" Doyle was not fooled; the doctor was trying to distract her about the shot. Doctors were wily.

"Dublin." She gritted her teeth as she felt the needle, her answer muffled by the sofa back.

"A fine place—I was at Trinity College for a Fellowship."

"Never been inside." She realized she was being rude and temporized. "I'm sure they are very friendly." She wasn't certain what a Fellowship was.

Acton, bless him, interceded. "How are you, Tim? I've been remiss."

"Not to worry; you've been distracted." The doctor was amused and thankfully was taking his vile needle away.

"Yes," agreed Acton, who was also amused.

He is pleased Timothy is here, Doyle realized—I must pull myself together. "How do you know Michael, Dr. McGonigal?"

"Timothy, please. We suffered through school together, although I suffered a great deal more than your husband."

Bemused, Doyle tried to imagine Acton in his youth, having a friend like Timothy and attending class, but she failed in the attempt. Having only known him in his formidable adulthood, it was impossible to imagine formative years, anything other than the man beside her. Just as well; she would have been in grade school wearing a plaid skirt and braids.

Acton said, his voice somber, "You've heard about Fiona?"

"Yes," said the doctor, and the two men were grieved. A mutual friend, Doyle realized.

Timothy continued, shaking his sandy head, "It was so senseless—I think that makes it worse."

Acton said nothing, nor did Doyle; it was not so senseless to them.

"How does Caroline?" Acton asked.

"Good; saving the world. She'd love to see you—speaks of you often."

"We must find time to visit, then. I will see to it."

It was true, and if Doyle were not so sleepy, she would be faintly alarmed at the prospect of meeting more of Acton's friends; although this one did not seem to be hiding any dismay upon making her acquaintance. A peaceful lassitude was stealing over her and she asked, "Is Caroline your wife?"

"My sister. I am unmarried."

"And you such a kind man," she observed in wonderment. "It's a wretched shame, it is."

"Not everyone is as lucky as your husband."

Touched, she said, "I thank you for the compliment." She was having trouble keeping her eyes open and so decided to close them. "You are very good."

She was dimly aware that the doctor placed a shallow tray under her leg and then inserted another needle near the wound, but this one did not seem as objectionable. He gave some instruction to Acton, asking him to hold her leg a certain way. She then lost interest but could feel some tugging that bordered on the uncomfortable. As she murmured in protest,

Acton stroked her forehead. "Hush, Kathleen; it will be over soon."

She dozed while the doctor continued his ministrations, but then recalled herself enough to tell Acton, "Munoz let me stay at her flat."

"Did she? Did you break anything?"

"I did not," proclaimed Doyle, unable to open her eyes. "We were very civil."

"Shall I have her promoted, then?"

"No," she said firmly, and the doctor laughed.

Falling asleep, she dreamed strange and disturbing dreams. She was trapped in a basement. Peering out a narrow window onto the street, she saw Acton searching for her and she tried to call out but found she had no voice. Pounding on the window with the heel of her hand she could see that Acton had given up; a limousine came for him and he left. A woman who looked remarkably like the queen but who was Acton's mother told her to stop making such a fuss, she would wake the baby. Doyle tried to explain that she had been shot and Acton must be told, but the woman walked away in disgust. Taking out her mobile, she attempted to dial a number but it never seemed to connect no matter how carefully she dialed. I must get out, she thought, and kept trying, trembling with frustration.

Doyle awoke later and took a moment to orient herself. Her leg was numb and propped up on pillows, with something cold wrapped around it. She was having a hard time focusing. Acton's flat; Owens dead.

Acton was standing by the windows, watching her with his hands in his pockets. The doctor had left and the flat was dark. "I'm awake," she said to him. "The drugs are a rare crack."

He approached. "Good. Try to keep still."

"I wasn't wearin' my ring, Michael. Timothy will think we aren't really married."

"No. He knew we were married."

"I showed Layton my ring."

At that, he sat beside her, his feelings somewhere between amused and amazed. "Did you indeed?"

"I killed him. Not Layton; Owens."

"I know. Try to rest, Kathleen."

She wanted to smile, but it seemed too much of an effort. "I like it when you say my name."

Running a finger along her wrist, he replied, "I like to say it."

"I kissed you first, remember?"

"Yes; I'll not soon forget."

"I was afraid of the ring, so I put it in my rucksack. I didn't lose it—I put it in the zipper compartment. I was very, very careful." She couldn't emphasize this enough.

He took her left hand and held it pressed between both of his. "You needn't wear it if you don't want to." He meant it. Knocker.

"That's a pint full o' ridiculous." She dozed for a minute, and then added, "I think I will buy you a ring."

"I would like that very much."

"The receptionist at Layton's must see that you have a ring," she said firmly.

"I will be certain to show it to her."

She slept again, fitfully, and then awoke with a start to wonder if she was having another nightmare—the man who had shadowed her now stood by the windows where Acton had stood, watching her. She gasped and sat up, reaching instinctively for the weapon that was no longer on her leg.

"It's all right, miss," the man said in alarm, and called out, "Chief!"

Acton strode into the room. "Easy, Kathleen, he's with me."

She sank back, slightly dizzy and her heart still pounding. "You should have told me, Michael. It would have saved me a lot of worryin'."

His brows drew together. "I'm sorry; I thought he was competent and you would be none the wiser."

The man had the grace to look ashamed and so Doyle interjected, "It was only luck that I twigged him."

Acton said nothing and Doyle added, "If I had known he was with us, I would have let him shoot stupid Owens."

"He would have to stand in line."

"It's ironic, is what it is." Doyle leaned back again and closed her eyes. "I told you that you shouldn't go about killin' people and then I am the one who does."

But Acton would not allow her to bear a tinge of guilt over the events of the evening. "You were perfectly justified and I'll not hear another word about it."

"Just the same," insisted Doyle, "it's ironic."

Opening her eyes, she saw Acton make a gesture to the other man, who nodded and moved into the spare bedroom. Acton leaned over to kiss her. "Stay here, we'll be back shortly. Promise me you won't move."

"What will you do with him?" asked Doyle, who, although her faculties were not fully restored, knew very well what was afoot.

"I'm afraid that's none of your business."

Doyle decided this was grossly unfair, given the situation, but found she was too sleepy to protest.

CHAPTER 38

HER EYELASHES WERE DARK AGAINST HER PALE CHEEKS. SHE looked so vulnerable; she had suffered so much. He tried to force himself to stop thinking of it.

Doyle awoke during the night in a cold sweat, filled with a nameless dread and wondering where she was. She tried to leap up but her leg hurt and she gasped. Acton was beside her, his arms around her. "Hush, it's me."

"Bad dream," she explained, wincing as she sat again. "Wretchedly sorry." She realized that he had been drinking, which, all in all, was not a surprise.

"How's the leg?"

"Hurts," she said succinctly. "What's your poison?"

"Scotch."

The room was illuminated by the lights from the street below, shining in through the expansive windows. He had been sitting in the large leather chair pulled next to her sofa and on the side table was a half-empty bottle of expensive scotch and a small glass. It was apparent that heavy inroads had been made.

"May I have a taste?"

"You don't drink," he said shortly. He was in a foul mood but was trying to hide it. Small wonder, poor man.

"Just a sip, to see what it's like."

She held out her hand and he hesitated, thinking to refuse, then handed her the glass. Tasting the amber liquid, she couldn't conceal her extreme distaste and handed it back. "Ach, that's foul. You're on your own, my friend."

"Just as well. You are supposed to take some antibiotics and another pain pill." He rose, heading to the kitchen to get the pills and a glass of water.

She made a face. "I don't like the pain medication—I think it gave me bad dreams."

Leaning against the counter, he thought about it. "The pills may not do so—they'll put you to sleep, which is probably beneficial at this point."

A compromise was in order. "All right; I'll take them only if I can sleep in your bed. With you. And you may bring the scotch."

Tilting his head, he countered, "Only if you will not demand sex from me again."

"Done."

As she dutifully swallowed the pills, she rested her gaze on the bare floor where Owens had fallen. "You will need a new rug."

"*Christ.*" A world of anger was contained in the word.

"You shouldn't blaspheme, Michael," she admonished gently. She shouldn't be so hard on him, he was struggling—she could feel it. "Come here and sit with me, please." She held out her hand.

He sat beside her, his hand still clasping hers, and met her gaze. "We needn't live here if you'd rather not. I'd understand."

She stared at him incredulously. "Michael, have you *seen* your view? Don't be daft, man. Besides, I don't believe in ghosts."

"And you call yourself an Irishwoman."

She laughed, and he rose to walk to the kitchen to wash his hands and splash water on his face. Watching him, she offered, "Please don't sober up on my account. I completely understand, and besides, I will be asleep in a matter of minutes."

"You are a very commendable wife." Toweling his face, he returned to sit beside her on the sofa.

"Well, I confess I am not much of a cook. However, I am handy with a gun, which as it turns out, is the more useful talent."

This, however, appeared to be the wrong thing to say. He met her eyes in all seriousness. "Perhaps you should consider a different career path."

Surprised, she didn't know what to say for a few moments. "Michael," she said gently, "I am a good detective."

He dropped his head, stubbornly refusing to look at her. "It is too dangerous."

She blinked. Mother a' mercy, was he going to be all lord-and-master and put his foot down? Remembering that he was bosky, Doyle proceeded with caution. "Look, I know this has been very difficult for you—"

He lifted his head to interrupt her, his eyes blazing and his words clipped. "For me? Don't say it; not with your blood all across the floor." Unable to contain himself, he stood and paced. She had a glimpse of white-hot rage; then it was gone.

Although she was taken aback, she kept her voice steady. "It is true, Michael. You would wear me around like a coat if you could—I understand how miserable this is for you."

He paused in his movements and she could see that he had mastered his momentary loss of control. The words were quiet. "You could be brought in out of the field."

This idea was nothing short of alarming, particularly in light of how miserable she had been the past two days whilst out of the field; impossible to consider such an assignment stretching out endlessly. "I want to work with you, in the field. I am good at it, Michael—we are good together." She tried not to sound like she was pleading; she knew instinctively that if she pleaded with him, she could get whatever she wished and that was not the way she wanted to deal with him.

Fingering his glass, he did not look at her. She reached up to wrap her fingers around his forearm. "I'm quite the hardy banner, y'know. Thank the holy saints for you and your illegal weapon; I swear I will wear it every day until I am eighty."

He changed the subject. "Timothy will return tomorrow to check on you. He said you are to rest."

"Readily. I'll call Habib in the mornin' and tell him I'm home sick."

His eyes met hers and there was a challenge in them. "I have a better idea; I will call Habib and tell him we will not be coming in because we are new-married."

Nodding, she replied in a steady voice, "Fair enough." Perhaps he would capitulate on the work issue if she capitulated on this. Her two weeks were not up yet, but she had always heard that marriage was full of compromises. "Now, help me into bed."

He slid his arms behind her shoulders and under her knees and carefully lifted her; she put her face into his neck and breathed in—he smelled of scotch. It was a novel experience; she felt like the heroine in a romance except that she was worried about forensics. "Owens was in the kitchen. Should we wipe it down?"

As he carried her to the bedroom, he put his cheek against her head. "Why would we do that?"

"Prints and epithelials?" she ventured.

He seemed amused as he lowered her into the bed. "Why would anyone be checking my kitchen for prints and epithelials?"

"Oh. I see what you mean. Will anyone wonder what happened to him?"

He took off his shoes, slid into bed beside her, and pulled the comforter around them, avoiding her leg. She noted he hadn't brought the scotch. "I really don't care."

Although she was getting drowsy from the pain pills, she knew, strange as it seemed, that he was not telling the truth.

They lay quietly for a few minutes. "Security cameras," she said suddenly.

"Taken care of. Try to sleep."

Breathing in his scent, she slid her hand over his chest, then between his shirt buttons. After unbuttoning a button, she leaned over to gently kiss his exposed skin, her hair falling around her face. She could feel his intake of breath.

"I thought we made a bargain."

"I missed you," she said softly.

"Kathleen, we will make you pregnant if we keep this up."

"Right you are." She lay back down. "I'm a wicked temptress, I am."

His arms tightened and he said nothing.

"I'm a murderess, too. I'll have to go confess."

He said carefully, "Do you think that's wise?"

"Very wise," she said sleepily. "You'll see."

"Why—exactly—did he decide you were next in line?"

An alarm went off inside Doyle's befuddled head. As though speaking to a child, she said, "He was nicked, Michael." That, she thought, and the semi-pornographic snaps you have of me in your mobile, which I must pretend not to know about. Apparently Section Sevens were thick on the ground in London; they should post a warning or something at the city limits.

"Did he tell you why?"

She had the certain conviction that he had waited until the drugs were working to ask these questions. He was a wily one, he was.

Doyle struggled to focus. She wouldn't tell him; the irony was a little too sharp and she was still stinging from Owens's comments. And Acton would be guilt-ridden, thinking he was at fault for her ordeal. Best leave the whole thing dead and buried with Owens—that would be the end of it.

"What did he say to you?"

Making an effort to string a coherent sentence together, she said vaguely, "I tried to keep him talkin', to give me a chance to get a shot off." She paused and added, "Like in those mysteries—Agatha Christie." And the scheme had actually worked, she realized. Huzzah. Along with the fact that he had been reluctant to kill her to begin with—it really does pay to be nice to

everyone just as the nuns taught you. She thought of something she was willing to tell Acton. "He said he killed my father."

"Yes. What was his purpose, do you know?"

"Michael, he just did. He was sorry."

"Why was he sorry?"

To throw him off, she managed to dredge up the name of a
scapegoat. "He said he worked for Solonik."

There was a pause. "Did he indeed?"

CHAPTER 39

He was tired but he lay awake, planning.

Doyle awoke in the middle of the morning, which was late for her. Stretching her arms over her head, she flinched as she moved her leg and was reminded of her wound. Acton was up already, of course—the man was like a cat, needing little sleep. She wondered if he was hungover. Carefully swinging her legs over the side of the bed, she tested her weight on the right one. Not too bad, she decided, and stood. Hopping over to the master bathroom, she shut the door, taking a few seconds to figure out how to turn on the elaborate shower. She was wrapping a small towel around the dressing on her calf when Acton knocked on the bathroom door. "Are you all right?"

"Perfectly." She pronounced it 'Paarfectly.' "How do you ever bring yourself to get out of this shower?"

"Don't wet your leg," he warned.

"I won't, but I will die if I don't wash my hair in the next two minutes."

She took a steaming hot shower, keeping her right leg out of the water as best she could. Then, wrapped in a towel, she opened the bathroom door and discovered he was sitting on the bed, watching the door. His eyes ran over her towel, and she could see that divertive tactics would be needed.

"Do you have a shirt I can borrow? I don't want to wear those clothes again. Ever."

He went to his wardrobe and pulled out a crisp, boxed shirt. She retreated back to the bathroom to put it on; the sleeves hung over her hands, and so she rolled them up. As she combed out her wet hair, she paused for a moment, regarding herself in the mirror. She opened the door and leaned out. "Do you have a thermometer?"

He smiled at her. "Let's give it one more day—we can do it if we put our minds to it."

"If you say," she offered dubiously, and was rewarded with another smile. He put his arm around her to assist her hopping progress to the kitchen, and she took the opportunity to assess him. He was out of the dismals, and a good thing; hopefully there would be no more discussions about the decedent's motivations. He seated her at the kitchen table, the weak sunlight intensified through the windows so that it was warm on her back. Her leg throbbed a bit, but she didn't want to take any more pills and so she ignored it. She wondered if she had set the standard now—no matter what happened to her, she could always think that it was nothing like getting shot up.

"What would you like for breakfast?"

"Do you have frosty flakes?" This had to be the longest she had ever gone without.

Leaning against the counter, he shook his head with regret. "No. But I'll put them on the list for Marta."

"Oh—does Marta live here?"

"No, she comes in three days a week to keep house. She's very efficient."

Wait until Marta was informed of the latest news, she thought with some misgiving. Not to mention that I am not one who would be comfortable with a servant seeing to me. Ah, well; things had changed. Understatement of the century.

In fact, things had changed so much that it hadn't occurred

to her until just now that it was well past the time she was usually at work. "Did you call Habib?"

"Yes." He said nothing more and she could see that he was hiding a smile.

"Unsnabble, wretched man—what did he say?"

Acton thought about it. "He said all that was proper."

"Poleaxed," she guessed.

"Yes." Acton smiled his rare smile. "I quite enjoyed it."

She buried her face in her hands. "I will be a freak at the circus." She peered at him covertly through her fingers. "It is just as well I will be leavin' the CID."

"No." He was serious again. "You are not leaving."

"I have quite made up my mind, Michael," she said firmly. "I cannot put you through this."

"No," he replied, and just as firmly. "I was drunk and inconsiderate. I apologize."

They regarded each other and much was unspoken. "We are at an impasse." Another vocabulary word—honestly, soon she would be spoutin' them off like Shakespeare.

"You are a good detective."

"I'd rather be good to you." She was almost surprised at herself—the personal was apparently more important than the professional, after all. Mental note.

He bent his head for a moment, thinking. "I can control what assignments you take; I may avoid those I believe are most dangerous."

"Done."

"I now know that you are capable of defending yourself."

"Indeed." She vowed he would never know how lucky the shot was. Best get to practice; she'd never be that lucky again.

He met her eyes. "You have a tendency to be reckless."

This seemed unfair. "I will try to be more careful, Michael, but recall that we would not be married and havin' this fine conversation, else."

He bowed his head in acknowledgment. "Touché."

She wasn't certain what this meant but let it pass.

There was a pause. She knew he would worry about her, but what were the chances something like this would ever happen again? Slim to none. "Are we finished having yet another tedious discussion? I'm a hungry casualty, I am."

He made toast and jam and then joined her to eat. Despite everything, she was very, very happy, sitting here with him with the warm sun on her back. This is a good place, she thought, I can feel it. She marveled at the difference twenty-four hours could make; just yesterday she had realized she was being shadowed, and now she sat with her new husband having breakfast, her old life abandoned without a second thought, all corpses efficiently disposed of, all wounds bound. "I suppose today is our honeymoon, only without the sex."

"Tomorrow," he assured her, "there will be an excess of sex."

Blushing, she laughed and thought he seemed very much at ease with her. We are compatible, just as he had pointed out when he made his proposal on that fateful night. Now my task is to see to it that he does not descend into any more black moods. "When is Doctor Timothy due?"

Apparently, Acton liked strawberry jam as much as she did, as he reached for another. "He has surgeries this morning, so he will phone this afternoon when he is available."

"Do you think that I could have you fetch some other clothes from my flat?" She didn't want to be meeting the good doctor in nothing more than Acton's shirt; the man must already wonder how on earth this had all come about. She couldn't let him think Acton was taken in by a brasser.

"We can look on-line and then order some clothes from the stores near here; they will deliver."

Bemused, she reflected, "I am like Cinderella, except for the gunshot residue."

He lifted her hand and kissed the palm. "No. You are more along the lines of a *deus ex machina,* or I suppose more properly a *dea ex machina.*"

She regarded him for a moment. "I don't know what that means," she confessed.

"Just as well. You're better off."

"I'm better off betterin' myself, I am."

"You couldn't be better."

He meant it. Amazing man, she thought. Truly nicked.

They ordered her some clothes and then she made a list of items she would need immediately before she was able to fetch things from her flat. Acton explained that the building's concierge would send someone to buy the items for them, and after they had dispatched this commission, she asked thoughtfully, "The gentleman who was my shadow—who does he work for?"

He was going to be coy, she could feel it. "Not CID."

"Huge surprise, Michael. Are you goin' to be tiresome about this?"

He thought about it. "Yes."

And there would be no more said on the subject, she knew. Interesting—she'd best be learning how to bake a cake.

His mobile rang and he checked the ID but didn't pick up. Reminded, she informed him, "I'll need to fetch my old mobile. And I need to give Layton's assistant his tablet back."

He observed her for a long and silent moment in the way that she used to think was disconcerting but now she realized was just a symptom of his condition—he was studying her. He finally said, "I think I would like to hear about everything you did yesterday."

"It's a grand tale, Michael." And she told it to him.

His mobile vibrated again and this time he answered it—it sounded like it was his assistant at headquarters. He listened for a moment and then said, "Thank you."

Every man jack is going to be congratulating him, Doyle realized—he'll not like all the attention given to him these next few weeks. I will have to cheer him along even though I feel the same way—we would rather be left alone. There's nothin' for it; we'd best get our story straight.

Acton gave some instruction about cases that needed attention and then listened again. He said he would be into the office for only a brief time tomorrow afternoon and that no meetings should be scheduled. His eyes moved to Doyle, who knew exactly what he was thinking and blushed. He then ended the call, and she realized he had received bad news.

Standing, he walked over to look out the windows, his hands in his pockets. "Fiona's funeral is the day after tomorrow. I'm to give the eulogy."

"I will come with you."

He was uncertain and glanced her way. "You may not be well enough."

"Nonsense," she said stoutly. "I am comin', whether you want me or no."

"Thank you."

She hoped she could conceal any limp. It would not do at all to appear at the funeral newly married and limping. Munoz would never let her live it down.

EPILOGUE

*H*E WAS DRINKING MORE THAN HE OUGHT. HE NEEDED TO DRINK TO *sleep, and even then he did not sleep well. He supposed a therapist would say he was clinically depressed, not that he would ever see a therapist. He found he did not want to speak to anyone outside of work; he had simply lost interest. Old friends were concerned, but he could not muster up enough emotion to mollify them. He spent long hours at work and there was little else.*

He was in the habit of having his assistant come in early to go over his appointments for the day. He would reassess the priority of the cases and decide what needed to be done. His assistant had indicated, in the way that women do, that she was available to him. He was not interested; he had little interest in sex anymore.

He stood at his window listening to the schedule for the day and drinking coffee. It was early and commuters were coming in off the St. James's Park station. He spotted a girl holding a tall cup and walking briskly as though she was cold. Scots or Irish, he thought, with that hair. Pretty. He watched her approach on the sidewalk and realized she would enter the building. She must work here, he thought; she moved very gracefully.

The next morning he stood at the window at the same time, refusing to admit to himself that he was watching for her. The girl made the same route at the same time—it was drizzling and she had her coat collar turned up.

He told his assistant she could come in a half hour later the next morning, and when the time came he pulled his binoculars out of his field kit. There she was. He could see her face clearly and the curve of her throat as she lifted the cup to drink. There was a tightening in his chest, making it hard to draw breath. Don't be a fool, he thought; she is probably married with children. She was wearing gloves, so he couldn't see if there was a ring. Look up her personal file and be done with this.

For the first time in months, he was eager to go home, and he left work early. He could obliterate any record of delving into her file, but it was safer to do so from home. He usually poured himself a drink when he walked through the door, but today he made straight for his desk. He pulled up CID personnel and typed in "red" and "auburn" for a search. Fourteen names came up; ten were women. He found her on the second try.

He looked at the photograph and the information on the screen and had to smile at the irony; it was the worst possible result. Kathleen Doyle, Detective Constable. She was aged twenty-four. Single, never married. He drew back from the desk and rubbed his face in his hands. Essentially, she worked for him. Unthinkable that he could openly pursue a relationship with a DC. A discreet affair would be equally impossible; there had already been a few sexual harassment lawsuits and it would be madness—an invitation to blackmail. And she was only twenty-four years old. There was a thirteen year difference between them—almost fourteen. Impossible. And the worst was the fact that she was single, which made him want to disregard everything else.

The next day he decided he would not watch her come in just to see if he could. He couldn't. It was raining and she held an umbrella, so that he couldn't see her well; he felt cheated and decided he would watch her go home instead. He hacked into her laptop and monitored it from time to time. She was working on assault cases, compiling statistics. Any emails were work-related. His assistant had to come in to remind him he was late for his meeting with the DCS.

She worked late and logged off at 8:00 p.m.—she put in long hours, then. It would probably be too dark to see her when she left. He watched with his binoculars anyway and saw a glimpse when she passed a streetlight.

This was too unpredictable and too frustrating; he contemplated his options, alert to possibilities and turning them over in his mind. He concluded the solution would be to try to work alongside her, even if it was just for a day. He would discover that she was young and vapid and there would be an end to this ridiculous infatuation. The thought of being alongside her brought a rush of adrenaline and a stirring of sexual feelings long dormant.

He met with the other chief inspectors on a weekly basis to set up inter-team conferences, discuss trends, and touch base. He asked a representative from HR to attend, as they would soon have to do performance reviews for the DIs and DSs—the DCIs had little direct contact with the DCs. He had nevertheless found a way to introduce the subject.

"I am thinking about teaching a class at the Academy on interrogation." He was well-known for his superior interrogation technique; the others hid their surprise that he was offering to teach a class. "I am concerned there is little skill among our rank and file." The others generally agreed and expressed the conviction that more training was indeed needed. Acton waited for the HR representative, who was very defensive, to defend her department's hires. She rose to the bait.

"We have several DCs who actually do quite well in interrogation situation training."

He looked interested. "DCs? Who?"

"Williams," she said. "And Doyle is exceptional."

Acton made a show of jotting down the names and said nothing further on the topic.

He waited until the next appropriate case arose and when it did— an early morning homicide call—he impatiently watched her arrive. He then made his way over to her building, to her cubicle, his heart pounding. It was early enough that the rest of her floor was nearly deserted. When he appeared in the entrance to her cubicle, she looked up and then stood so quickly she nearly knocked over her chair.

"Detective Constable Doyle, I am Chief Inspector Acton." He offered his hand.

She controlled her surprise. "I am pleased to meet you, sir."

The accent was a shock. Dublin, he thought—he hadn't known she had an accent. "I wonder if you would spare some time to accompany me on a homicide investigation," he said, trying to breathe evenly. He could still feel her touch on his hand.

"Certainly, sir." She gathered up her rucksack and followed him.

He briefed her in the car and she took notes. He took in every detail of her appearance, relishing the opportunity to observe her at close quarters. She was left-handed; she wore no jewelry. Her skin was luminous, he decided, was the correct word. He had to train his thoughts back to the matter at hand before his body betrayed him.

"A minor official from the Home Secretary's office has been found in the river. In light of the recent scandals"—he glanced at her and she nodded in acknowledgment—"it may be suicide, or it may be someone who didn't want him deciding to tell what he knows." There had been allegations of bribery, and it wasn't clear whether other high-ranking persons were involved in the scandal. It was an interesting, high-profile case.

She accompanied him to the crime scene and didn't blanch at the unpleasantly bloated body. She helped him turn it over to investigate for marks.

"What do you think?" he asked.

"Shot in the back with a small-caliber weapon from less than two feet. Either didn't know the killer was standin' behind him or had no anticipation that the person was wantin' to kill him."

They proceeded to the man's home, and he sought to question the new widow, who was nearly collapsing with grief. Poor woman, he thought; one blow upon another.

He gently asked her about her husband's last hours—where he had gone, how he had seemed. Had he received any calls that upset him? This was difficult for her to answer, as he had been very upset for the past few days from his other troubles. The woman sobbed into a tissue.

"Sir," Doyle said. "May I speak with you for a moment?"

He was very surprised she would interrupt; thus far she had been reserved and careful in his presence. She took him outside and glanced around to make certain they would not be overheard.

"What is it?" He tried to curb his impatience.

"She's lyin', sir."

They stared at each other. Beautiful brown eyes, he thought. He ac-

tually forgot where he was and what he was doing for a brief moment. He pulled himself back with an effort. "Why do you think she's lying, Constable?"

She was nervous but stuck to her guns. "I just know, sir. It's hard to explain." She added, "She's actually very, very happy."

He regarded her for a moment, trying to decide what to do. The woman appeared genuinely grief-stricken and to haul her in for questioning would seem cruel and unwarranted. On the other hand, there could be no better opportunity for a disgruntled wife to dispatch her husband, while all suspicion was diverted elsewhere.

He asked that the wife be brought in for questioning, much to the astonishment of everyone else present. By the time he had her seated with a solicitor in the interrogation room, she was already breaking down. He had a confession within twenty minutes; the newspapers had a field day.

He thought about it after he went home, sitting at his desk and staring out the window, the scotch untouched. She was extraordinarily intuitive, he decided. He would have to be very careful to guard himself when he was near her. Because he would continue to be near her, of course—he was completely fascinated by her, every aspect, every detail. She was intelligent, although not well educated. She was willing to work hard and seemed devoted to her job. She had tried to rein in her accent early in the day, but as she became more relaxed around him, it became stronger and he found it enchanting. She had a reserve, a dignity that masked, he was certain, her vulnerability. He glanced idly at his laptop screen, which displayed her personnel photograph. He needed a better photograph—he would have to take one when she was unaware. He couldn't wait for tomorrow.